I0640028

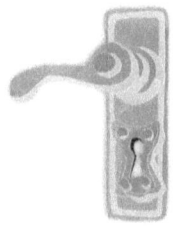

LOCKED WITHIN

AN EMMA WINBERRY MYSTERY

HELEN MACIE OSTERMAN

LOCKED WITHIN by Helen Macie Osterman

Copyright© 2017 by Helen Macie Osterman

Cover design by Robyn Hyzy

Interior layout by Ellie Searl, Publishista®

ISBN-10: 0998685208

ISBN-13: 9780998685205

LCCN: 2017939393

PEBBLE CREEK PRESS
HOMER GLEN, IL

In memory of my lifelong friend, Delores Mikos.

ACKNOWLEDGMENTS

I WISH TO THANK THE member of my writer's group, The Southland Scribes, for their invaluable input; and to Lynn Schoorl, always my first reader.

CHAPTER 1

"THAT WAS PERFECT!" THE DIRECTOR exclaimed wiping perspiration from his brow. "We'll run through the second act after a fifteen-minute break. Supers, you're on in scene two."

Emma Winberry and Nate Sandler walked off the stage of the Performing Arts Center, and toward the community room for a refreshing drink. They had been supernumeraries, extras, for the Midwest Opera Company for a number of years and felt at home in the grand old building on Chicago's north shore that dated from the 1920s.

"Do you want a cup of tea?" Emma asked.

"I think I'll have coffee," Nate answered.

"You never drink coffee in the afternoon." Emma frowned.

"I just feel in the mood." He poured himself a cup and added three sugars. Emma took a cup of herbal tea.

They sat in a corner and began discussing the opera. They had met five years ago as supernumeraries rehearsing this very opera, Giuseppe Verdi's, *A Masked Ball.*

"Remember the last time Midwest put on this production?" Emma asked, a coy tone to her voice.

"Of course I remember. Marcantonio Speranza sang the lead role." His lips twitched as he tried to suppress a smile.

"What else?" she asked.

He thought for a moment. "I seem to remember you tripped over something."

"Oh Nate, you old fooler, that was the year I first became a supernumerary and met you."

"Emma, my love, I shall never forget meeting you and everything that has happened since." He took her hand and pressed it to his lips.

She sighed. "You called me Sparrow, because I was so skinny," she said, laughing.

"I still call you that, but you have filled out nicely since we've been together." He examined her thin, but shapely figure with an appreciative nod.

It hadn't taken long for them to fall in love and, for the past four-and-a-half years, they had been living in a deluxe six room condo on Chicago's Lakeshore Drive. Since they were both in their sixth decade of life, they saw no reason to marry. Emma was a widow and Nate, divorced. Their grown children approved of the arrangement and between the two of them, they had seven grandchildren.

"Hello there," a deep contralto voice called out. They looked up to see the robust form of Delia Armanetti, a member of the chorus. She had been singing for the Midwest for quite some time, but during the past year, she and Emma had become close friends. She was much younger than Emma, but their relationship was close.

"Hi, Dee," Emma said warmly. "Come sit with us." Only Emma and a few other friends dared to shorten her name. To everyone else, she insisted on, Delia.

Nate gave her his seat and was about to pull up another chair when Dee's eyes implored him. "Nate, I'd like to have a little talk with Emma—girl to girl. Okay?"

"Sure. I want to have a few words with the super captain anyway. See you ladies later." He sauntered off whistling one of the arias.

Emma sat back and waited for her friend to begin the conversation. She noticed that Dee was clutching her lucky stone. The woman rubbed it between her fingers when she was nervous and she was rubbing it rhythmically now.

"You remember that I told you my older son, Mike, got a divorce?"

"Yes, about three months ago, right?" Emma wondered where this was leading.

Dee slowly shook her head. "Nice Italian woman. I liked her." She gazed down at the stone in her hand. "He got married again, last week." The woman's round face contorted in a frown, the heavy dark brows almost meeting in the center.

"That's rather quick." Emma wondered if they had to get married, but, these days a pregnancy outside of marriage bore no shame.

Dee's voice lowered to almost a whisper. "They went to a Justice of the Peace: no church, no family. I wasn't even invited." A tear escaped her eye and sneaked down her plump cheek.

Emma took her hand. "I'm so sorry, Dee. Maybe she'll be a good wife to him." It sounded lame but she didn't know what else to say. "Give her a chance. You need your family."

"I don't like her. She's too flashy and spends money like water." She shook her head and continued rubbing the stone.

"Now, Dee, you can't be sure of that."

"Eh, I think he had that bimbo on the side for a long time. You know his veterinary practice is good, and he makes a nice living. I think she's after his money. Besides, she smokes too much." Dee took a deep breath and rubbed her hand across her forehead.

What's the matter?" Emma asked. "Do you have a headache?"

The woman nodded. "I been getting a lot of them lately. I think my blood pressure is too high."

Emma's antennae went up. She noticed the woman's face flushing and perspiration breaking out along her hairline. "Have you been to the doctor?"

Dee shrugged. "He gave me some pills, but I don't think they're working. Sometimes I feel dizzy."

"Now listen to me," Emma said, a stern tone to her voice. "You call the doctor tomorrow and find out what's wrong."

"Eh, what good does it do? He'll only give me more pills, and they make me tired. And I have to go to the bathroom so much. That's not good during a long opera."

"My friend," Emma said forcefully, "if you have a stroke, that will be the end of your career. You don't want that, do you?"

Dee lowered her eyes. "Would anyone care?"

"I care," Emma almost shouted. "Stop feeling sorry for yourself. You have a great voice and many friends here, and two fine sons."

"Mike is so busy all the time and now he has this new woman. And Sam—he's all the way in California. I see him maybe once a year."

Emma grimaced. Her children were so caring. It hurt that her dear friend didn't have the same relationship with her sons, and she knew the woman had no siblings. She held her hand. "Promise me you'll see the doctor."

Dee nodded.

At that moment they heard the stage manager call all chorus members and supers to the stage. Emma watched her friend out of the corner of her eye as they started walking. She seemed a bit unsteady. The short dark hair around her face appeared wet with perspiration. Of course it could be from the lights. Many of the performers complained about the hot bright lights. And Dee was at least twenty pounds overweight. But Emma felt a gnawing inside.

She had been plagued with a sixth sense all her life and frequently knew when something unpleasant was about to happen. Now she had that feeling about Delia Armanetti.

* * *

Emma and Nate walked the four blocks from the Performing Arts Center to their condo. As the cold March wind hastened their steps, Emma shivered and grasped Nate's arm.

"I'm worried about Dee."

"Now what? You're always worrying about someone. What's with her?" He put the key rather forcefully into the lock on the door of their building.

"I don't think she's well."

"What makes you say that?"

"She's complaining of headaches and occasional bouts of dizziness," Emma said, following him inside.

"Then she should see a doctor."

"I told her that."

Nate punched the sixth-floor button on the elevator and turned to Emma. "That's all you can do. The rest is up to her."

She didn't respond to that statement but promised herself to keep after the woman and check up on her.

Oh, why am I always trying to watch over people? But she knew the answer. It was her way, and there was nothing she could do about it.

Emma stretched as she walked into the large atrium facing Lake Michigan. The turbulent waves mirrored her unease. Clouds skittered across the full moon. Their reflection bounced on the waves in a wild dance.

Oh Guardian Angel, why do I feel fear for Delia? Is she in some kind of danger? She will need your friendship in the coming months, her inner voice said.

Emma heaved a sigh. She had been conversing with her Guardian Angel all her life. The celestial voice always responded in her head, and she heeded the warnings.

"Are we having dinner tonight?" Nate called from the kitchen. "Or are you putting me on a diet."

"I'll be right there." She gave one more glance at the moon's bizarre dance on the lake, looked around at her beloved plants that thrived in the atrium, then reluctantly walked toward the kitchen.

* * *

When Emma questioned Dee about the doctor a few days later, the woman was evasive, said she couldn't get an appointment for two weeks. But she insisted she was taking her medication and felt better.

"No more headaches," she said.

Emma had to admit that Dee did look better—no flushing of the face, no compulsive rubbing of her stone.

But still, she worried and kept a close watch over her friend.

* * *

The rehearsals continued without incident until the night of the dress rehearsal. This was exactly like the performance, including an audience, except that the stage director or the conductor could halt the action at any time for a comment or correction.

In the brief intermission between scenes in Act One, Emma searched for Dee. The woman was certainly behaving strangely ever since her son remarried. Emma knew that the pain went deep and that she did not approve of her new daughter-in-law.

Emma spotted her in a corner rubbing her stone in one hand and what appeared to be rosary beads in the other.

"Dee?" Emma approached her, a concerned expression on her face.

At first there was no response. She kept rubbing the stone and slipping the beads though her fingers.

"Dee, are you all right?" Emma grasped the woman's shoulder.

"Huh? Oh, Emma, I didn't see you."

Emma noticed the flushed face and a pulse bounding in her temple. There was also a slight drooping of her right eyelid. "I don't think you're well. Did you go to the doctor?" She sat next to her friend and put her arm around her shoulder.

"I got an appointment—I think—maybe tomorrow."

Her halting speech frightened Emma. "You'd better go home or, better yet, right to the emergency room. Something is wrong."

Dee looked at Emma and squeezed her eyes shut. "It's okay. After the performance, I go home." Her shoulders sagged and she let out a deep sigh. "I'm so tired."

"Dee, you shouldn't sing." Emma tried to hold her friend back, but the woman pulled her arm from Emma's grasp.

"I sing." She stood and grasped the back of the chair. "It is my *life!*"

The stage manager called the chorus members onstage. Emma watched with trepidation as Dee straightened herself, took a deep breath and, with halting steps, walked toward the stage.

Oh Guardian Angel, something is going to happen. I feel it. And I'm powerless to stop it.

Emma followed and watched from the wings as Dee took her place among the other members of the chorus.

The curtain rose, the music began; Emma clenched her fists and watched. The scene was dark. The fortuneteller, *Ulrica,* stirred a cauldron and began an incantation.

Emma craned her neck to see her friend. She stood in the back with the taller chorus members. The music continued and the principals sang while Emma's eyes never left Dee. The chorus sang snatches between the tenor and the soprano. Suddenly Emma noticed commotion on the stage.

"Help!" someone called out.

The conductor tapped his baton; the stage director ran out and flipped open his cell phone as the curtain descended rapidly.

By now Nate was beside Emma, restraining her from running onstage. "Easy," he said. "You don't know what happened."

"It's Dee, I know it is."

"Everyone back," the stage manager ordered. "Let the doctor through." A man dressed in evening clothes, most likely a patron, followed him.

A short time later, the paramedics arrived. Three men hurried onstage: two pushing a gurney and one carrying a pack of equipment.

"Who is it?" Emma begged.

"One of the chorus members fainted, that's all. Now clear the stage. We'll resume the dress rehearsal shortly," the stage manager said.

But Emma knew it was Dee and that it was much more serious than a fainting spell. Nate pulled her as far away as possible, but she fought him with every step. When she saw the gurney rush by and Dee's ashen face covered by an oxygen mask, she gasped and buried her face in Nate's shirt. "If she had only listened to me and not gone on."

"Stop blaming yourself," Nate commanded. "You are not responsible for other people's lives. When are you going to realize that?" He gently pushed her away and cradled her face in his hands. "Sparrow, whatever happened is not your fault."

"I guess you're right, but if she had listened . . ." She left the sentence unfinished.

"The outcome might have been the same anyway," he said.

She nodded and looked down at the floor. Something familiar sat in a corner. She picked it up and realized it was Dee's lucky stone. Emma clutched it for a moment. Was that a vibration she felt? Carefully she put it in her pocket.

CHAPTER 2

THE FOLLOWING DAY THE FIRST performance of *A Masked Ball* was a complete success. Emma went to her son-in-law, James', office to ask about Delia. He was an executive for the Midwest Opera and the one who had encouraged her to become a supernumerary in the first place.

The office door was slightly ajar as she heard her son-in-law talking on the phone. Inching her way in, she saw him motion her to a chair. She noticed how his hairline had receded in the past few years. His was a job filled with stress and last minute changes.

Emma smiled at the picture on his desk of her daughter and their two sons.

When he completed his call he greeted her with a grin. "Hi Emma, what can I do for you?"

"I just wondered if you had heard anything about Delia Armanetti, the chorus member who collapsed yesterday." She held the woman's lucky stone in her hand and absently rubbed it.

James frowned. "Let me call the chorus master." He picked up the phone and punched in the numbers then waited through a number of rings. "He must have left already. All I know is that the paramedics took her to Northwestern Hospital. If it was merely a fainting spell the doctors may have released her already." He gave Emma an encouraging nod.

"No." She shook her head. "It was more than that. I feel it."

"Knowing you, it most likely was." He got up from the chair, stretched and yawned. "I'm ready to go home. Aren't you?"

"Yes. Nate is waiting for me in the lobby."

"No he's not." James smiled as Nate walked into the office.

"Come on, Emma. Security wants to lock the place up. Time to go home."

"I'm ready." She gave her son-in-law a peck on the cheek. "Give my love to Sylvia and the boys."

"I will."

They left the building together, James heading for his car and Emma and Nate walking the four blocks home.

"What was so important that you had to bother James on opening night?" Nate asked with just a bit of annoyance in his voice.

"I wanted to know if he had heard anything about Dee." Then in a defensive tone she added, "She is our friend, and I'm concerned."

He grunted. "Did you find out anything?"

She let out a frustrated breath. "No, he tried to call the chorus master but he had apparently left. I'll call Northwestern Hospital in the morning. If they admitted her, I may be able to visit."

"That's a plan. Now put it out of your mind."

* * *

Emma's attempts to call Delia's home were met with the answering machine. Finally she called the hospital. The only information they gave her was that Mrs. Armanetti was in Intensive Care. When she asked about visitors, the response was, "Family only."

Oh Guardian Angel, what am I to do? What happened to her? How can I find out? Call her son's place of business, came the answer.

Now why didn't I think of that? She pondered, annoyed with herself. But where does he work?

She called James' office and spoke with his secretary. "Joanne, this is Emma Winberry. Do you have any information on the chorus members?"

"What are you looking for?" the woman asked.

"Well, you know that Delia Armanetti collapsed during the dress rehearsal."

"Yes, I heard that. Is it serious?"

"She's at Northwestern Hospital in Intensive Care, but that's all they'll tell me. When I call her home all I get is the answering machine. Do you, by any chance, have her son's business number?"

"Hmm, let me look that up. I know we have next of kin and we should have home and business numbers. Hang on a minute."

Emma paced as she waited. Nate was downstairs in the exercise room going through his daily ritual. He had decided that he was definitely getting too paunchy and, since Emma continued to bake her delicious muffins and pies, he would work off the extra calories. He was rewarded with compliments from friends for his new look.

"Emma, sorry I took so long," Joanne said. "Here is his work number." She read off the ten digits as Emma scribbled them down.

"Thanks, Joanne. I'll call right now."

"Do let us know what you find out."

"I will. Bye."

Emma immediately punched in the numbers.

"Paws and Claws, veterinary practice, may I help you?"

"Yes, I would like to speak with Mr. Armanetti, please." She heard a dog yapping in the background.

"You mean Dr. Armanetti. Did you wish to make an appointment?"

"Sorry, I meant Dr. Armanetti." Of course he was called Doctor, Emma chided herself and grimaced at the correction by the receptionist. "I'm a friend of his mother and am concerned about her."

"One moment please. I'll see if he can speak with you."

Another pause, then a male voice came on the line. "Dr. Armanetti here."

"Oh hello, my name is Emma Winberry and I'm a supernumerary at the Midwest Opera. Your mother is a friend of mine. I called the hospital and, of course, they gave me no information. How is she? I'm extremely worried."

"Thanks for your concern, Mrs. Winberry. I remember my mother talking about you." He hesitated for a moment. "I'm afraid she's had a rather severe stroke and is paralyzed on the right side." More hesitation. "This is so difficult for me. She's always been strong and self-reliant. Now, to see her like this—so helpless." Emma heard the tremor in his voice.

He managed to control himself and continued. "The medical team had trouble getting her stabilized at first, but I just spoke with the doctor and he said that she's doing better. They will probably move her to the step-down unit shortly. That's the next step before she goes into a private room."

"What's the prognosis?" Emma was almost afraid to ask.

He hesitated for a moment. "It's guarded, which means, they don't know." He let out a breath. "We'll just have to see how she does in the next few weeks."

Emma heard the sorrow in his voice. "Thanks. Here's my number. Please let me know when I can visit."

"I will, and I'll tell her you called."

"All right. Good bye." Emma pressed the phone to her chest and uttered a prayer.

"Who are you going to visit?" Nate asked.

Emma jumped. "Oh you scared me. Don't sneak up like that."

"I wasn't sneaking anywhere. Now what has you so upset?" He took the phone out of her hands, replaced it on the charger, and took her in his arms.

She snuggled close relishing his masculine smell, a combination of after-shave and sweat. In halting tones she repeated her conversation with Delia's son.

He shook his head. "Doesn't sound good."

"No it doesn't. If she had only listened to me."

"Don't start that again. You have no control over another person's actions. Clear?"

"I suppose."

"Now get that grim expression off your face. I'll take a quick shower and we'll go for a walk along the lakeshore. Okay?"

"Okay."

For the rest of the day, Emma's thoughts were never far from Delia. What would happen to her? Singing was her life. If she didn't recover …

Guardian Angel, how can I help her? What can I do? Be there for her. She will need a friend.

That wasn't much of an answer as far as Emma was concerned. Her modus operandi was action, not just being supportive. She blew out a breath and watched the waves dancing on the placid water of Lake Michigan. Without realizing it, she kept rubbing Dee's lucky stone.

CHAPTER 3

EMMA TRIED TO GO ABOUT her daily routine, yoga in the morning, a walk along the lakeshore with Nate, weather permitting, and checking in with the children, but Dee was always on her mind.

Finally, when she hadn't heard from Dr. Armanetti in three days, she again called the hospital.

"Mrs. Armanetti has been moved to a private room. Visitors are permitted," she was told.

Emma was peeved that Dee's son hadn't called her, but realized he probably had more important things to do. She decided to go that very afternoon.

"Nate, I'm going to visit Dee. Do you want to come along?"

He grimaced. Emma knew how he felt about hospitals. They had entirely too many occasions to visit them in the past few years.

"You go," he said, "and give her my best."

It was the answer she expected. "Okay, be back later." She gave him a kiss, slipped on a jacket, and put Dee's lucky stone in her pocket. The woman would surely need it.

As Emma walked out of the building, the late March wind swirled about her legs. She pulled her jacket tighter around her slim body as she hurried toward the bus stop, shivering. But, no matter what the weather was like, she loved living here, in this bustling city, and in this luxurious condo with Nate. She still kept pinching herself to make sure she wasn't dreaming. So much had happened in her life in the past few years, that, when she looked back, it seemed as though she were watching a movie and she was merely one of the actors.

She took a deep breath of the invigorating air as her bus arrived.

* * *

Every time Emma entered a hospital, she hesitated, remembering her own experiences, one just last year abroad. However did she get herself into so many scrapes and near death experiences?

Guardian Angel, I am only visiting a friend this time. There is no way I can get into any trouble. And I'm counting on you to see to that.

All her life Emma had relied on her Guardian Angel's assistance. In her mind the angel was female and was always there to guide her. But, on occasion, she seemed to be taking the day off.

She gave her head a vigorous nod and walked up to the desk. "Where can I find Delia Armanetti, please?"

The woman smiled, looked up the room number and directed Emma to the appropriate bank of elevators. When she approached the room, Emma stopped for a moment, filled with apprehension. What would she find?

You'll only know when you walk inside, her inner voice said.

Emma held Dee's lucky stone in her hand and rubbed it vigorously. A pitiful moaning sound greeted her as she entered the room. A young nurse was urging Dee to take her medication. Dee shook her head from one side of the pillow to the other.

The nurse glanced at Emma, a look of frustration on her face. "She's not very cooperative, I'm afraid."

"I'm a good friend of hers. Let me try," Emma said, sitting on a chair by the bedside. "Dee, it's Emma, from the Midwest. Do you know me?"

The woman turned her face toward the voice. "Ma," she whispered grasping out with her left hand. "Ma."

Emma swallowed the lump in her throat as she noticed the drooping eye as well as the entire right side of her face. This poor woman was a far cry from the self assured, lusty, mezzo-soprano she knew.

"Take your medicine, please," Emma prodded as she held the cup to Dee's lips. The woman swallowed, some of the red liquid spilling from the right side of her mouth. Emma grabbed a tissue and wiped it away.

"That's better than I've done all day," the young nurse said. "Maybe we should hire you."

"We're good friends," Emma said feeling the grasp of Dee's left hand. She noticed the right arm lying limp and useless on the bedclothes, a splint on her hand holding the fingers straight. "Is she getting therapy?" Emma asked.

"Oh yes, twice a day, both physical therapy and occupational therapy. Speech therapy will start soon."

"Why the splint?" Emma asked.

"Well, at this point, she has no control over her right side. We're trying to keep the fingers from contracting into a fist." Then she turned to her patient. "But we're going to work hard to get that control back, aren't we, Mrs. Armanetti?"

Emma felt disheartened when there was no response from Dee. She merely turned her head away.

When the nurse left, Emma let out a sigh. "Can you speak at all, Dee?" she asked.

Garbled sounds issued from the woman's throat as she tried to form words. Then she began to cry. "Ma—Ma—Ma," she repeated over and over.

This isn't getting me anywhere, Emma thought. "I have something for you." She pressed the lucky stone into Dee's left hand and noticed her eyes brighten, just a little.

"Nos—nos," Dee said, grasping it and rubbing as hard as she could. Emma saw a look of gratitude in her eyes.

"I found it on the floor after they took you to the hospital."

"Ah, ah, ah," Dee kept repeating as she rubbed the stone.

I have to make sure the staff knows how important this is to her, Emma thought. "I'll be right back, Dee."

She walked into the hallway and looked for the nurse who had been caring for her friend.

She found her standing at the desk thumbing through some papers. Quickly Emma explained the importance of the stone to Dee and how superstitious she was.

"How can we be sure that no one throws it away?" Emma asked.

"I'll make a sign and put it above her bed. We do that to alert the staff to anything special to watch for or any particular needs."

"Thank you," Emma said.

Within a half hour a sign in large printed letters was fixed to a bulletin board next to Dee's bed.

> Patient has smooth stone that helps her to relax.
> Please see that it is with her at all times.

"That's perfect," Emma said. Then, turning to Dee, she kissed her cheek and said, "I'll be back tomorrow. You do what the nurses tell you so you can get back on that stage."

Dee gave her what passed for a smile as a tear escaped her eye. Emma wiped it away, turned, and left the room.

* * *

Delia Armanetti lay staring at the ceiling, frightened and confused, clutching her lucky stone.

Wrong with me—can't move arm—leg—can't talk—all jumbled up— tired—sleep—

CHAPTER 4

A S SOON AS EMMA WALKED into the condo, Nate knew the visit hadn't gone well. She plopped on the couch, letting out a deep sigh. He sat next to her and cradled her in his arms. "Tell me about it."

She buried her face in his shirt desperately trying to control her emotions. "It was awful," she whispered. "She couldn't even communicate with me—just made pitiful sounds." Emma looked up into his caring face. He wasn't a handsome man, but his eyes shone with love.

He held her close, rubbing her back. "Strokes can be pretty devastating."

"But I didn't think it would be *that* bad. The only time she tried to smile was when I put her lucky stone in her hand."

Nate caressed her face and smoothed her unruly hair. "Did the nurses tell you anything?"

"Oh you know how they are with all those privacy issues. Unless you're a family member, they tell you zip." She stood up and began to pace.

"Why don't you call Bertie," Nate suggested. "She may be able to tell you about this sort of thing. After all she is a social worker and I'm sure she's worked with a lot of stroke patients and their families."

"Good idea. Why didn't I think of that?" Emma was annoyed with herself for not considering her daughter-in-law immediately. She could probably tell her all she needed to know. Emma picked up the phone, punched in the numbers and soon heard Bertie's cheery voice.

"Hi, Emma. How are you and Nate?"

"We're fine. And how is little Robin?" Her youngest grandchild was just a year and a half and getting into everything.

Bertie sighed. "She just went down for a nap. Cutting another tooth and keeping me up at night."

"What about Martin? Isn't he helping you?"

"Huh! That man can sleep through anything. He claims he never hears a sound."

Emma laughed. "He was like that growing up, too. I had to literally pull him out of bed in the morning to get him to school on time." She smiled, remembering how difficult her younger son had been.

After a momentary pause, Emma got down to the reason for her call. "One of the members of the opera chorus had a stroke and I'm really worried about her."

"I'm sorry to hear that. Strokes can have many different symptoms. Is one side of her body affected?" Bertie asked.

"Yes, the right. And she can't seem to articulate. She tries to speak but it comes out all mixed up. She appears to know what she wants to say but can't form the words."

"That sounds like Broca's aphasia," Bertie said. "There's a particular area of the brain that controls speech and, if that's damaged, the result is either inability to speak at all or what you just described. It's very frustrating for patients and caregivers alike."

In the background Emma heard a small voice beginning to cry.

"Oh, there she goes. I thought I would have a little respite, but it doesn't appear so." The crying grew louder.

"You'd better go, and thanks." She had so many more questions, but now was not the time to ask them. She said goodbye and put down the phone.

"You're making faces," Nate said when Emma returned to the couch.

"Well, Robin is cutting more teeth and is fussy so Bertie couldn't tell me too much. Maybe you can look it up on the computer." She smiled and batted her eyelashes at him.

"Never mind the coaxing. What do you want to know?" He walked into the study and fired up the computer.

"She said it was probably Broca's aphasia."

"Great. Now how would I spell that?"

Emma shrugged. "I haven't the foggiest."

Nate deftly Googled stroke then tried various spellings until he hit the right one. "There you go." His brow furrowed as he began to read. "Says it's caused by damage on the left side of the brain."

Emma felt perplexed as she leaned over his shoulder and studied the screen. "How can that be? Her entire right side is paralyzed."

Nate gave her a smug look. "Well, my dear, there is a crossover of functions in the brain. Damage to the right side affects the left side of the body and vice-versa."

"How do you know that?"

He shrugged. "I remember reading it somewhere. Brain function is so complex that researchers are still learning new things every day."

"Humph!" she said sitting on a chair.

"I'll print this out. There's lots of material here." He pushed the print button and pages began spitting from the machine.

Emma put on her reading glasses and picked up a page. "Look, it says there is such a thing as Melodic Intonation Therapy. Some patients can sing the words even though they can't speak them. Isn't that strange?"

Nate took the paper from her hand and read on. "It says here that singing capabilities are stored in the right side of the brain. Since Delia is a professional singer, I would imagine that therapy might work well for her."

"Oh, I hope so," Emma said. "Singing is her life."

Nate took her hand in his. "Give it time, Sparrow. Just be there for her." Strange, Emma thought, that's just what her Guardian Angel had told her.

CHAPTER 5

THAT NIGHT EMMA TOSSED AND turned, her sleep interrupted by confusing nightmares. By early morning, she slid out of bed, unable to relax. Her dreams always meant something; someone was in trouble. Sometimes she didn't know who it was, but this time she knew it was Delia.

When she came out of the bathroom, she saw Nate sitting on the side of the bed rubbing his face with his hands.

"Why are you awake so early?" she asked, glancing at the clock.

"Only a deeply drugged person could sleep through all your muttering and kicking, my dear. I'm probably black and blue all over."

"Oh Nate, I'm so sorry." She hurried to the bedside, sat down beside him and cradled his head in her arms.

"Umm, that's nice," he said nestling between her small breasts. "Come back to bed," he whispered, pulling her on top of him.

She gently pushed him away. "Sorry, dear, but *amour* is far from my mind. I can't think of anything but Dee. She's in trouble, and I have to help her."

"Spoilsport," he said, relaxing back on the bed. "Of course she's in trouble. She's had a stroke. Now how do you intend to fix that?"

"It's more than that," Emma said, furrowing her brow. "I just haven't figured out what."

"All right, you go work your magic while I'll catch a few more winks." He turned over and within minutes was asleep.

Emma quietly made her way into the kitchen and put on a pot of coffee. When it was brewed, she poured herself a cup, added a little milk, and walked into the atrium. This was her favorite room in the house: filled with her beloved plants, floor to ceiling windows, a fabulous view of Lake Michigan, and, to the south, the Ferris wheel at Navy Pier. She took a sip of coffee then sat in her comfy lounge chair gazing across the lake. The sun was just peeking over the horizon, sending its rays across the unusually still water.

All right, Guardian Angel, these dreams mean something. What am I supposed to do to help Dee and what sort of danger is she in?

Be observant. When the time comes, you'll know what to do, her inner voice said. Well, that was pretty vague. I suppose I'll just have to wait and see.

* * *

Later that afternoon Emma felt an overpowering need to visit Dee again. She always listened to her inner voice and its bidding.

"Nate, I'm going to see Dee. Do you want to come?"

He hemmed and hawed then simply said no. She understood. She kissed him and promised not to stay long, just felt the need to see how the woman was progressing.

When Emma arrived on the ward, she heard some commotion coming from Dee's room. Quickening her step, she hurried into the room where a nurse and an aide were struggling with their patient.

"Oh—oh—oh," Dee kept shouting.

Emma ran to the bedside. "What's wrong? Can I help?"

The nurse turned to her with a frustrated expression and blew out a deep breath. "You're the woman who brought her that damned stone," she said in a less than friendly tone. "She won't let go of it for a minute, not even to feed herself."

Emma took a step back and gazed at the pleading look on Dee's face.

"Ma—Ma—Ma," she moaned.

"Is she having any difficulty swallowing?" Emma asked, remembering something she had read in the pages about stroke patients.

"No," the nurse answered. "The therapist has done studies and there is nothing wrong with her swallowing reflex. She simply refuses to cooperate."

"Let me try." Emma sat on the side of the bed and gave her friend a hug. Tears rolled down the woman's face.

Guardian Angel, tell me what to do. I made things worse by giving her the stone. No you didn't, her inner voice said. *Think of a way.*

"Delia," Emma said in an authoritative tone. "Give me the stone so you can eat your lunch." Dee shook her head and clutched it harder.

"It's no use," the nurse said. "She won't give it up. She's going to the rehabilitation ward tomorrow and, believe me, they won't put up with this. They'll simply take it away from her."

"No, no," Emma said. "You have no idea what it means to her. She carries it with her whenever she performs on stage. It gives her confidence and a feeling of security."

"Well, we have to come up with a solution, and soon."

"I'll feed her," Emma said.

"That's not the point. She must learn to feed herself with that left hand."

"Let me try to work with her," Emma pleaded.

"All right." With a sigh, the nurse and the aide left the room.

Emma felt their hostility toward her. After all, she had caused this problem. She gave her friend a stern look. "Did you hear what the nurse said?"

Dee clutched the stone to her chest.

"Let me hold it for you while you eat your lunch." The woman rolled her head from side to side.

"Come on now, you want to get well, don't you? You have to eat," Emma urged.

She held a spoonful of tepid soup up to Dee's mouth. Reluctantly the woman swallowed it.

After an hour of cajoling and pleading, Emma had gotten half of the food into her. But that wouldn't solve the problem. She gazed at her friend, now fast asleep, still clutching the stone.

Suddenly Emma remembered something. "Yes, that should work," she said aloud as she made her way to the nurses' station. "I have a solution. I'll be back in an hour. Please don't take the stone away from her."

The harried nursed glanced at Emma in disbelief. "Did she eat anything?"

"Yes, more than half of her lunch." Emma refrained from telling her that she had fed Dee every bite.

"That's some progress." The nurse turned to answer a ringing phone as Emma walked toward the elevators.

She knew that the stone meant more to Dee than mere superstition. Her parents had been singers in Milan and, when their older son, a promising tenor, died in a tragic accident, they turned their aspirations to Delia. Her contralto voice did not have the necessary timbre to capture major roles, but she was able to sing in the chorus. Her mother gave her the stone for luck, said it was blessed by the pope. Delia carried it everywhere. Said it gave her confidence and she felt her parents' presence.

Guardian Angel, now you must help me to find what I need.

* * *

When Emma opened the door to the condo, she practically ran into the bedroom and began searching through drawers.

Nate stood at the doorway, arms folded across his chest, a questioning expression on his face.

"Now where is that?" she mumbled. "I know I put it in here somewhere." She pushed items from one end of the drawer to the other, tossing some on top of the dresser.

"To what do we owe this frenzied search?" Nate asked.

"Oh." Emma jumped as she turned to him. "Don't sneak up on me like that."

"I didn't sneak anywhere, my dear. You came barreling through the door and started throwing things around in that drawer."

"I'm looking for something."

"That's obvious. If you tell me what it is, I may be able to help you."

She took a deep breath and stopped for a moment. Nate took her hands in his, led her to the bed, and sat her down.

"You'll think I'm crazy," she whispered.

The edges of his mouth twitched. "I already know that, so why don't you tell me something I don't know?"

All right." She recounted the episode at the hospital and the threat that the stone would be taken away.

"Hmm." Nate's brow furrowed. "She's so superstitious that might be disastrous."

"So you agree with me."

"Yes, but I still don't know what you're searching for."

Open the bottom drawer and find the box with the souvenirs, her inner voice said.

"Oh my God!" Emma jumped off the bed. "My Guardian Angel just told me where it is." She pulled out the bottom drawer and retrieved a metal box. With trembling hands, she laid it on the bed and lifted the lid. Inside were nick-knacks from various trips she had taken and on the bottom she found a small leather pouch. She gave Nate a triumphant grin.

"And what, pray tell, is that?" he asked.

"I bought it on an Indian Reservation years ago. It's to be worn for protection." Carefully she opened the pouch and poured out the contents on a handkerchief she took from the drawer.

"What is all that stuff? Voodoo?"

"No, silly. This is one kind of weed to ward off evil spirits, a few sacred rocks and some beads. Don't you see? We can put Dee's stone in this pouch and the leather thong goes around the neck. That way she will have her left hand free for therapy."

Nate shrugged. "It might work, if she'll let go of the stone."

"She'll have to. I *will* convince her."

"If anyone can, you can." He watched her fold all the items from the pouch in the handkerchief. "And what do you plan to do with all that stuff?"

"I'll put it back in this box. Never know when it might come in handy. Now I have to get back to the hospital. I promised the nurses."

Nate raised his hands in a submissive gesture. "Come on, I'll drive you. Let's get this over with."

She threw her arms around his neck and kissed him hard. "You're a dear."

"I know, and don't you forget it."

* * *

When they arrived on the ward, Emma sought out the nurse and told her the plan she had devised.

The nurse shrugged and gave her head a slight shake. "I hope it works. She must learn to use that left hand. Her son said that she's right-handed so, to change that to left hand dominance, takes a lot of work and determination." The woman frowned at Emma as though she were to blame.

"I understand," Emma said, "and I'll help as much as I can." She grabbed Nate's hand and hurried to Dee's room.

A woman Emma didn't recognize sat at the bedside speaking in a subdued voice. Emma noted that Dee turned her face away. Was this the daughter-in-law that Dee had told her about? Emma could feel her friend's dislike for the woman. She frowned at the bleached blond hair, dark roots showing at the center part. The left side hung down to her chin while the right side ended below her ear. Asymmetry seemed to be in vogue. Her tight sweater plunged in front showing ample cleavage. It hardly seemed appropriate attire for visiting a hospital. Her left leg was crossed over her right knee. The short skirt rose to what Emma considered an indecent level.

Emma especially noticed her long curved fingernails painted blood red. They looked more like talons than natural nails. Were they fake? Of course.

Nate stayed at the door while Emma walked in.

"Excuse me." She extended her hand to the visitor. "I'm Emma Winberry, one of the supernumeraries from the opera. Dee and I have worked together for quite some time." She gave the woman her most engaging smile.

She smiled in return, but, to Emma, it didn't appear genuine. "I'm June Armanetti, Delia's daughter-in-law."

Emma noticed her lips were extremely thin, the lower one barely visible. She used lip liner to accentuate it, but it didn't look natural. Her clothes smelled of cigarette smoke. Emma remembered Dee's remark about her smoking too much.

June took Emma's hand half-heartedly, then quickly released it.

Dee's eyes opened wide at the sound of Emma's voice. "Ma—Ma—Ma," she mumbled.

Emma grasped her friend's left hand, noting that it was firmly clutching the stone. She gave her a hug and sat on the side opposite the daughter-in-law.

"She won't let go of that stone," June said, "and the staff can't proceed with therapy. I wish I knew who brought the damned thing. I say we simply take it away from her." Her voice took on a harsh tone.

Emma cringed. If she only knew I was the guilty party. "Oh, oh, oh," Dee moaned.

"Just a minute," Emma said. "I have a solution to the problem." She looked intently at her friend as she took the leather pouch from her purse. "Now Dee, listen to me carefully. In order to get well, you *must* learn to use your left hand."

Dee moaned and moved her head from side to side.

"I know how much that stone means to you. Here is a leather pouch that I got from an Indian Reservation. They put their most valued possession in the pouch and wear it around their neck for protection." She noticed that Dee was listening intently.

"Now, you put the stone in this pouch, and we'll put the leather thong around your neck. That way you can wear it all the time for protection and leave your left hand free for therapy."

Emma sat back and let her words sink in. She glanced at June from the corner of her eye. June Armanetti let out a harsh sound and fiddled with an unopened pack of cigarettes, then she began cracking her knuckles. Emma felt a definite negativity emanating from her. No wonder Dee didn't like her.

Slowly Emma loosened the leather thong that held the pouch closed. She held it out toward Dee. The pain in her friend's eyes brought tears to her own. Gradually Dee loosened her fist and let the stone fall into the pouch. Emma pulled the thong tight then placed it around Dee's neck. The pouch nestled between her breasts. Dee gave Emma a crooked smile and extended her left hand. Emma grasped it and held it for a long time, their eyes saying what words could not.

June Armanetti got up from her chair. "Well, you're very clever, Mrs.— ah?"

"Winberry. Just call me Emma. You'll be seeing a lot of me."

"I'm sure I shall," the woman said between clenched teeth. She leaned over Dee and brushed her lips across her cheek, leaving a lipstick smear. "Goodbye, Mother D, I'll be back soon."

Dee grunted as the woman left the room, her high heels clicking on the tile floor her, hips swaying provocatively.

Emma wiped the red stain from her friend's face and frowned. She noticed Nate's eyebrows rise as he rubbed the cleft in his chin. She would be sure to mention his reaction to June later.

Emma and Nate said their farewells then Emma stopped at the desk for a moment and told the grateful nurse of her success. Afterwards she and Nate walked toward the elevators.

"I watched that whole scene," Nate said. "There is no love lost between Dee and her daughter-in-law. That was obvious."

"No," Emma agreed. "I could feel the negative vibes. And, I saw you staring at her backside as she walked out."

"I couldn't help it. There she was clicking and swaying. Her face isn't much, but she makes the most of her figure." He chuckled. "She wasn't too crazy about your interfering, either."

"That's just too bad, because I am going to help as much as I can, whether she likes it or not."

Watch that woman, her inner voice said. *She will cause trouble.*

Emma frowned. She would heed her Guardian Angel's warning. She always did.

* * *

Delia caressed the pouch holding her lucky stone as she tried to make some sense out of what had happened to her.

Doctor said stroke—why I can't move arm and leg—can't talk. Don't want June here—only Emma.

Have my lucky stone—help me to get well. Try hard for Mike and Emma, and Sam, too.

CHAPTER 6

THE NEXT TWO PERFORMANCES OF *A Masked Ball* were a huge success. When the curtain came down and the cast took their bows, everyone breathed a sigh of relief. They all knew they had done a good job. Everyone anticipated glowing reviews in the newspapers.

Emma and Nate met James as they were leaving the Center. "What are you two going to do before the next opera in the fall?" James asked.

Nate gave Emma a critical look. "I guess I'll spend the summer keeping you out of trouble." He grinned and chucked her under the chin.

'Emma lifted her head and lowered her eyes in a theatrical pose. "I do not intend to get into any trouble. I will spend the summer tending my plants, visiting my children and grandchildren, attending the concerts at Millennium Park, and enjoying all the city has to offer." With those words she gave her head a decided nod.

"I haven't seen that yet," Nate said. "This may be a first." They said goodbye to James and walked home.

"You think I can't stay out of trouble, don't you," Emma said, swinging her arms.

"I think it's your nature to seek out problems and try to solve them." He lifted his hand to ward off her protest. "That's all well and good, but you put yourself in danger too many times."

Emma pouted and said nothing. He was right. Every time she tried to help someone, she stumbled into a perilous situation. Not this summer, she promised. Not this summer.

* * *

Mike Armanetti sat with his arms on the table, his head hanging down.

"What's the matter, baby?" June asked kissing him on the neck. "I'm here, remember?" Her long nails slid carefully down his shoulders.

He let out a sigh. "I know I've been neglecting you, honey, but I'm so worried about my mother."

"She's in good hands at that hospital and I visit whenever I can." She let the corners of her mouth pull down in an expression of concern.

"I know and I appreciate it," he said sliding his arm around her and patting her backside. "The doctor said they'll be transferring her to the rehab section soon. He said she's making some progress but not as much as she should."

He looked at his wife and thought for a moment. "When they discharge her, I'm thinking of having her move in here, with us."

June's eyes opened wide. "With us?" She swallowed hard then sucked in her lower lip.

"Don't worry. It won't be for a long time yet, but I want you to know that I intend to take care of my mother, even if I have to hire someone. She worked hard putting me through school and I won't desert her now. Understand?" His expression indicated that the subject was not up for discussion.

She forced herself to smile, kissed him on the cheek, and walked out of the room.

* * *

June sat in a chair in the living room looking out over the pristine yard. A man was mowing the lawn, another trimming the edges. She clenched her fists. Married less than two months and now I have to contend with a sick old lady. She remembered how she had to kick and scratch for everything when she was a kid. All the mistakes she made had cost her dearly. Now she had a chance at a real life, but this was not what she had bargained for. Mike promised her nice vacations, clothes, dinners in up-scale restaurants. She had no intention of playing nursemaid to his mother. The woman didn't like her from the very beginning.

She got up and stretched. It was too soon to concern herself with such things. Maybe Mother Dee. wouldn't ever recover enough to come home. He could always put her in a nursing home. But he would want only the best for his *precious mother* and that would cost a lot of money. She bounced her fists on the windowsill. She would figure something out, kill the old lady with kindness. For now, she would go shopping. She opened a pack of cigarettes, lit one, and took a deep drag. As the nicotine entered her blood stream, she felt instant gratification. She took another drag and another as she walked to the car.

* * *

Emma sat curled up on the couch, so engrossed in what she was reading, that she didn't hear Nate come in.

"Is that a new mystery that has your rapt attention?" he asked walking toward her.

"Oh, I didn't hear you." Her eyes never left the page. "It's a book titled *Stroke,* that I got from the library."

"Why, are you planning on having one?" he asked suppressing a smile.

She turned to him. "Don't be ridiculous. I'm thinking of Dee." Then she spotted the bag with the hardware store logo. "What did you buy now?"

"Wait until you see this." His enthusiasm was almost contagious.

Emma knew how he loved to browse through all the useless gadgets that filled the shelves.

She had a drawer full.

He took her hand and led her into the kitchen. "Just get a look at this." He put the bag on the counter and pulled out what looked like a wine bottle opener.

"But we already have at least two wine bottle openers," she said cocking her head.

"Aha, but not like this one. This actually re-corks the bottle after you open it." He preened.

"Doesn't the cork swell when you pull it out of the bottle?" Emma asked.

"It does. And this gadget forces it back into the neck keeping the remaining wine air tight."

Emma didn't see how it could be air tight after it had been opened, but she chose not to mention that fact. "What about that lovely cut glass stopper you bought last month?"

He frowned. "We can use it when company comes over. Now I'm going to try this out."

"You do that and I'll go back to my book." Emma knew from experience that she would rather not be in the room when he tried out something new. She sat back on the couch, picked up her book and resumed reading.

It wasn't long before she heard some grunting sounds followed by a few expletives. She snickered but refrained from investigating. Soon Nate stomped out of the kitchen, his fists clenched, a determined expression on his face, and walked into the study.

Emma put the book down and tip-toed into the kitchen. The wine bottle sat on the counter, the cut glass stopper protruding from the neck. She saw no sign of Nate's new purchase. Quietly she returned to the living room and picked up her book.

CHAPTER 7

L ATER THAT DAY AS THEY walked along the lakeshore, Nate asked, "Did that book answer all your questions?"

Emma shook her head. "It just raised more. The brain is very complicated and once it's injured all kinds of things can happen. Did you know that sometimes other areas of the brain can take over the functions of the injured part? It's amazing."

"Well, don't get too caught up in it, my dear." He snaked his arm around her trim waist. "There's nothing you can do about it." He hugged her close.

"Knowledge is power," she said planting a kiss on his cheek. He smirked and said nothing.

"I don't like the daughter-in-law," Emma said. "She appears solicitous, but something doesn't ring true about her."

"She didn't impress me much, either. But, Emma, please listen to me for once in your life." He stopped walking, took both her hands in his, and looked straight into her huge gray eyes. "You can't interfere in other people's lives. In the past your, so called, "sixth sense" has gotten you into all sorts of trouble. I want a nice quiet summer, understand?"

She blinked, pursed her lips, and took a deep breath. He was right, of course. Her meddling had almost cost her life, more than once. She would listen to Nate and only be supportive this time.

But you can't can you? Her inner voice asked.

Emma raised her chin, kept her eyes forward, and chose to ignore the voice this time.

* * *

When she next visited Dee, Emma was told that the patient was transferred to the rehab ward. She got the room number and directions to the proper elevator. She found the room empty and the bed neatly made with proper hospital corners. Emma noticed the sign above the bed instructing the staff to have Dee's stone in the pouch around her neck at all times. She smiled in satisfaction. At least she had done something helpful.

She walked out to the desk and saw the ward secretary hard at work. "Excuse me, can you tell me where I can find Delia Armanetti?"

The woman consulted a schedule. "She's in physical therapy right now."

"May I go there?" Emma asked innocently.

"Are you a relative?"

She hesitated, hated to lie, then blurted out, "I'm her cousin."

The woman gave her a dubious look then directed her to the therapy departments.

Emma took the designated elevator crowded with wheelchairs and visitors. She scrunched into a corner and got off in the basement and pushed open the door to the room marked **Physical Therapy**. The department was extremely large and appeared to be well staffed. In one corner a woman lay on an examining table exercising her knee; a man was slowly pedaled a stationary bike, grimacing in pain; others were walking with the assistance of a therapist. Each patient was carefully supervised.

"May I help you?' an older woman asked. Her name tag read Ellen Baxter, RPT. "I was looking for Delia Armanetti," Emma answered. "I'm her cousin."

"She's working in the parallel bars," Ellen Baxter said. "Please don't disturb her during therapy."

"I won't," Emma promised. "May I sit in this corner and observe?" She indicated a folding chair tucked in an out of the way spot.

"That will be all right. When she's finished, you can take her back to the ward if you will. We're a little short handed today and transport has been very slow."

"I'd be glad to." Emma smiled and sat unobserved on the chair. Her heart ached as she watched Dee trying to walk. The last time she had talked with

Mike, a few days previously, he said she had regained some use of her right leg but the muscles were still very weak. The woman she watched bore no comparison to the robust, self assured singer that Emma knew. Her frame appeared shrunken, as if the weight had melted from her body; her head hung down.

"Look up, Delia," the therapist instructed. She gripped a security belt around Dee's waist for support. "That's it. Hold on to the bar with your left hand and move your feet."

Dee took a mincing step with her left foot and dragged the other behind her. Emma noticed a plastic brace on her right lower leg sliding into the orthopedic shoe she wore. Her right knee buckled.

"No, no!" the therapist scolded. "Hold yourself up."

An assistant walked behind the patient pushing a wheelchair. The therapist signaled to her and they eased Dee into the chair. Tears streamed down her cheeks and she moaned pitifully.

"Don't cry," the therapist said. "You did much better this afternoon than you did this morning. You're making progress."

Dee simply moved her head from side to side.

"We'll send you back to your room and see you tomorrow."

Emma rose from the chair and walked toward them. "I'll take her. I've come to visit."

At the sound of Emma's voice, Dee perked up. "Ma—Ma—Ma," she said reaching out with her left hand.

"You certainly got a rise out of her," the therapist said.

"We're very close," Emma clasped her friend in her arms. "I'll take you back to your room, Dee, and we can visit."

"Ma—Ma—Ma," Dee said, nodding.

"Thanks," the therapist said. "This is the first time I've seen any response from her."

"I'll try and motivate her," Emma said directing the wheelchair out of the room and toward the bank of elevators.

By the time Emma got to the nurses' station, Dee was listing precariously to the side. Even though she was strapped in, Emma feared she might fall.

"We'll get her back to bed," the nursing assistant said taking the chair. Emma breathed a sigh of relief to hand over her burden.

"Come on, Mrs. Armanetti, you have company waiting for you." The woman motioned for a male attendant and pushed Dee into her room.

Emma wondered who the company might be and whether she should leave. But her curiosity got the better of her and she followed them into the room. She took a step back as she saw June Armanetti pacing back and forth before the window. She turned abruptly at the sound of the wheelchair and the voices. Again she was dressed in a skirt much too short for a woman of her age and a sweater so tight that Emma wondered how she fit it over her head.

"Uh, uh, uh," Dee moaned.

"Here's your daughter-in-law," the aide said.

"Ah!" Dee shouted and slammed her left hand on the arm of the wheelchair.

June frowned when she spotted Emma.

"What are you doing here?" she asked, none too politely.

Emma forced a smile. "I just stopped by for a brief visit."

After Dee was settled in bed, June approached her and said, "Look what I brought for you, Mother D, a CD player and some of your favorite songs."

Dee's eyes brightened. "*Antac, antac,*" she said reaching for the pile of discs and knocking them to the floor.

"Look what you did," June reprimanded her. "You're so clumsy!"

Emma quickly picked up the discs. "She didn't mean to. Her coordination is still poor."

June scowled. "What the hell is she saying anyway?"

Emma shrugged then turned to Dee. "What would you like to listen to? How about the one you made singing famous mezzo arias."

"Atnac, atnac," Dee said again, a crooked smile crossing her face.

"How considerate of your daughter-in-law to bring these." Emma found the disc and slid it into the player.

The first aria was from *Samson and Delila,* one of Emma's favorites. When Dee heard her own voice singing, she began to hum along.

Emma looked at June. "This is wonderful," she said.

The other woman frowned. "Not my kind of music." She sat in a straight-backed chair and began tapping her foot impatiently and cracking her knuckles.

Emma cringed. She hated that sound.

Before long Dee began to nod and was soon asleep.

"Turn that damned thing off," June said, reaching for the machine with her red talons.

Those nails reminded Emma of a predator, ready to pounce on its unsuspecting prey.

"Why don't we simply turn the volume down," Emma suggested. "The familiar music may help relax her."

June got up, and began walking toward the door. Emma adjusted the volume and followed. As the two women waited for the elevator, Emma's inner voice said, *Invite her for coffee.*

Emma frowned momentarily then blurted out, "How about a cup of coffee? There's a shop in the lobby."

June gave Emma a surprised look, then shrugged. "Why not?"

Guardian Angel, why did you do that?

The more you know about her, the more prepared you will be. Prepared for what? Emma wondered.

When the crowded elevator stopped at the first floor, they made their way to the coffee shop.

Neither one had said a word. They chose a table near a window away from others and each ordered only coffee.

"How about a pastry?" Emma asked.

"Oh no, I must watch my figure. I'm an actor, you know." She preened.

"I didn't know that." Emma exaggerated her surprise. "I'm certainly impressed."

"It's only community theater, but one never knows who might be sitting in the audience." Her voice took on a haughty tone.

"True," Emma said taking a sip of the hot beverage. She glanced at the woman's mouth and watched her bite her lower lip, again accentuated with liner. Not much theatrical potential there, she thought.

"My mother-in-law hates me," June whispered.

"Oh no," Emma said. "She hasn't had a chance to get to know you yet."

June shook her head. "She liked Mike's first wife because she was Italian." She spat the words out with venom.

"Give her some time," Emma said.

June shook her head. "It'll never work. Now Mike wants her to come and live with us—that woman in my house."

"It's much too soon to think about that. Dee is just beginning to use her right leg. Who knows, in time she may regain everything she lost and be able to live independently." Emma tried to sound upbeat but doubted her own words.

"I wish," June said. Then her expression changed. "Why am I telling you all this? I don't even know you." A deep furrow appeared between her almost colorless eyes.

"I'm a good listener," Emma said.

"Hmm." June took a swallow of coffee. "I wish I could smoke in here. I need a cigarette right now and I think I'm getting a migraine. I get them once in a while, you know."

"No, I didn't know. Do you take anything for them?" Emma asked.

"Sometimes I have to go to the emergency room they get so bad. The doctors say I am a very unusual case. They might even write about me in a medical journal." She appeared to be bragging about her condition.

Emma wasn't impressed. There's something not quite right there, she thought.

June closed her eyes momentarily and put her hand against her head. Then she brightened a bit.

"You know, there are these great places I read about called adult day care centers. I'd drop off Mother D in the morning and pick her up again in the evening. Real convenient." She bit down harder on her lip. "Then Mike can get somebody to come in on the weekends and I'll be free as a bird."

She has it all figured out, Emma thought gritting her teeth. It took a lot of effort to keep her face expressionless. I'd better change the subject before I say something I might regret.

"I really like your hairstyle. It complements the shape of your face." Emma didn't believe that, but it sounded like the right thing to say at the time.

"You think so?" She fluffed the left side with a hand sporting a huge emerald ring. "I can give you the name of my stylist. She could do *wonders* with your hair."

Emma ignored the sarcasm in her voice and managed to plaster a smile on her face. "I'm sure she could."

June looked down at an ornate watch. "Oh goodness. I'm gonna be late for rehearsal. Gotta go. I'm sure I'll see you again." She slid off the chair, gave Emma a nod, and walked quickly away, clicking her heels and swinging her hips.

Emma let out the breath she had been holding.

That woman is going to be trouble, her inner voice said.

Oh Guardian Angel, show me how to protect my friend.

CHAPTER 8

SOMETHING ABOUT THE WAY JUNE had referred to dropping Dee off at a day care center bothered Emma. She had sounded so flippant about it.

"Nate," Emma called from the atrium. She was on her hands and knees busily tending to her tomato and herb seedlings prior to putting them on the roof garden, but that wouldn't happen until the weather was more settled. The sun shining through the atrium windows was deceiving. She would continue to pamper her tender seedlings for the next few weeks.

"Do you need help?" he asked.

She examined him with approval. Working out every day had certainly toned him up—no more paunch.

"You look great," she said.

"You didn't call me out here to tell me that, did you?" He tightened his biceps and assumed a body builder's pose.

"No, I didn't. Now you can stop showing off." She sat back on her heels and slipped off her gardening gloves. "Did you ever hear of an adult day care center?"

His brow furrowed as he thought about it. "Can't say that I have. Why do you ask?" She told him about her conversation with June the previous day.

He let out a breath and shook his head. "I can see trouble in that marriage if Dee moves in with them. No new bride wants to take care of a debilitated woman."

Emma stood up and put her hands on her hips.

"How do you know Dee will be debilitated? You're jumping to conclusions, just like June. In time, she may regain all, or most, of her abilities," Nate said.

She pursed her lips, lifted her chin, and frowned.

He took her hands in his. "Only time and the proper therapy will tell." He paused for a moment. "Sparrow, stop worrying about it. You have no control over what happens in other people's lives. How many times do I have to tell you that?" He heaved a sigh of frustration.

She puffed out her cheeks. "I think I'll call Bertie and ask her about these centers. She should know."

When she placed the call, her daughter-in-law's cheery voice came on the line. "Good morning, Emma. Isn't it a lovely day?"

"You sound chipper," Emma said, smiling.

"Robin finally cut that molar and is sleeping through the night again. I feel rejuvenated."

"That'll do it." Emma remembered the sleepless nights when her children were teething. She had felt like a zombie for days.

"I must tell you what Robin did yesterday," Bertie said, a note of excitement in her voice. "I was looking for the small daily planner that I keep in my purse. I remembered writing an appointment in it but forgot where I put it. I'm absolutely lost without that thing."

Emma felt a tingling up her spine. She knew what Bertie was going to say next.

"You know, that child came walking into the living room and handed it to me. Without my saying a single word, she seemed to know exactly what and where it was. Isn't that amazing?"

"Bertie," Emma hesitated a moment, "I did the same thing when I was a child. I think she has inherited my—abilities. My Grandma Lizzie had it, then me, and now, Robin. So don't let anything she does surprise you."

"Hmm," Bertie said. "It will be interesting raising a precocious child, quite a challenge."

"Yes it will be, especially for Martin. He used to think I was a witch." They both laughed. "Now I need to ask you something. What do you know about adult day care centers?"

"Why do you want to know?"

Again Emma repeated her discussion with June.

"Sounds like she's eager to get rid of Dee before they even know the outcome. Not a very caring woman."

"She isn't," Emma agreed.

"Most of the adult day care centers I visited were extremely well run, staffed by a registered nurse, a physical therapist and a recreational therapist, plus ancillary personnel. Of course, it all depends on funding. Some are for profit, others non-profit. The cost can be pretty high if the participant needs special treatment. I was impressed by the ingenuity of some of the staff members in keeping the participants stimulated."

Emma breathed a sigh of relief. "So they're not just places to 'dump off' someone to get them out of the way."

"Absolutely not! There are guidelines they have to follow, and, I believe, most are licensed by the state."

"That does relieve my mind," Emma said. "Thanks, my dear. You're a fount of information."

As Emma pondered what she had learned, she realized that Dee would probably be better off in a place like that, if the necessity arose. She went back into the atrium and continued to tend to her plants while Nate went downstairs to pick up the mail.

* * *

"Emma," Nate called as he walked in the door. "Have you decided about our trip to Florida?"

Oh dear, Emma thought. I forgot all about it, Nate's brother's sixtieth birthday celebration. She knew he really wanted to go and she should be with him, but her concern for Dee had driven the trip right out of her mind.

She smiled as he took her in his arms and planted a kiss on her neck. That always sent goose bumps down her arms.

"Of course we must go. He's your only brother and sixty is a milestone."

"Good. I was afraid you might balk because of Dee."

"No." With hesitation, she said, "Our friend is in good hands and there's nothing I can do."

He breathed a sigh of relief. "At last, a sensible observation. I do believe you're beginning to realize that you can't help everyone." He turned toward the study. "I'll go online and order the plane tickets."

Emma walked into the atrium. *Oh Guardian Angel, I pray that nothing will happen to Dee while I'm gone. It's only for a week.*

There was no reply from Emma's inner voice. She always found that disturbing.

* * *

Emma arranged for their next-door neighbor, Claude, to care for her plants while they were gone. He was a fastidious man and relished the responsibility.

When she visited Dee and told her she would be gone for a week, the woman had cried and carried on so, that Emma wanted to cancel. But she couldn't disappoint Nate.

She called all her children and gave them the phone number in case any emergency should arise.

"We're only going to be gone a week," Nate said as he packed a suitcase.

"I know, but unforeseen things happen. Remember last year when we were in the UK and Susan was injured in that auto accident? We had to make a quick trip back."

"Don't remind me." He shut the case with a loud click. "Are you packed? You don't need all that stuff, you know. We're not going to any remote area. They do have washers and dryers in Naples, Florida."

"All right." She removed a few items and closed her suitcase. "Oh, I forgot my hairbrush." She hurried into the bathroom and returned with the item.

"Why are you snickering?"

He shook his head and ran his hands through her hair. "No matter what you do, my Sparrow, your hair always insists on doing its own thing."

"Maybe I should shave my head," she muttered as she shut the case for the second time.

Soon the limo arrived and they were on their way to O'Hare Airport. Emma vowed to leave all her concerns behind.

CHAPTER 9

"DR. ARMANETTI," MARGE, THE RECEPTIONIST called, peeking into the examining room.

"Yes?" He looked up from his work, a frown on his face.

"Sorry to bother you, but Animal Control is bringing in a severely injured dog. Said he was hit by a car."

"All right. Ask my assistant to come in here, now."

A muscular woman with small cat-green eyes, set a little too close together, entered the room. "You wanted me, Doctor?" Her voice was brusque. She stood with one hand on her hip.

"Yes, Frances, we have an emergency coming in. I won't know how serious until I examine the dog. Please take care of any animals waiting for injections. We may need to reschedule the others."

She nodded and walked out of the room. He finished removing the sutures from a cat that had required minor surgery, and smiled at the anxious owner.

"She should be fine, Mrs. Owens. If you notice any swelling or redness along the suture line, bring her back in."

"Thank you, Doctor. You have such a great way with animals." She bundled the cat in her arms and left.

Mike walked out into the waiting room wiping his hands on a paper towel. "Marge," he said to the receptionist, "please go next door and see if Dr. Espinosa might be able to help if this injury is really serious."

Marge hurried to the vet next door and returned just as two men carried in a large dog covered in blood. Only an occasional whimper indicated that he was alive.

"In here," Mike directed them.

"Dr. Espinoza will be right over," Marge said, averting her eyes from the injured animal. The waiting clients' expressions' mirrored their concern. One woman began to cry.

After a cursory examination, Mike determined he would have to do major surgery in an attempt to save the animal's life, but he didn't hold out much hope.

"Why don't you just put him down?" Frances said, as she roughly washed away the blood. "Be careful there," Mike said. "Gently. I'm going to talk to the owner."

Marge escorted a near hysterical woman into one of the examining rooms. "Doctor, can you save my Samson? I recently lost my husband and my dog is all I have." She held her hands together in an attitude of supplication.

"I'll do my best. The vet from next door will assist me. We'll keep you informed of our progress, but I can't give you any guarantees. He's lost a lot of blood."

She lowered her eyes and let out a deep sigh that sounded more like a moan. "I understand. Thank you."

Mike turned to his receptionist. "Marge, can you make a cup of tea for this lady and reschedule all the other patients except for those that Frances can attend to."

"Yes, sir." She left the room as Mike went back to the mangled animal.

As the two doctors worked with precision and patience over the dog, Marge rescheduled those who needed the vet's care, then she attempted to console the distraught owner. She had been with the Mike since he opened the clinic. There was nothing she wouldn't do for him.

At that moment June Armanetti walked into the office and insisted on seeing her husband immediately.

"I'm sorry, Mrs. Armanetti, but he's operating right now," Marge responded.

"Well how long will it take?" June demanded, tapping her foot.

"I have no idea. The dog is badly injured."

"Huh, an animal is more important than his own wife," she muttered and stamped out of the office.

The few clients who remained showed their distaste by shaking of heads and frowning. They held their own pets closer and stroked them lovingly.

* * *

While Frances gave the routine care of vaccinations, nail clippings and ear cleaning, Marge sat with the distraught owner of the injured dog.

"Is there anyone I can call to be with you?" she asked.

The woman shook her head and wiped away a tear. "My daughter lives in Seattle, and, as I told the doctor, I'm a widow." She whispered the last words.

"How about friends?"

"I don't want to bother anyone." She took a deep breath, leaned her head back, and closed her eyes.

Marge took her hand. "Come with me."

She led the woman into a lounge the employees used for breaks. It held a small refrigerator, a coffee machine, and a couch.

"Lie down and rest. I'll let you know how things are progressing."

The woman smiled gratefully, then did as she was told, too shocked and hurt to protest.

Marge tucked a pillow under her head and covered her with a light blanket. She pulled the door closed as she left the room.

Frances stood there, her arms folded across her chest. "What if I want to get a cup of coffee or something from the fridge?"

"The poor woman is all alone. Can't you give her some consideration?" Marge frowned.

There was no love lost between the two of them.

"Oh my, little 'Nancy Nurse,' or is it 'Mother Teresa'?" Frances said with scorn.

Marge turned to her with clenched fists, her eyes wide. "You would never understand. Why are you even tending to animals? I know you don't like them." She stood her ground as Frances moved closer.

"Just stay away from me, you twit. I'm doing my job and getting paid. That's all I care about."

Marge pursed her lips and held back the words on the tip of her tongue. The ringing phone pulled her away.

* * *

Frances watched her with scorn. What a gutless wonder. She would scrub the floors if Doc asked her to. Bet she stays here as long as he does. Why not? Who would be interested in her anyway with that mousey hair and those thick glasses? If I cared, I would tell her to spruce up her wardrobe, get her hair styled and some designer specs. But I don't care, about her or anyone else.

* * *

After four grueling hours, the vets had done all they could. The dog was alive but it was questionable whether he would survive. Mike thanked Dr. Espinoza and dragged himself into the lounge where the owner waited, sipping a cup of coffee.

"Doctor, how is Samson?" she asked, her eyes wide and imploring.

"Please, sit back." He sat next to her, grasping her hand. "We've stitched him up as best we could and gave him some blood and fluids. There was a lot of damage, but I think we managed to repair most of it."

"Oh, thank God," she said with relief.

"He's not out of the woods, yet. I'll stay with him tonight and we'll reevaluate his condition tomorrow. Now, I suggest you go home and get some rest." His reassuring smile seemed to put her at ease.

"May I—see him?"

"Certainly." He took her arm and led her to a large cage where the animal slept peacefully, an intravenous line sneaking out through the bandages.

"He's not in any pain, is he?" she asked stroking the large head.

"No. He's still under the effects of the anesthetic. I'll keep him sedated all night," Mike assured her.

She turned eyes bright with tears to him. "How can I thank you, Doctor? The people from Animal Control said they didn't think anything could be done."

"Don't thank me yet. He still may not survive. You must be prepared for that."

Even though the prognosis was not good, the way he said it seemed to ease her fear. She followed him out of the room. "You will call me if anything happens?"

"Absolutely."

After she left, Mike dropped into a chair, weary and exhausted. Then he noticed that Marge was still there. "Why didn't you lock up and go home?" he asked.

"I thought you might need me."

"Where's Frances? Gone I expect." He let out an exhausted breath.

"Oh yes. After she finished the injections, she took off. Said she had an appointment."

"Hmmm."

"I ordered some take out," Marge said. "I knew you wouldn't leave that dog."

"Marge, you're a jewel. Remind me to give you a raise."

She giggled. "You said that last week, Doctor."

"Did I?"

"Oh, by the way, your wife stopped in. Wants you to call her ASAP."

"All right. Go home, Marge, and enjoy your evening."

"You're sure you won't need me? I can stay."

"No, thank you. Go home."

After she left, he checked on Samson then nibbled on the Chinese food Marge had ordered for him. He didn't feel hungry but knew he had to eat something. The jangling of the phone made him jump. He decided to let the answering machine pick it up, but when he heard June's voice, he answered.

"Why are you still there?" she demanded.

"Sorry honey, but I just finished a four hour operation on a badly injured dog."

"Well, how soon can you get home?"

"I won't be coming home tonight. I can't leave this dog."

"What about that assistant, Frances. Isn't she supposed to do those things?"

"She's not skilled enough to care for a critically ill animal."

"Oh for God's sake, it's only a dog!" she shouted into the phone.

"June, this is my livelihood. Each patient is important to me or I wouldn't have gone into veterinary practice." He was too tired to argue with her.

"Tonight's the opening night of the play. Don't you want to see me onstage?" Now her voice took on a childish whine.

Oh hell, he thought. I forgot all about it. "I'm sorry but I won't be there. I'll see the next performance, I promise."

"It's not the same. Opening night is special."

"June, my practice is more important than your play. Now I must get back to my patient."

He shook his head as he stumbled back to the treatment room. Did I make a mistake in marrying June? She's a high maintenance woman. And now I have to care for my mother, too.

He checked the IV, the dog's breathing and heart rate and decided the animal was stable.

Only then did he sit down in a chair to wait out the night.

CHAPTER 10

EMMA CLUTCHED NATE'S HAND AS the plane touched down with a lurch then bounced a couple of times.

"Easy, Sparrow. That landing was a little rough, but we're on the ground now, so relax."

"I don't like it when the plane bounces like that." She let out the breath she was holding.

He gave her a hug and, as they arrived at the gate, stood up to retrieve their carry-on luggage from the overhead compartment. Since most of the airlines began charging for checked luggage, he decided they would travel light.

As they left the secure area, Nate's brother, Sol, called out to him. "Over here, Nate."

"Come on, Emma, there they are."

The brothers shook hands then embraced patting each other on the back, while Emma hugged Sol's wife, Rachel.

"You two don't come down here often enough," she scolded. "You could be spending the cold winter months here in the Florida sunshine—the men golfing and fishing, and you and I swimming and gossiping." She poked Emma in the ribs and laughed.

Emma smiled. What woman didn't like to gossip? But a steady diet of Rachel was more than she could handle.

"One problem is that we're involved with the opera during the winter," she explained.

Rachel waved her hands. "In retirement you should relax and enjoy life. Who knows how long we have left?"

If she only knew how many scrapes I've been in during the past few years, Emma thought. But she wasn't about to share them with this nosey woman.

When they reached the house and stored their belongings, Sol took Nate out into the backyard to look at the new barbecue pit while Rachel showed Emma around the spacious house. The living room resembled a model home: a flowered patterned couch with a chair to match, throw pillows in green and yellow, a glass topped table with a vase of fresh flowers in the center, prints strategically hung on the walls. The room was lovely, but sterile.

"I know what you're thinking," Rachel said. "It looks like nobody lives here." She held up her hands in a supplicating gesture. "It's a house, not a home. When my children were young the furniture was lop-sided, toys all over the floor. I was always picking up after them and scolding. Now, I wish … " She left the sentence unfinished.

Emma felt uncomfortable, so she decided to ask about the son and daughter. "Do your children visit often?"

Rachel shook her head. "Our daughter, the business woman, refuses to settle down. She travels all over the world for some international Internet company. I don't know what she does, but she makes a lot of money. She doesn't want to settle down with a husband and a bunch of noisy kids."

As Rachel continued to complain about her daughter, Emma tuned her out. Her thoughts reverted to Dee. She had only been gone a few hours and, already, she worried about the woman, wanted to pick up a phone and call. I must stop this, she scolded herself. I owe it to Nate. Enjoy this week, that is, if Rachel ever stops talking.

"So what do you think about that?" Rachel asked.

Emma looked at her through glazed eyes and thought for a moment. "Whether we like it or not, I think we must let them live their own lives."

"Huh, that's what Sol says, but am I to have no grandchildren?"

Emma furrowed her brow. "I thought your son and his wife had a child."

Rachel shrugged. "Sara couldn't have any of her own. After five miscarriages, Abe said, no more. So—they adopted." She hesitated.

"There's nothing wrong with giving an unwanted child a loving home." Emma wondered why Rachel sounded disappointed.

"She's Chinese."

Help this woman accept this child even though she is different, Emma's inner voice said. "Rachel." Emma took her hand and gazed into her eyes. "Just because the little girl doesn't resemble her adoptive parents, has no bearing on how much she needs them and, how much they need her. They wanted a child to love and I'm sure it makes no difference to them."

Rachel looked out the window. "That's what Abe says, but it's hard for me."

Emma saw the pain in the woman's eyes. "Inside people are all the same. Someday, I hope we'll accept these differences as only superficial. Love the little girl. She needs her grandma."

Rachel forced a smile. "You're a wise woman. No wonder Nate loves you so much. Come on, let's get dinner started. Tell the boys to fire up the new pit. I got some lovely steaks."

* * *

The next day Nate was eager to see his son and grandchildren. They only lived a few miles away.

I wonder how Dee is doing, Emma pondered as she struggled with one of her earrings. I'll call later.

"Emma, we're ready to leave. What's taking you so long?" She heard the impatient tone in Nate's voice.

She hurried out and climbed into the car beside him. "Had trouble with my jewelry."

"You don't need to fuss down here. Remember, we're on vacation."

She rewarded him with a smile and a kiss on the chin.

When they arrived at Nate, Jr.'s house, Emma recognized the younger replica of his father waving to them.

"Nate, he looks just like you," she said.

"Yeah, poor guy. Alec resembles his mother but Ed got most of my genes."

"Why do you call him Ed?"

"I told you earlier. His middle name is Edward. It was too confusing having two Nates in the family and no kid appreciates being stuck with Jr. as his name, so—Ed." He gave Emma a look of annoyance.

She nodded. "Of course. I remember." But she had completely forgotten.

Emma pulled her thoughts back to the present. She had been thinking about Dee. Had to stop that. She smiled as she watched father and son shake hands and then embrace in a man hug. A trim, attractive blond woman hurried out of the house and kissed Nate.

"Emma," he called. "Come and meet my son and his wife."

Emma hurried toward them and clumsily tripped over a tree root as she walked toward the group. Nate reached out and grabbed her arm.

"That's one of her charms," he said with a twinkle in his eye. "She stumbles a lot."

"This is my son, Ed, and his lovely wife, Marsha, who never ages a day. Bottle that, my dear, and you'll make a fortune." He gave his daughter-in-law a hug and kiss on the cheek.

Emma greeted them graciously as Rachel and Sol came with more hugs and kisses. Two rambunctious boys ran from the swimming pool in a race to greet the guests.

"I won."

"No, you cheated. Started out before me. No fair."

"Hey, you two, cool it," Ed scolded. "Say hello to your grandpa and his friend, Emma."

"Hi Grandpa," the younger one said, wrapping his wet body around Nate's legs. "Tommy, you rascal. I swear, you've grown a foot since I last saw you." Nate tousled his blond curls.

He turned to the older boy, who resembled his father. "Billy, Tommy, I want you to meet Emma."

"Hello, boys." She extended her hands to them.

They hesitated for a moment, then took them and said "Hi."

"Are you like—our Grandma?" Billy asked.

"Sort of. You can call me Grandma Emma or just Emma, whichever you like."

They thought for a moment, then said together, "Okay." With that they waved to Sol and Rachel and ran back to the swimming pool.

Ed and Marsha's house was the antithesis of Rachel and Sol's.

"See?" Rachel said. "This is what a home is supposed to look like: clothes and books all over." She picked up a sneaker, then put it down again and let out a deep sigh.

Marsha and Emma exchanged glances, but said nothing.

"Did you bring your suits?" Marsha asked. "It's a perfect afternoon for a swim." They all agreed and quickly changed into swimwear.

While the others were changing, Emma quickly placed a call to the Armanetti home. "Hello," June's flat voice answered.

"Hi, this is Emma Winberry. I'm in Florida and wondered how Dee is doing."

"She's okay. I'm busy now and can't talk." With those words, she disconnected the call. Miserable woman, Emma thought angrily.

"Emma, where are you?" Nate called.

"Coming." She quickly slipped into her bathing suit and joined the others.

* * *

Later in the waning afternoon, as everyone relaxed by the pool, Tommy came up to Nate. "Grandpa, guess what."

Nate frowned. "Since I'm not a mind reader, you had better tell me."

"Dad's friend bought a sailboat—a huge one—and he's gonna take us sailing. Isn't that cool?"

Nate turned to Ed. "How big?"

"A forty-nine-footer," Ed answered raising his eyebrows.

"Whew, that's what I call a boat. I'd love to go aboard something like that. I always wanted to go on a real boat."

"My friend, Arthur, and his wife took courses in sailing and are ready to do some serious navigating on the ocean. He's promised to take me and the boys for a day's sail."

"Sounds great." Nate gazed at the ocean with a gleam in his eye. "Sol, remember when we went sailing on Lake Michigan with the Sullivans?"

"Sure do," his brother answered. "What were we, early twenties?"

Over a few beers, the brother reminisces about their early years together.

Emma watched his reaction. She wasn't keen on the idea of spending time on a boat where there was no land in sight, unless, it was a cruise ship. She joined the women who agreed that sailing was a guy thing. They passed a pleasant evening with girl talk. Emma made a real effort to be engaging. She could feel Nate's eyes on her. He walked up to her and handed her a drink.

"I've been watching you. Can you, at least, make an effort to join in the conversation?" A deep crease formed between his eyes.

"I'm so sorry, but I can't stop thinking about Dee." He puffed out his cheeks and walked away.

* * *

"By the end of the week, Emma was eager to get home. She had called the hospital twice and, each time, received the same answer.

"We can only give information to the immediate family."

She forced herself to become immersed in the conversation with Nate's family to his looks of approval.

* * *

As the plane took off on its way to Chicago's O'Hare airport, Emma watched the satisfied expression on Nate's face.

"Did you really enjoy yourself?' he asked.

"Oh, yes, after I pushed Dee to the back of my mind. Your family is delightful."

He laughed. "Even though Rachel talked your ear off?"

"I think she's a lonely woman who doesn't have many friends."

"She has acquaintances," he said, "but no friends like you and Gladys."

You must visit more often, her inner voice said. *Nate spends time with your family.*

Emma felt a pang of guilt. Every time in the past that Nate had suggested a trip, something intervened.

"You know, Nate, we have to go and see your family more often."

"Really? I didn't think you liked Florida."

"Well not in July, but we can certainly squeeze in a week or two in the winter months between operas."

"We'll do just that." He planted a kiss on her cheek, leaned back in his seat and smiled.

CHAPTER 11

A S SOON AS EMMA AND Nate entered the condo, she headed straight for the atrium to check on her plants. True to his word, their neighbor, Claude, had taken excellent care of her babies.

"I swear," Nate said, "plaster could be falling from the ceiling, but you would still run for your plants."

"Is plaster falling from the ceiling?" she asked walking into the living room.

"No, but there are six messages on the answering machine."

"Hmm." She scrunched her nose at him and depressed the play button. The first two were hang ups. The third was from Sylvia reminding them of a cook out the following weekend.

Emma listened intently to the fourth message.

"Mrs. Winberry, this is Mike Armanetti. I'm concerned about my mother's slow progress. Please call me at your earliest convenience."

Emma frowned. Why would he call her? She had never met the man, but he did know that she and Dee were good friends and she had left her number with his receptionist.

The other two messages were pleas for money. Emma turned to Nate. "Did you hear that call from Dee's son?"

"I heard. What does he expect you to do?" His voice reflected his annoyance.

"Haven't the foggiest." She shrugged her shoulders. "Let's get unpacked, then I'll go next door and tell Claude that we're back and thank him for taking care of my plants." She let out a breath. "Then, I'll call Mike Armanetti."

* * *

By the time Emma got around to calling Mike, it was eight o'clock and she wondered if he would still be at the veterinary clinic. She punched in the number and got a recorded message saying that the clinic was closed and giving an emergency number.

Next Emma called his home. "Hello," a woman answered.

"This is Emma Winberry calling. I received a message from Dr. Armanetti. Is he at home?"

"Oh, this is his wife. I remember you." Her voice was flat and without any inflection.

"How are you?" Emma wasn't in the mood to make small talk with June but didn't want to sound rude.

"I'm okay," she replied.

"Is Dr. Armanetti in?" Emma repeated.

A sigh. "I'll get him."

Obnoxious woman. What did he ever see in her? Her seductive hips, I suppose.

"Mrs. Winberry, I'm so glad you called." Mike sounded breathless.

"I would have called sooner but was out of town. What's going on with your mother?"

"She's not cooperating with the therapists." He blew out a breath. "I've spoken to her numerous times, but she's being stubborn. Keeps talking gibberish. No one can understand what she's trying to say."

"Is she working with the speech therapist?" Emma asked.

"Oh yes. The woman is patience personified, but Mom isn't responding as she should." He stopped for a moment. "They're suggesting permanent nursing home placement." His voice dropped to almost a whisper.

"Oh no!" Emma said. "I'll go there tomorrow and talk with her. She's always responded to me."

"That's why I called you. I do have power of attorney, since my mother is unable to communicate her wishes. I gave the hospital administrator your name as a person they can share information with."

"I'll do all I can to help," Emma said, feeling a burden placed on her shoulders.

"Thanks. I really appreciate it. Let me know if you make any headway."

"I will. Bye."

"Now what are you getting yourself into?" Nate asked, his brows furrowed, his hands on his hips.

"I'm simply trying to help a friend. I wouldn't call that 'getting into' anything. Dee's not cooperating with the therapy and I'm going to see if she'll listen to me." She pursed her lips and lifted her chin.

"If the professionals can't do anything with her, what makes you think you can?"

"I can try. She's cooperated with me in the past. Maybe she will again."

* * *

The following day Emma walked into the rehab center with feelings of trepidation. Would Dee listen to her? Was she going downhill? Had she given up hope? No! Emma didn't believe that. The Delia she knew was a strong determined woman and that person was still there—locked within—somewhere. If Emma could only reach her.

As she approached the nurses' station, Emma saw June Aramantti talking with a woman wearing street clothes. The social worker perhaps? She stood far back enough so as not to be noticed but was able to catch a few words of their conversation.

" ... not cooperating ... certain requirements that must be met ... "

June shook her head and said something inaudible followed by, "nursing home."

That was all Emma had to hear. With determination, she walked into Dee's room. The woman lying in the bed was a shadow of the robust singer Emma knew. Her hair was disheveled, remnants of food dribbled down her chin.

"Dee," Emma said, grasping her friend's hand. "It's Emma."

The eyes opened a sliver, then wider. "Ma—Ma," she whispered.

"Yes, I'm here." Dee gripped Emma's hand with a strength that belied her appearance. Tears streamed down the dejected face.

Emma searched for the box of tissues but found it empty. She frowned and groped in her purse for one. She dabbed at Dee's face and, when the tissue was soaked with tears, wiped the food from her chin.

"Now, let go of my hand so that I can comb your hair. It's a little messy."

Dee let go of Emma's hand but clung to her arm. With some difficulty, Emma opened the drawer to the bedside table and found the hairbrush. She extracted herself from Dee's grasp and tackled her hair. From the looks of it, no one had bothered for quite some time. Emma was becoming upset with the care her friend was receiving.

"There, that's better," she said brushing the last strands from Dee's face.

"What are you doing here?" an unfriendly voice asked.

Emma knew immediately who it was, but turned slowly and smiled. "Visiting my dear friend."

"Oh, that's right. Mike called you," June said approaching the bed, her tone softening. Dee waved her hand at her daughter-in-law in a dismissive gesture.

"Now Mother D, you know I always try to help you," June said in a condescending manner. She grasped the bedrail with her red claw-like nails.

I can see that, Emma thought.

"She let you brush her hair," June said. "Won't let me touch her."

She bent her head close to Dee. "You know, Mother dear, if you don't start making some progress pretty soon, this place will boot you out. Understand?" She turned and waved at both women. "Bye now." Then she walked out of the room, cracking her knuckles and clicking her heels on the tile floor.

"Miserable woman," Emma muttered. She sat forward and turned Dee's face toward her. "Don't pay any attention to her. I'm going to help you work hard."

Dee didn't acknowledge whether or not she comprehended Emma's words.

Emma look around for the CD player and found it sitting on a small table on the far side of the room. A lot of good it did over there. She got up from the chair and walked over to the player.

"Ma," Dee called out in alarm.

"I'm not going anywhere." Emma retrieved the player, placed it on the bedside table, and searched for an electric outlet. "You need your music," she said, reaching down and plugging in the player. "Now, where did they put the CDs? I swear, there's no organization in this place."

"What are you looking for?" an aide asked, pushing in a wheelchair. "I was looking for the CDs for this player," Emma answered.

"Her daughter-in-law took them home. Said she didn't need them." The woman shrugged then turned her attention to her patient. "Hi Delia, it's time for physical therapy. How about showing your friend how well you're doing."

Emma turned to the woman, puzzled. "I thought she was regressing. That's what her son said."

"It all depends on who's working with her. Some folks around here," she lowered her voice, "especially the one who just left, don't seem to want her to improve." She gave Emma a conspiratorial wink then addressed Dee.

"How about it, Delia. Let's do a nice transfer for this lady." Dee gazed at Emma with a half smile.

"Can I help?" Emma asked.

"No. She has to do it with minimal assist."

Emma watched as the assistant helped Dee sit on the side of the bed, put the brace on her right leg, then her shoes. She secured a safety belt around Dee's waist. Emma was ready to spring into action, but saw it wasn't necessary.

"Now grab the arm of the chair with your left hand," the assistant instructed, "put your weight on your left leg, and there we go."

Taking most of Dee's weight with the belt, she eased her into the chair, strapped her in, and put her feet onto the foot rests. "Much better than yesterday."

Dee looked at Emma.

"That was great! I'm proud of you." Emma swallowed the lump in her throat. "May I go with her to therapy?" she asked.

"Sure. Come along."

* * *

When Emma returned home, she found Nate chopping vegetables. He smiled at her. "Thought I'd surprise you and make a stir fry. I *can* cook, you know."

She threw her arms around his neck and kissed him soundly. "You are a dear."

"Watch the knife," he warned laying it out of reach. "Your enthusiasm may get you stabbed, my love." He sat down on a kitchen chair and pulled her onto his lap. "Now, tell me about Dee."

"All she needs is understanding and encouragement. She's walking in the parallel bars, with some difficulty of course, but there is movement returning to her right leg. The therapist said that's a good sign. She's sometimes difficult to work with, but definitely has potential."

"So what's this talk about a nursing home?" Nate asked running his hand gently down Emma's back.

"Umm. That's nice." She nuzzled up to him for a moment then pulled away. "If you ask me it's all a ploy by her daughter-in-law to get her out of the way. She even took away the CDs and put the player out of reach."

She screwed up her face. "I wonder if the good vet realizes who is undermining his mother's progress."

CHAPTER 12

JUNE ARMANETTI PACED FROM ONE end of the huge living room to the other, absently stroking the expensive furnishings. She recalled her talk with the social worker. The woman told her that it was too soon to consider permanent placement, but nursing home was sounding better and better. The ringing phone irritated her. She didn't want to talk with anyone right now.

"Hello," she said, grabbing the instrument.

"Mrs. Armanetti?"

"Yes, who is this?"

"Frances Pullman, your husband's assistant."

"Oh? What do you want?" Why is *she* calling me? June wondered. She was irritated but, curious.

"I thought you and I might go out for lunch. There's something I need to discuss with you, something very important." Her voice sounded friendly enough but there was a threatening tone to it.

"Can't you tell me what it is over the phone? I don't have time for this."

"I don't think that's a good idea." Again, the menacing tone. "Better that we meet, say lunch on Saturday? It's my day off."

June didn't like this one bit. She didn't know France well, but, maybe, she should listen to what she had to say. Her gut told her something about this wasn't right, but, on the other hand, it might be nothing. "All right, but how about brunch. I have a performance in the evening and want to be rested. I'm an actor, you know."

"So I've heard. How about The Cozy Nook at eleven?"

"I suppose."

"And, Mrs. Armanetti, it's to the benefit of both of us that you be there."

"I will. Goodbye." What did the woman want? Worse yet, what did she know? Nothing.

Mike had said he was having trouble with her and was thinking of giving her notice. She probably wants me to put in a good word with him. Still, she felt uneasy about this meeting.

* * *

"Nate, I have a plan." Emma cozied up to him on the sofa.

"Oh, oh. When you act like this, I'm suspicious." He gazed at her, his eyebrows raised in a question.

"Just hear me out. If I go to therapy with Dee every day for, say a week or two, she may make better progress. She really responds to me." Emma gave him her most enticing expression.

"Let me get this straight. You want to spend two or three hours every day at the rehab center with Dee. Am I correct?" His face remained expressionless.

"Well, yes." She snuggled closer.

"And what, pray tell, am I supposed to do while you're gone?"

"You can work on your articles for the investment journal," she suggested.

"I could. Or, perhaps, I can get acquainted with that widow who just moved in on the second floor. Remember when she introduced herself to us? What was her name? Oh yes, Yvonne Simmons, right?" The sides of his mouth began to twitch.

Emma clearly remembered the middle-aged attractive woman who graciously introduced herself, eyeing Nate with apparent interest. She panicked and her eyes widened as she grasped his arm.

"Nate, you wouldn't, would you?"

He burst out laughing. "Oh Sparrow, don't be so gullible. I was just pulling your leg. I'm not interested in any other woman, understand?" He tweaked her nose, then gave her a kiss that reinforced his words. "You go ahead. I know that these initial weeks are critical. I'll behave myself."

"Nate, meeting you changed my life, in a way I never imagined."

He smoothed her unruly hair. "Never fear, my dear, you did the same for me."

* * *

June walked into The Cozy Nook and immediately spotted Frances Pullman seated at a private table in a corner. She approached cautiously trying to read the woman, but sensed nothing.

The smile that greeted June was obviously forced. Frances' eyes were almost slits in her face. Had June never noticed that before? Why should she since she had little contact with her.

They exchanged stiff greetings as she sat and the waitress poured her a cup of coffee. "Would you ladies care to order now?"

"Later," Frances said without taking her eyes from June's face. She sniffed. "You smell of smoke. Does the doc approve? You should quit, you know. It's bad for your health."

"Mind your own damn business. Now cut the crap. What do you want to see me about?"

Frances opened her purse and took out copies of a half-dozen newspaper clippings. She slid them across the table.

As soon as June saw them, she stiffened, feeling the blood drain from her face. Her pulse pounded at her temples and her breathing quickened.

"Where did you get these?" She tried desperately to control the panic in her voice.

"Does it matter?"

June felt herself deflate. "I suppose not."

"Does your husband know about your past?" Frances asked, her manner almost casual.

June said nothing, just sat there biting down on her non-existent lower lip and clenching and unclenching her fists.

"I'm sure you know that the Internet holds a wealth of information, if one knows where to look. I learned all about you. Changing your name and hair color was a pitiful attempt at hiding your true identity." Frances' face remained expressionless.

This frightened June more than anything else. "What do you want?"

"Now that's better, nice and business-like." Frances' voice became low and threatening. "I need $10,000."

"You must be out of your mind." June almost shouted the words.

Frances motioned with her hand to lower her voice. People at nearby tables were staring. "I didn't mean all at once. You can pay me in installments. And don't tell me your husband doesn't have the money. I know how much his practice brings in. Ten grand is nothing."

June seethed inside. How dare this woman threaten to destroy her life? If Mike knew about her past, he would divorce her, of that she was certain. And, she had signed a prenup. She would be left with almost nothing. She did have her private stash that Mike knew nothing about. He gave her a generous allowance and she had carefully saved some of it.

Right now, she saw no way out but to pay Frances. But, what was *she* hiding? Cunning bitch! Well, she could play this game, too.

"Do we have a deal?" Frances asked sipping her cold coffee.

"Do I have a choice?"

Frances laughed, an ugly, guttural sound.

"Yes, we have a deal," June said through gritted teeth. Her coffee cup sat untouched. She wanted to throw it at Frances but decided that would not be prudent. "I'll send you a check before the end of the week."

Frances shook her head. "No checks, cash only. Meet me here next Saturday, same time , with $500."

June could barely contain herself. She wanted to jump across the table and gouge the woman's eyes out, but thought better of it. What had the psychiatrist told her? Take deep breaths. See yourself in a peaceful place. At all times keep control of your emotions. She simply nodded.

"And one piece of advice," Frances continued. "Be good to the old lady. The doc dotes on his mother. Kill her with kindness."

How ironic, June thought.

Without another word, Frances slid out of the booth and walked away.

The waitress came up to June. "Did you wish to order now?"

"No, I'm not hungry." She paid for the coffee and stood up. Her legs felt like rubber. She grasped the edge of the table, took two deep breaths, and managed to walk outside. She sat in her car for a long time, smoking cigarette after cigarette, before she was calm enough to drive home.

CHAPTER 13

FOR THE NEXT WEEK, EMMA accompanied Dee to all her therapies, sitting at the side, observing. She saw the gratitude in her friend's face and it gave her a real sense of satisfaction. Dee seemed content to let her lucky stone hang around her neck without having to grasp it in her hand. Emma took that as a sign that the woman felt more confident.

In physical therapy Dee continued to improve, gaining some control over her right leg. Her walking grew steadier each day as she navigated the parallel bars. The therapist still walked with her, holding a safety belt around her waist.

"Very good," the therapist said. "Soon we'll try you with a quad cane."

Emma felt a lump in her throat as she watched Dee's triumphant smile. A little bit of the old determination showed through.

She was learning to feed herself with her left hand and assist with dressing. The only area where she made no progress was speech. Emma pushed the wheelchair into the therapy room.

"Good morning, Delia," Terry, the speech therapist, said. She was a motherly woman, slightly overweight, with graying hair, and a bright, cheerful demeanor.

When Dee's chair was positioned at the table, Terry brought out five square blocks. "Let's start out with counting today."

"One," the therapist said, pushing a block toward Dee.

She examined it, frowned, and appeared to be attempting to repeat the word. "OO," she said. Terry didn't seem daunted. "All right, let's try two."

Again Dee made the same facial expressions. She finally said, "OO—d."

Sue looked at Emma and shook her head. "I get these same responses every day." She sighed in frustration. "How about three." She pushed a third block toward Dee.

After an internal struggle, Dee said 'e-r', rolling the 'r.

"Just a minute," Emma said. An idea had suddenly come to her. She knew it was her Guardian Angel. "How about trying the numbers in Italian."

"I don't speak Italian," the therapist said.

"But I do," Emma replied. "Dee, listen. " She held up one block. "*Uno. U—no,* "Emma repeated drawing out the word.

Dee smiled. "OO," she said. "OO."

Very good," Emma said. "Let's try two. "*Due, du—e.*" Again she drew out the syllables. "OO—d, OO—d."

Emma frowned. This wasn't working.

"It's backwards," her inner voice said.

"Yes, that's it," Emma said clapping her hands together. "She's saying the words backwards." She turned to her friend. "Dee, say *due.*"

"OO—d, OO—d."

"Excellent," Emma praised her. She was excited now. They had made a breakthrough; a small one, but one that showed some progress. "Let's try three. *Tre, tre.*"

"E-r," Dee repeated, rolling the 'r'. "E-r."

"Very good, Delia," Terry said.

"Do you have a pad of paper and a felt tip pen?" Emma asked.

"Certainly." The therapist procured the requested items.

Emma printed in large letters, *UNO, DUE, TRE,* each beneath the other. The she lined up a number of blocks on the table. "All right, Dee, watch."

Emma pointed to the first word and said, *"Uno."*

Dee nodded and smiled, then picked up one block and put it next to the word.

"Due," Emma continued.

Dee placed two blocks alongside the word.

"Tre," Emma said.

Again Dee understood and placed three blocks in the appropriate spot. "*Brava*!" Emma said, clapping her hands. "Va—va—va," Dee joined in.

Terry smiled at Emma. "Mrs. Winberry, do you want a job here?"

Emma laughed. "I was a primary grade school teacher many years ago. Now I just want to hear my friend sing again."

"*Atanc, atanc*," Dee said enthusiastically.

The therapist turned to Emma, a question on her face. "She's saying, *canta*. That means sing in Italian."

"Ah, ah," Dee said rocking back and forth. Then she began to hum an operatic aria.

"I do believe that, thanks to you, Mrs. Winberry, we *have* made a breakthrough. Can you come again tomorrow?"

"Absolutely," Emma said. She gave Dee a hug. "I'll see you *domani.*"

Dee smiled and nodded.

* * *

As she lay in bed, Dee screwed up her face trying to make sense of what had happened to her.

Now Emma understands me. But why can't I say the words right? They sound right to me. I must try harder. Domani, domani-tomorrow. I must say it.

CHAPTER 14

EMMA OPENED THE DOOR TO the condo calling, "Nate, Nate, are you here?"

He walked calmly out of the bedroom. "I'm here. Where did you expect me to be?"

"I wasn't sure. Thought maybe you went for a walk or to the hardware store." She didn't mention the widow on the second floor, but noticed the grin spreading across his face.

"Come here." He took her in his arms and kissed her passionately. "I spent the time thinking up ways to drive you crazy in bed." He patted her backside and held her tight.

"You dear sweet man." She swallowed the lump in her throat.

"Come on," he said. "Let's have a cup of tea and you can tell me how things went." As she heated the water, Emma excitedly related the session with the speech therapist.

"Isn't it rather odd that she would verbalize words backwards?" he asked as he poured out two cups of boiling water and dropped a tea bag in each.

"The therapist said it happens. What confused her was that Dee was speaking in Italian."

"Uh huh. So that's where my little linguist came to the rescue." He reached over and caressed her cheek. "You really are a good woman, Sparrow."

Emma looked down as she spooned a half teaspoon of sugar into her tea. "Sometimes I seem to be in the right place at the right time, that's all." But she knew better.

"Why don't we go out to dinner tonight?" Nate suggested.

"Good idea. You know, that session was exhausting." She stifled a yawn. "I think I'll take a little rest after I finish my tea."

"You do that. Remember, you're not a young woman anymore."

Emma hated when he said that. Knew he did it on purpose. "I'll let it slide, this time," she said, but it was true and she should slow down a bit, but that wasn't her way.

CHAPTER 15

THE FOLLOWING DAY EMMA MADE her way to the rehab center with a lighter step. *Oh Guardian Angel, I feel that Dee has turned a corner and is on her way to recovery.*

Watch closely, her inner voice said. *She will need you more than ever in the coming months.*

Emma frowned. What was that supposed to mean?

As she approached Dee's room, she heard someone talking to her. Presuming it was the nurse, she knocked before entering. She was surprised to see June brushing Dee's hair and mumbling something.

"Oh, hello," Emma said.

June stiffened as she saw who it was, then a smile crossed her face as she nodded and continued to arrange Dee's hair with a red bow.

"Ma—Ma," Dee called pushing June away and reaching out to her friend.

Emma gave her a hug, then turned to the other woman. " I didn't mean to intrude, but I've been accompanying Dee to her therapies and she seems to be making real progress."

"Yes, so the nurse told me. I couldn't be happier. Doesn't she look nice?" June admired her handiwork.

Emma thought the bow seemed childish, but said nothing.

"I'm going to be here every day now," June said. "So you won't have to bother coming."

What was this sudden change? Immediately Emma became suspicious. "That's great, but the speech therapist asked me to come because Dee is beginning to verbalize in Italian and I speak the language. Do you?" Emma couldn't refrain from a bit of sarcasm.

"No, I don't," June answered, gritting her teeth. "I'll tell you what. I'll go to the other therapies and you can take speech. How's that?"

"Fine," Emma said. This woman had a hidden agenda. She felt it. Why this sudden change of heart? She had better heed her Guardian Angel's advice.

* * *

When Emma returned home and told Nate about June's sudden change in her demeanor, he examined her critically.

"If I didn't know better, I would think you're jealous. You're not, are you?"

"Of course not. If Dee's daughter-in-law has decided to take part in her therapy, that's great. After all, she will be living with them when she's discharged." She frowned. "It just seems so sudden, that's all."

"Do you feel that you won't be needed anymore?' he persisted.

Emma thought for a moment. She did feel as though June was trying to shut her out. "The speech therapist wants me to continue working with her."

Nate took her in his arms and held her close. "My little Sparrow, always remember that I need you, too. Okay?"

She looked into his eyes, smiled, and nodded.

* * *

During the next two weeks, Dee made significant progress. She was able to walk with a quad cane and a brace on her right lower leg. Her arm, however, remained paralyzed. June was there every day just as she promised. Emma frequently saw her leaving as she came in for the speech sessions.

The therapist had begun Music Intonation Therapy and Dee's response was dramatic. As she heard the familiar tones of an Italian folk song played on the piano by one of the assistants, Dee began to sing. Her voice was soft and hesitant at first, but gained assurance and volume as she continued.

Emma listened at the doorway. Dee was verbalizing most of the words correctly and her voice was regaining its melodic tone.

"Isn't this great?" the therapist whispered to Emma. "She's doing much better than I expected. She still says her words backwards, but they are more complete and she is managing to make herself understood. Her self confidence is returning."

As Emma listened to her friend, she felt tears stinging the back of her eyes. "Do you think she will ever be able to speak normally?"

"I do. Today she said the word mass. I asked her if she wanted to go to church, but she shook her head. I printed out the word and she pointed to the letters SAM, her son's name."

"Yes," Emma said. "I believe he lives on the West Coast."

"Her older son said he has been traveling for work but he's on his way here to see his mother."

The woman took Emma's hand. "You have been invaluable in helping us communicate with this patient. We're having a staffing tomorrow to plan for her discharge home."

"That's wonderful," Emma said. "Will she have home therapy?"

"Probably. The daughter-in-law seems eager to take over as much as she can. We'll discuss everything with the family and set the wheels in motion. Now I think she's seen you and would like a visit."

Emma gave Dee a hug as the woman acknowledged her. "Ma—Ma— atnac—atnac."

"Yes, I heard you singing. It was lovely."

"You can take her back to her room if you like, Mrs. Winberry. We're finished for today."

As Emma wheeled Dee toward the elevator, she felt uneasy about the discharge. What would happen when she was left in June's care? Had she really changed in her attitude towards Dee? No, leopards can't change their spots. June has another agenda. But how can I remain involved when Dee's at home?

Guardian Angel, now what?

But there was no answer this time.

* * *

On Emma's next visit to the rehab center, she found Dee's room empty. Anxiously she hurried to the nurse's station.

"Excuse me," she said to the occupied ward secretary. "Delia Armanetti's room is empty. Has she been transferred?"

The woman blinked then pulled the name up on her computer. "She was discharged yesterday."

"Oh," Emma said, taken aback. "Can you tell me where she went?"

"Sorry, I don't have that information."

Emma turned away, disappointed and uncertain of her friend's fate. Can I call June? She wondered. Will she tell me anything or say mind your own business. The latter, most likely. She heaved a sigh and went back home.

You've done all you can for now, her inner voice said.

I suppose, Emma agreed with her Guardian Angel, but she wanted to be part of Dee's recovery. That was the real issue. She felt left out and she didn't trust June.

Wait—you will be needed.

CHAPTER 16

THE FOLLOWING WEEK EMMA CALLED the Armanetti home. After five rings, June answered. "Hello, this is Emma Winberry. Sorry to bother you at home, but I wanted to know how Delia is doing."

"Oh, it's you. She's fine. A therapist is here working with her now. I can't talk. Lots to do. She doesn't need your help anymore." With those words, she disconnected the call.

"You're making faces," Nate said. "I presume the lady June did not appreciate your call."

"That's putting it mildly. She was downright rude. Said Dee didn't need my help anymore."

"Uh huh."

"What's that supposed to mean?" Emma was annoyed at his complacency.

"It means, my dear, that she has her own plans and doesn't want you to interfere." That did not satisfy Emma at all. She wanted to be sure that Dee was all right.

Call her son, her inner voice said.

Good idea. Emma picked up the phone and punched in the clinic number. She was told that Dr. Armanetti was busy and couldn't talk with her at the present time.

"Can you ask him to call me back?" Emma said. "Is it about your pet?" the receptionist asked.

"No, I'm a friend of his mother. I called the house, but Mrs. Armanetti was busy and couldn't speak with me." Emma noticed a pause from the other end.

"Excuse my saying so, but you won't get much from that one. Give me your name and number and I'll have the doctor call when he has a break."

"Thank you so much." Emma gave her the requested information and replaced the phone on the charger. Now all she had to do was wait. But waiting was not her forte. She decided to bake a batch of muffins, even though she had a dozen in the freezer.

As she loaded the ingredients onto the counter, Nate came into the kitchen. "What's up?" he asked.

"I'm waiting for a phone call."

"What does that have to do with all this?" He indicated the items she had lined up. "I can't just sit and wait. I have to do something, so I'll bake some muffins."

"Do you intend to take them to the food pantry? We already have a freezer full as well as that pie you made yesterday."

"Oh Nate." She put her arms around his neck and leaned her head against his cheek, relishing the masculine smell of his aftershave, and told him about her call to the vet's office.

"You can't do any more than that. Now put all this stuff back and come into the living room. Let's watch that new movie we got from Netflix. Okay?"

"Okay."

Nate helped her put everything away, and, as they were walking into the living room, the phone rang.

Emma hurried over and grabbed the instrument. "Hello."

"Hi, Emma," a familiar voice said.

"Gladys, we haven't talked in ages." She settled in a corner of the sofa and prepared for a chat with her long time friend, Gladys Foster. The two had been friends since childhood and had remained close throughout the years.

"I know," Gladys said, her usually ebullient voice devoid of emotion.

"What's wrong?" Emma knew by her tone that there must be something bothering her friend.

Gladys hesitated, then blurted out, "Cornell wants a temporary separation. Said he needs some space."

Emma was speechless. Her friends had been happily married for ages. This couldn't be happening. It was unthinkable.

Holding her breath, she asked, "Why?"

"He isn't giving me any reason, just says he needs time to think and make some decisions."

Emma heard a sniffle. "That's nonsense." She hesitated for a moment, then asked, "Is there another woman?" She was afraid of the answer. Cornell was not the type, but still ...

"I asked him that and he said no, but I suspect there might be someone. He's been quiet and withdrawn lately."

For once in her life Emma had no words of wisdom or consolation to give. "What shall I do?" Gladys asked, sounding like a child seeking direction. There was so much pain in her friend's voice that Emma fought back tears.

Ask her to come to you, her inner voice said.

Good idea. She glanced at Nate who was watching her quizzically.

"Just a second, Gladys." She put her hand over the mouthpiece. "Nate, would you mind if Gladys came for a visit?"

"Of course not. She and Cornell are always welcome."

Emma held up a hand and turned back to the phone. "Why not come here for a while; give you both time to think things over."

"I don't know what good that will do," her friend answered, sobbing.

"Give it some thought and let me know."

"All right. I'll get back to you."

After terminating the call, Emma sat staring at the wall.

"I take it there's trouble in Paradise," Nate said, sitting down beside her. She told him what Gladys had said, shaking her head in the process.

"Cornell? That sure doesn't sound like him. Did he say why he wants a separation?"

"No."

Nate let out a breath and slowly shook his head. "I thought that was a solid marriage."

"So did I."

"Is Gladys coming?"

"She'll think about it."

Nate put his arms around her. "I know how close you and Gladys are, even though she lives far from here. I like her, too. I like them both." Before either one could say any more, the phone rang again.

Emma absently picked it up. "Hello."

"Mrs. Winberry? This is Mike Armanetti."

"Oh, I'm so glad you called. Sorry to bother you at the clinic, but I'm trying to get some information on your mother's progress. Your wife didn't have time to talk to me."

"Yes, she's really devoting herself to Mom. I couldn't be more pleased." Emma didn't believe that for a minute, but listened politely.

"Next week Mom will begin attending an adult day care center from Monday through Friday. That will relieve June of some of the burden."

"That sounds great. Where is it located?"

He gave Emma the name and address. "I thought you might want to visit her there, so I gave your name to the administrator. I told her how helpful you've been with Mom and her communication difficulties." He hesitated a moment. "Sorry, but I have clients waiting. Please stop by at the center when you have time. And, thanks for your concern."

Well," Nate said. "Where is what located?" He glanced at the name and address Emma has scribbled on the back of an envelope.

"An adult day care center. Dee will start going there next week."

Nate shrugged. "That sounds promising. She must be making progress."

"Yes!"

"You're making faces again," he said.

"At least she'll be away from June for most of the week. There's something that doesn't ring true about that woman. Her sudden devotion to Dee is suspicious. She certainly didn't show any of that in the hospital."

"Maybe she's had an Epiphany," Nate said holding out his arms.

Emma frowned. "And maybe she has something else planed. At least I'll be able to see Dee at that center. You don't mind, do you?"

"And if I did?"

"Oh Nate, don't tease."

He heaved a sigh. "Do what you must, my dear. I may even go with you." She threw her arms around his neck and kissed him hard.

"Nice," he whispered, holding her close. "Now what do you intend to do about Gladys?"

CHAPTER 17

E MMA WAITED A NUMBER OF days, but heard nothing further from Gladys. When she tried to call, all she got was the answering machine.

"No one there, again?" Nate asked.

Emma shook her head. "First she calls me for advice and now, nothing."

"Maybe the whole thing blew over and they're away on a second honeymoon," Nate suggested.

"She would have told me."

"All right," Nate said trying to placate her, "how about going to that day care center to see Dee."

"Oh Nate, really?" Emma immediately perked up.

"I know you're chomping at the bit, so comb your hair and let's go. And, on the way back, we can stop somewhere for dinner." He ran his hand over her unruly hair trying to smooth it down.

Emma hurried into the bathroom, vigorously brushed her stubborn locks, applied a little lipstick and decided that would do. On second thought, she changed into a colorful tunic top and a pair of beige slacks.

"I'm ready," she said prancing into the living room.

"Charming," Nate said. "Now where is this place?"

"The address, of course. Now where did I put that?" Emma began searching through pieces of paper stacked on the end table. Finally she found what she was looking for scribbled on the back of an envelope.

"Here it is."

Nate grimaced as he tried to decipher the words. "Can you please tell me what language you used to write this?"

Emma stared at the paper. "Um—it says—, I'm not sure." The name of the street was unreadable and she didn't remember what it was.

"Never mind. As long as I have the name of the place, I'll look it up on the Net."

"I'm sorry," Emma said trailing after him into the study.

Within minutes Nate had pulled up the site and written down the address and phone number. "Look, Emma, they have a virtual tour of the place. Pretty high end, if you ask me."

She watched as he maneuvered the mouse around the image. "I'm sure Mike Armanetti will insist on the best for his mother."

* * *

When Nate and Emma arrived at the address, they found a very modern one-story building, set on a large lot with a well-tended lawn and flower beds around the entrance. Picnic tables and a gazebo sat on one side of the property.

"Nice," Emma said alighting from the car.

Nate let out a whistle. "I'll bet this costs a bundle."

"Come on." Emma grabbed his hand and headed for the front door.

As they entered, a young woman greeted them. "Hello, may I help you?"

"I'm Emma Winberry and this is Nate Sandler. We wondered if we can visit with Delia Armanetti for a while."

"Oh yes. Delia's son told the administrator you might come. Since she's new here, a familiar face may make her more comfortable." She held out her hand. "I'm Sara Bolton, the activities director. The clients are all in the day room doing their exercises. It would be best if you wait until they're finished. Have a seat."

"Thank you," Emma said, taking the woman's dainty hand.

Sara directed them to a seating area near the door. "I'll tell Mrs. Carter, the director, that you're here." She bounded away toward an office.

"She's certainly bubbly," Nate said.

"I guess you have to be in a place like this."

Sara returned shortly. "Mrs. Carter would like to speak with you."

"Of course. Can Nate come along?" Emma asked.

"He'd better or one of these widows will be after him." She laughed, a pleasant, musical sound.

Nate frowned as he followed Emma into the office with Mrs. Carter's name on the door. A middle-aged woman, wearing designer glasses and a simple tailored suit, greeted them.

Emma recognized it as a Gucci design she had seen advertized at Nordstrom's, for an exorbitant price.

"How do you do." Mrs. Carter rose from behind her desk and shook both their hands as Sara introduced them. "I'm glad you're here. As Sara probably told you, the transition to a new place is sometimes stressful. With all the privacy rules, sharing information is limited. But her son, Dr Armanetti, listed your name as someone with whom we can discuss Delia's progress."

"I understand," Emma said, nodding.

Mrs. Carter rustled through a pile of folders and pulled out the one she sought. "It says here that she sang in the opera chorus." She looked at Emma for corroboration.

"Yes. Singing is her life. Nate and I are supernumeraries for the Midwest Opera and Dee has been a member of the chorus for a number of years. She has a lovely mezzo voice."

"As I'm sure you know, our biggest problem is communicating with her. According to this report from the speech therapist, she's trying to verbalize but the words come out backwards and in Italian."

"That's what she was doing in the hospital," Emma said.

"Unfortunately, no one here speaks Italian, so that does create a problem."

"I do," Emma said, then glanced at Nate to be greeted with a frozen stare. She ignored it and continued, "How often does the speech therapist come?"

"Twice a week."

"Perhaps I could come on those days and work with her. Would you allow that?" She felt Nate pinching her leg and pushed his hand away.

"That would be extremely helpful. You can come as a volunteer. We have a number of generous folks who spend time helping the staff," Mrs. Carter said with a relieved smile. "We must be able to communicate if we are to help these people. And, stroke patients can continue to improve for a long time, with the proper treatment."

"I'm sure that won't be a problem." She turned to Nate."Would you mind?" she asked sweetly.

He rolled his eyes. "Do what you have to do, my dear."

"I believe the exercise period is over, "Mrs. Carter said. She led them into a large multi- purpose room with chairs arranged in a circle.

Emma counted about a dozen participants, three men and the rest, women.

"All right everyone," Sara Bolton said to the group, we have visitors this afternoon, Delia's friends."

Dee looked up as she heard her name. Her eyes opened wide at the sight of Emma. "Ma—Ma," she said attempting to stand.

"Wait a minute," Sara said. "Let me help you."

With minimal assist, Dee rose from the chair, grasped her quad cane, and slowly walked over to Emma and Nate. A sling supported her right arm, but she had gained more control over her leg and her walk was steadier than when Emma had last seen her.

Emma waited until she was clear of the circle of chairs, then gave her friend a hug. "Ma—Ma," Dee said, her eyes filled with tears of joy.

Emma's heart broke as she felt the bony frame of the once robust woman. She had aged ten years in the last two months.

"You remember Nate, don't you, Dee?"

She struggled with the words, then blurted out, "*Tae, Tae.*"

'Hello, Delia, it's good to see you." He, too, gave her a hug.

"You came on a good day," Sara said. "The speech therapist will be here shortly and you can sit in on the session."

At that moment a tiny bird-like woman walked up to Emma and Nate. "Everyone must have a number," she said. "You are forty-five and forty-six." She pointed to each of them, then nodded in satisfaction.

"All right, Agnes, go along to the craft table," Sara said shaking her head. "She refuses to call anyone by name. She's assigned a number to each one of us and never forgets who's who." She laughed, again that musical sound.

"Are you a singer?" Emma asked.

"Why do you say that?"

"Your laugh is so musical."

"*Atnac—atnac,*" Dee said beginning to hum a song.

"We do have music therapy," Sara said, "and Delia is one of our stars, aren't you?"

Dee smiled and began to sing. The words were garbled, but Emma recognized the melody as an Italian folk song.

"Here comes Diane, the speech therapist," Sara said. "Let me introduce you."

"Diane, Emma and Nate are friends of Delia, and, Emma speaks Italian," Sara called out.

"Wonderful," the therapist said. "You're just what we need." She was young and shapely with blond hair and sparkling blue eyes in a heart shaped face.

Emma watched Nate's approving glance and felt a twinge of jealousy. She ignored it and spent the next hour with Dee and Diane. She noted there was little improvement in her word pronunciation.

"This is where our problem lies," Diane said. "But I think things will improve with your help. Will you be able to come twice a week for a while?"

"Yes, I certainly will."

Have some of Dee's friend from the chorus come to entertain, her inner voice said.

Good idea!

She turned to Diane. "What do you think about getting some of the chorus members together to, perhaps, put on a program for the clients?"

"Fantastic. I'll run it by Mrs. Carter, but I'm sure she'll approve. We may even invite the families to come." She gave Emma a grateful smile. "Mrs. Winberry, you are a jewel."

Emma felt her cheeks flush. "Not really and, please, call me Emma."

* * *

"What did you think?" Emma asked as they drove away from the center.

"Interesting place. While you were with the speech therapist, the number lady cornered me and showed me her art work. She had drawn a picture using only numbers connected to each other."

"Did it resemble anything recognizable?" Emma asked.

"Well, I've seen some abstract paintings that weren't as good. I asked Sara why the obsession with numbers. It seems the woman was a physicist before she was injured in an accident and sustained severe head trauma. That ended a brilliant career. Sad, isn't it?"

Emma watched a furrow form between his eyes and the edges of his lips turn downward. "We are so lucky," she said. "Every day is a gift and spending it with you makes it extra special."

"Let's not get maudlin," he said. "How about some dinner?"

"You're on."

CHAPTER 18

As JUNE DROVE TO HER meeting with Frances, she seethed at the audacity of the woman. How dare she threaten her. She gritted her teeth and relived her early years: an abusive father, an alcoholic mother, never enough to eat.

June and her sister had become adept at stealing what they wanted. It started with a candy bar, a bag of potato chips, then cigarettes. She smiled at the memory. They never got caught. Not until later …

Now she had to hand over $500 to Frances. But she knew it wouldn't end there. Her private stash would rapidly dwindle. Then what? She decided to confront Frances.

When they each had a cup of coffee, June said, "I don't know how long I can keep this up without my husband finding out."

Frances smiled, her eyes cruel and unyielding. "I'm sure you'll find a way. You can always pawn your jewelry, and I'll bet you have some nice rocks. You've got a good life. You don't want to jeopardize it, do you?"

June said nothing. She handed over the envelope and slid out of the booth. "See you next week," Frances said, giving her a two finger wave.

As June walked to the car, she pulled out a pack of cigarettes and began visualizing ways to dispose of Frances. It would have to appear accidental. I've done it before, she thought, but this time, I must be more cautious—almost got caught—can't afford that now—too much at stake.

CHAPTER 19

EMMA PUT DOWN THE PHONE and muttered something incomprehensible. "Now what?" Nate asked.

"Still no answer at Gladys' number."

"Like I said before, maybe they made up and went on a second honeymoon."

"No, Gladys would have called me." Emma was more than annoyed: she was beginning to worry.

Call her daughter, her inner voice said. "Why didn't I think of that?"

"Think of what? Sparrow, you really must stop talking to yourself like that. It confuses me."

"I was talking to my Guardian Angel."

"Oh, that explains everything." He held out his arms and gazed at the ceiling.

Emma ignored the note of sarcasm in his voice. "She told me to call Gladys' daughter."

"Great idea. Do you have the number?"

"It's in the address book in the top drawer in the kitchen."

"I'll get it," he said.

Emma grimaced as she heard a few choice swear words coming from the kitchen. She walked in to see Nate picking up scraps of paper from the floor.

"When are you going to organize this thing? How do you ever find anything?" He slapped the book and the papers on the table. "They're all yours."

Emma frowned and began riffling through everything discarding papers with unidentified numbers and saving the ones she needed. She heard Nate answer the phone but ignored it until he appeared in the doorway, instrument in hand.

"Gladys is on the phone."

Emma stared at him, her eyes wide with surprise.

"It's about time." She grabbed the phone and was about to chastise her friend, but Gladys started speaking first.

"Emma, I know you must be angry with me, but Tessa broke her arm and I went right over to help with the children."

Tessa was the oldest of Gladys' three daughters. "I'm so sorry, How did it happen?"

"She tripped over one of the kid's toys and landed on her right arm. I was so upset over everything that has been going on that I neglected to call you."

"Don't give it another thought," Emma said. "Family must come first." She hesitated a moment then asked, "And Cornell?"

"He came over to help, too, but nothing has changed. He's preoccupied all the time, as if he's struggling with something. He's so distant that I can't approach him. He won't even talk about it with the children. I almost don't know the man anymore." She took a breath and let it out slowly. "What am I going to do?"

"Have you considered coming here for a while?" Emma asked.

"Yes. Tessa thinks it's a good idea. Her husband is taking some vacation time, so, if it's all right with you, I'll be there next week."

"Absolutely. Nate and I both want you to come."

"Thanks, my friend. I'll let you know when I make my flight plans."

Emma sat, still staring at the papers strewn over the kitchen table.

Nate came over and kissed her on the back of the neck. "So, what happened?" She told him everything Gladys had said.

He shook his head. "Trouble always comes in bunches. We'll see what we can do to help her." He looked at the table. "How about we sort through this mess right now?"

* * *

The following week, Emma went to the day care center on Tuesday and Thursday to work with Dee and the speech therapist. She wished she was able to drive, but had given up that skill long ago. She had been a cautious driver, too cautious. When the police stopped her one time too many for driving too slowly, her children convinced her to sell the old car and rely on public transportation.

Now she had to board two buses to reach her destination and was glad she had only committed herself to two days a week.

When she returned, she was exhausted.

"Are you certain you want to do this?" Nate asked her. "You've worn yourself out. I'll make us a cup of tea."

She heaved a sigh. "It's a long way, but I'm seeing progress already. Dee is saying 'si' and 'no'. So that means something. The therapist is concentrating on counting. Her short-term goal is to get up to five verbalizing the words correctly."

"It sounds like a painstaking process," Nate said. "Oh, I almost forgot. Gladys called. She'll be arriving at O'Hare Airport on Friday afternoon. I wrote down all the flight information."

"Great." Emma was eager to see her friend. It was too long since they had visited and she hoped that, together, they could figure out what the problem was. Emma suspected Gladys would tell her, woman to woman, things she hadn't wanted to say over the phone.

As she sipped her tea and nibbled on a cookie, she felt Nate studying her. "Why are you looking at me that way?"

"You're making faces."

"I wasn't aware of that."

"When you're worrying about something, you always stick out the tip of your tongue and frown. What is it?"

"Dee has a bruise on her upper left arm."

"What happened?" Nate's voice took on a concerned tone.

"Nothing at the center. The administrator called June who told her that Dee bumped into the edge of the refrigerator."

"Sounds plausible." He finished his tea and took another cookie. Emma shook her head. "Maybe, but I don't trust that daughter-in-law."

"You don't think she would hurt Dee deliberately, do you?"

"I wouldn't put anything past that woman. By the way, she's appearing in a play at the local Lincolnwood Community Theater. I saw an announcement on the bulletin board at the center. I think we should go."

"Why?"

Emma shrugged. "Just want to see what kind of an actor she is, that's all."

"You don't fool me for one minute, Sparrow. You have an ulterior motive." Emma smiled, but said nothing.

"Okay, when is this thespian delight to take place?"

"Tomorrow night at eight. Do we have anything planned?"

"You know we don't." He picked up the tea cups and muttered to himself as he walked into the kitchen.

* * *

The following evening, Emma and Nate sat in the Lincolnwood High School auditorium for the final performance of a play written by a local play write.

"I hope the performance is better than the setting," Nate said.

The haphazard placement of furniture on the stage jarred Emma. She had expected a little more professionalism. But then, her reason for being here had nothing to do with the play.

"Nate." She grabbed his arm. "There's Mike Armanetti, Dee's son. I recognize him from the picture Dee showed me. Let's call him over." She waved until she caught his attention.

He looked at her quizzically, then walked over to them.

"Dr. Armanetti, I'm Emma Winberry and this is Nate Sandler. We spoke on the phone a few times. We're supernumeraries at the opera and have known your mother for a number of years."

"Of course. You've been so concerned. I'm grateful." He smiled and extended his hand.

"I recognized you from a picture your mother showed me of you and your brother. She's so proud of both of you." She gave him a disarming smile and returned the handshake.

"How nice of you to come to June's play. She's been working really hard with caring for mom and rehearsing. I don't know how she does it all." He cocked his head. "But how did you hear about the play?"

"There's a notice on the bulletin board at the day care center. I've been helping the speech therapist. Dee is making progress, but it's slow. I do believe her speech will return given enough time and effort by the staff."

"That's right," he said. "The administrator told me that you're volunteering there. I'm truly grateful." He squeezed Emma's hand.

"Dee means a lot to us, doesn't she Nate?"

"She certainly does," he agreed. "She's a fine singer and a very determined woman."

Mike laughed. "That describes her perfectly."

At that moment, the houselights dimmed and the play began. Emma had seen better performances put on by her children's high school. The two leads were mediocre actors, but June, in a subordinate role, did a poor job. A number of times she appeared to forget her lines and needed a prompt.

When the curtain came down, the audience applauded with enthusiasm. Emma was convinced they were all happy that it was over.

Mike turned to them. "Not exactly Broadway, huh?" He was obviously embarrassed.

"One doesn't expect too much from community theater," Nate said. "I think it's more for fun than anything else."

"There were some amusing lines," Emma said, although, at the moment, she couldn't remember any of them.

"You will stay and say hello to June, won't you?" Mike asked.

"Absolutely." That's why I sat through this fiasco, Emma thought. She smiled at Nate who returned her grin through gritted teeth.

Before long, the actors came out to greet their families and friends. When June spotted Emma and Nate, her smile turned into a frown.

Mike put his arm around his wife. "Wasn't it nice of mother's friends to come to the play?"

"How did you know about it?" she asked, still frowning and sucking on her lower lip.

"There was a notice on the bulletin board at the day care center," Emma said sweetly. "I've been working with the speech therapist. Dee is really making progress." She carefully watched June's reaction. Was that fear she saw in the woman's eyes?

"Isn't that great?" Mike said.

"It's too bad she bumped into the refrigerator," Emma continued. "That's quite a bruise on her arm."

Mike turned toward his wife with concern. "You didn't tell me mother hurt herself. How did it happen?"

"Uh, she lost her balance and tripped over the rug by the sink."

"June, they told us to get rid of all throw rugs. I thought you had." He frowned and fisted his hands, then seemed to remember where he was. "Please, toss it out. We can't have her falling."

The glare that June gave Emma spoke more than words.

She turned to her husband and the actor took over. "I will, darling. You know I want her to get well as much as you do."

* * *

As they drove home, Nate said, "The performance she gave after the play was much better than the one onstage."

"There's something devious about that woman." Emma pursed her lips. "I wouldn't be surprised if she hurt Dee deliberately."

"You have no proof of that."

"No, but you can be sure the staff at the center will be watching Dee closely from now on."

CHAPTER 20

JUNE SLAPPED THE THICK ENVELOPE on the table then slid into the booth across from Frances. "That's the last of my private stash," she said her, voice exuding venom.

Frances greeted her with a smile. "Good morning to you, too." Her eyes narrowed. "That only amounts to two thousand dollars. Far short of our goal."

"There's no 'our' in this. It's blackmail, and you know it."

"That's such an ugly word. I consider it a business agreement. I have something you want and am willing to turn it over to you when the proper payment is made."

"How do I know that you don't have copies and, later, will come after me for more money?" June examined the other woman's face but it remained passive.

"You'll have to take my word for it." Frances' eyes became slits, not unlike those of a snake stalking its prey. "Like I said before, pawn some of your jewelry. I'm sure you have many pieces like that rock on your finger."

June pulled back her left hand and put it in her lap.

Frances simply laughed, but the sound was harsh and unyielding. "Coffee ladies?" the waitress asked walking up to the booth. "Yes," Frances said, "and give the bill to my friend."

June could hardly contain her fury. She took a deep breath then blew it out, slowly. "There may be a problem."

"What?"

"The old lady is starting to talk."

"So, what can she say? You haven't done anything stupid, have you?"

"Well, I lost my temper and roughed her up a little. Told everyone she bumped her arm on the refrigerator." June clenched her fists then let them loose as the nails dug into her flesh.

Frances put her hands on the table and half lifted herself up, then sat back."I warned you about the doc and his mother. Don't screw this up because you're the one with everything to lose."

June shook her head. "I'll be extra careful from now on."

"You'd better be. There are laws against abuse of the elderly and disabled. The doc sees it with people abusing their pets and he has no mercy. Calls the authorities immediately. Do you think for one minute that he'll let you get away with injuring his own mother?"

"There's something else. This woman, Emma Winberry; she's a friend of my mother-in-law. She's working with the speech therapist because she speaks Italian."

"So what?"

"She showed up at my play last week and mentioned the bruise on Mama's arm in front of my husband. I covered it up the best I could, but I think she's suspicious."

Frances thought for a moment. "Maybe we can scare her off."

"What do you mean 'we'? She knows me."

"But she doesn't know me," Frances said. "Get me her address and phone number. Does she live alone?"

"No, she lives with a guy, Nate something or other. They're both extras in the opera."

Frances grimaced. "You're an actor. Can't you disguise your voice?"

"I suppose I could."

"Let's see what we can come up with," Frances said, a scowl on her face.

CHAPTER 21

EMMA PACED BACK AND FORTH at the baggage claim area waiting for Gladys. According to the arrival board, her plane was delayed.

"Emma," Nate said, "will you please sit down. You're making me nervous."

"I can't. I'm going to the ladies room."

"You just went a half-hour ago."

"Well, I have to go again."

When she returned and glanced at the board, she noticed that Gladys' flight had landed. "Great," she said, watching crowds of people headed for the carrousels.

Nate grabbed her hand and sat her down next to him. "Those passengers are from a flight that originated in Los Angeles. You know it takes time for everyone to deplane. Now take a deep breath and relax. Isn't that yoga that you practice every day doing anything for you?"

"You're right." She followed his suggestions and immediately calmed down. After the people from LA dispersed, another group came along.

"There she is!" Emma said, jumping up. "Oh Nate, look how thin and worn she looks." She hurried toward Gladys waving to get her attention. Nate followed.

Without a word, the two women embraced.

With a lump in her throat, Emma managed to say, "I'm so glad you're here."

"So am I." Gladys' eyes shone with unshed tears. "I had to get away."

Nate came up and gave Gladys a hug. "Which bag is yours?"

"That red one just coming out." Gladys pointed to a large bright red wheeled bag. Nate retrieved the piece of luggage and they were soon on their way to the condo.

Emma and Gladys sat in the back holding each other's hands. "How is Tessa?" Emma asked.

"She's a trooper, and her husband, Rick, is a big help. I'm worn out."

"I can see that. While you're here, Nate and I will see that you rest and we'll plan some fun things to do."

"Right now my life is topsy-turvy. I don't know what to do." She turned to Emma with so much pain in her eyes that all Emma could do was hold her close.

"Let's not talk about it now. First rest, then good food, then a walk along the lakeshore. That's my recipe for solving problems."

"You're good for me, Emma."

"We've always been good for each other."

* * *

While Gladys napped in the guest room, Emma and Nate discussed her situation.

"I read someplace that men go through a form of male menopause," Emma said. "Do you think that could be Cornell's problem?"

Nate shook his head. "I don't believe there's any such thing. I have a feeling it's something else."

"Like another woman?"

He frowned. "Maybe not. I don't see him as the type to go philandering around with so much to lose. I'm thinking, perhaps, it's something to do with the business."

"Hmm. Gladys didn't mention anything like that."

"He probably didn't tell her." Nate thought for a moment. "I think I'll wait a few days, then call him and see what I can find out."

"Oh Nate, you are becoming a top-notch sleuth."

"You're rubbing off on me, my dear." He slid his arm around her waist, kissed her neck, and made his way to her lips.

* * *

The following day Gladys reluctantly accompanied Emma to the day care center. On the long bus ride, Emma explained the situation to her friend.

Gladys sighed. "Everyone has problems of some kind. I have to stop feeling sorry for myself."

"You and Cornell have been married for ages, my friend. You *must* trust him. He has his reasons, and we'll get it all sorted out while you're here. I promise," Emma said.

Oh Guardian Angel, I hope I'm not making a promise I can't keep. It will all work out, her inner voice said.

When they reached the center, Gladys was surprised at the well tended exterior and more so at the amenities offered to the clients.

"This has to be expensive," she said.

"That's my thinking," Emma agreed. "And I'm sure Dee's daughter-in-law doesn't like that one bit. She's the kind that loves to spend money."

The bird-like woman came up to them taking mincing steps. "You're number forty-four. I remember." She pointed to Emma. Then she turned to Gladys. "You're new so you'll be number fifty." She nodded in satisfaction and walked away.

Emma laughed at her friend's quizzical expression. "She identifies everyone by number—head injury. Apparently she was a brilliant scientist at one time. When I asked her what her number was, she replied, "Why one, of course"."

"How sad," Gladys said, grimacing.

"There's Dee." Emma took her friend's arm and walked into the day room.

"Ma, Ma." Dee reached out her left hand; a purple bruise covered the top and reached halfway down the fingers. She winced as Emma took the hand in hers.

Emma gritted her teeth. "What happened to your hand?"

Dee made a backhand motion as if she were hitting something.

At that moment, Sara, the activities director, came up to them. She pulled Emma aside and whispered, "Her daughter-in-law had quite a shiner when she brought Delia in this morning. Said Dee hit her then tried again, but smacked her hand against the wall."

"I wonder what June did to provoke that," Emma said.

Sara shook her head. "We have a call in to her son, but the receptionist said he was busy and would call back."

"What do you do in a situation like this?"

"We usually get social work involved, but Mrs. Carter wants to talk to Dr. Armanetti first."

Emma and Gladys tried to get Dee involved with the exercises, but she was too upset to participate.

When Diane, the speech therapist arrived, she, too had a difficult time with Dee. Gladys helped with the exercises while Emma tried to work with Diane, but Dee couldn't or wouldn't repeat any of the words. She kept saying one group of letters over and over, "*a'-g-e—a'-g-e*," and became more agitated as she continued.

"Mrs. Winberry, Diane asked, "can you make out what she means?"

Emma thought. *Guardian Angel, what is she saying?*

Remember, her inner voice said, *Italian and backwards.*

Emma wrote down the letters, A-G-E, then reversed them, E-G-A. "E g-a?" she asked Dee.

"*Si , si, a'-g-e, a'-g-e*"

"Apparently that's only part of the word," Emma mused as she tried to think of what Dee was trying to say. Suddenly the word materialized in her mind.

"Dee, are you trying to say, *strega?*"

"*Si, si, a'-g-e, a'-g-e.*" She nodded and pounded on the table with her left hand, then winced.

"What does it mean?' Diane asked.

"It means witch. She's apparently calling June a witch. There's a lot of animosity between those two." Emma shook her head.

"I'll tell Mrs. Carter to inform the son. Delia may have to be removed from that home." Emma shook her head. She rubbed Dee's back and tried to calm her, but, by now, tears coursed down the woman's cheeks and mucus ran from her nose. Emma grabbed a bunch of tissues and wiped her friend's face.

When she and Gladys were ready to leave, Dr. Armanetti hadn't yet called back. Emma knocked on the administrator's door.

She was greeted with a tired smile. "Come in, Mrs. Winberry."

"Delia is really upset today," Emma said.

"That's not unusual with stroke patients, but something must have happened this morning."

"May I call you tomorrow?" Emma asked.

"Legally I'm not supposed to give out information to anyone but the immediate family, but you have been instrumental in this client's progress and the client's son did give us written permission to treat you like family. I'll tell you what I can."

"Thanks." Emma nodded. As she walked out of the office, she heard someone playing the piano in the dayroom. Then Dee's melodic voice rose above the other clients who were trying to sing.

Gladys sat at the piano playing old favorites to the delight of clients and staff alike. She was a natural, couldn't read a note of music, but played everything by ear.

Emma inched her way to Gladys' side and sat on the bench next to her. She whispered, "Play *Santa Lucia.*"

Gladys nodded, then, with a fanfare, began playing the familiar melody.

Dee's eyes opened wide as she stood up, held onto the piano with her left hand, and sang loud and clear. She sang in Italian, but Emma recognized the words verbalized correctly.

Diane was thrilled. "My God, a breakthrough." Even Mrs. Carter came out of her office.

Everyone applauded and Dee attempted a bow, but Sara grabbed her as she began to totter forward. Still, her face was wreathed in smiles.

Gladys played two more familiar Italian songs and Dee sang. By then she was visibly tired and the music session concluded.

"We will definitely add more intense music therapy, immediately," Diane said. "What a voice!"

* * *

When they returned home, Emma told Nate what happened.

"Sounds like a volcano rumbling. Who knows when it will erupt."

"Nate," Gladys asked hesitantly. "Were there any phone calls for me?"

"No, but there was a hang up. I hate it when people get a wrong number and just disconnect without apologizing."

He winked at Emma. "It sounds like you girls have had a rough afternoon. How about we go out for pizza?"

"That's a plan," Emma agreed. She turned to Gladys. "Okay with you?"

"Sure." She did a poor job of hiding her disappointment that Cornell hadn't called.

Emma was the last one out the door. Nate and Gladys were already in the elevator. She heard the phone ringing but decided to let the answering machine pick it up.

* * *

That night as Dee lay in bed, her mind began to clear a little.

Hit her … hit her…

June is strega. Tell Mike to send her away. Nice to sing again. Canta … canta … canta.

CHAPTER 22

JUNE WALKED INTO THE COFFEE shop and spotted Frances waiting for her.
"Who gave you the shiner?" Frances asked without any greeting whatsoever.
June slid into the booth. "The old lady."

"Why?"

"Because she hates me."

"Come on, you must have said or done something to provoke her."

June gritted her teeth and pursed her lips. "She slopped oatmeal on her top and I had to change her before she could go to the day care center. I guess I was a little rough."

"Uh huh," Frances said. "And what did the doc have to say about that?" June didn't answer but remembered the tirade with her husband.

He sat them both down. "You two will have to get along, do you hear me?" He had pounded his fist on the table.

"June, all you have to do is help Mom get dressed, get her breakfast, and take her to the center. Is that too much to ask?"

"She fights me every step of the way." June had tried to defend herself.

Mike turned to his mother. "Mom, can't you cooperate with June? She's only trying to help you."

"No, no!" She had waved her bruised hand around, then began to cry.

Mike, as always, had taken his mother's side. "Now listen closely." His eyes bore into June's. "If I have to hire a live-in to care for my mother, the cost will come out of your allowance. In fact, there'll be no extra money to give you. Is that clear, my dear wife?"

"That's not fair. I do my share around here."

"Like what? Prepare an occasional meal? Usually you order out."

"You could put her in a nursing home." June had made the mistake of verbalizing her wishes.

He turned to her, nostrils flaring, eyes filled with anger. "Never!"

He stomped out of the room leaving the women staring daggers at each other.

June clenched her fists, wanting to throw a punch, but she had to contain herself. She would find a way, and soon.

"You're not going to tell me, are you," Frances said bringing June back to the present.

"It's none of your business." She took the envelope from her purse and slid it across the table.

"Coffee ladies?" the waitress asked coming up to them.

"Yes," Frances said sweetly. After she walked away, Frances focused on June. "There's something I'm sure you haven't thought of."

"What?" June was both interested and fearful of what the other woman had to say. "I'm sure she takes medication."

"Yes."

"How about doubling up on some, like tranquilizers?"

June shook her head. "Wouldn't work. I already thought of that. If the prescription runs out too soon, the pharmacy won't refill it and Mike will surely ask questions. I can get away with dropping the bottle once, but that's all."

"You're not very imaginative," Frances said, sipping her coffee. "Why don't you go to the doctor and get something for your nerves? After all, you're under a strain, and you get those migraines" She hesitated for a moment. "Then just put some in her oatmeal in the morning. Maybe she'll have an accident at the center. No one will be able to blame you for that."

June half smiled. "You are devious. Perhaps I'll think about it." Without another word, she left wondering if she might be able to slip something in Frances' coffee. But the woman was too clever and too sharp. June would have to think of some other way to dispose of her.

CHAPTER 23

EMMA CALLED HER SON-IN-LAW, JAMES, at the Midwest Opera Company. "Hi, Emma, how are you and Nate?" he asked.

"We're fine, James, and I presume Sylvia and the boys are okay or I would have heard from her."

"Absolutely. What can I do for you?"

She heard him shuffling papers so decided to get right to the point. "I've been visiting Delia Armanett. She's attending an adult day care center and doing quite well. I'm working with the speech therapist, because Dee is responding in Italian." She heard a laugh on the other end of the line.

"You're just the one to get results," he said.

Emma continued excitedly. "Yesterday Dee was singing to piano accompaniment and the words were clear! It's strange. She can sing but can't speak intelligibly. The therapist said that singing is controlled by a different area in the brain. Isn't that amazing?"

"It certainly is," James said. "But I don't think you called just to give me that piece of information."

"Of course not. I know I'm taking up your valuable time. What I would like to do is arrange for some of the chorus members and an accompanist to put on a program for the clients at the center. The administrator is all for it. The staff has an event planned next month for the participants and their families: a picnic lunch and various activities. It would be a perfect time for the entertainment."

"Sounds good," James said. "I know the chorus master and members have been concerned about Delia. Give me the date and I'll run it by him and see what we can do."

"I knew you'd come through." She gave him the information including the address. "Give my love to Sylvia and the boys and we'll have to visit soon."

"Okay. Bye."

Emma felt satisfied with her efforts and optimistic that Dee would recover enough to be independent. She wasn't expecting her to return to the operatic stage. That would require a miracle.

"Are you finished monopolizing the phone?" Nate asked. "Sorry, I was talking to James."

"I know. I heard part of your side of the conversation. Now I want you to take Gladys shopping. I'm going to try and get a hold of Cornell and find out just what's going on."

* * *

"Come on, it's a lovely day and we'll just take a look around the shops. Might find some good sales."

"By the way," Gladys said, as they walked along Michigan Avenue, "with all that's going on in my life, I forgot to ask about your cataract surgery. How did that go?"

"Marvelous! It's amazing what modern medicine can do. Instead of replacing my lenses with ordinary ones, the doctor used corrective lenses for folks like me who are very nearsighted."

Emma grinned. "I remember the day Nate took me to the Out Patient Clinic for the first implant. I was so nervous, I almost tripped on the step. Nate grabbed me and reminded me what the doctor had said. 'It's a piece of cake.'

"Yes, but he wasn't the one having someone poking around in his eye. I thought I was going to faint." She stopped for a moment and snickered.

"Nate, as usual, told me to take deep breaths, as if I didn't know that. But he did hang on to me until I had control of myself."

"That's typical of him," Gladys said, a faraway look in her eye.

"It only took a few minutes to get me settled on a litter, an intravenous solution running in my arm. The nurse gave me some tranquilizers that gave me a nice buzz."

She shrugged. "Before I knew it, the procedure was over. Immediately I was able to see out of that eye. I tell you, it was so easy that I had the other one done as soon as possible.

"Now I don't need to wear hard contacts anymore nor those thick glasses I wore when my eyes were tired. I just use designer specs for reading. I'm proud to say I have 20-20 vision."

"That's great! You never could see, even when we were kids." Gladys smiled for the first time since she arrived. "I remember one day Johnny Carlson waved at you from across the street and you didn't know who it was."

Emma giggled. "Yeah, and I had such a crush on him. I think he ignored me after that."

They stopped in front of a shoe store. "Let's have a look in here," Emma said scanning the window display. "Maybe something will jump out at us and scream, *buy me.*"

Gladys let out a Humph. " I doubt that." She turned to Emma. "It's been good for me to be here, but I really want to go home."

"I know—soon. Oh look at those brown shoes! How about we try on a pair or two?"

Reluctantly Gladys went along and did buy a pair of shoes, but Emma knew her heart wasn't in it. No matter how Emma tried, she couldn't lift her friend's spirits.

When they returned home both women were tired and Emma had exhausted all attempts to entertain Gladys.

Nate greeted them at the door, a smug expression on his face. "Gladys, sit down and listen to what I have to say."

They both gave him a quizzical look. "May I listen, too?" Emma asked.

He nodded. A pitcher of iced tea sat on the coffee table and he poured a glass for each of them.

"I spoke to Cornell earlier." He held up his hand as Gladys opened her mouth to speak. "You have nothing to worry about. There is no other woman."

"Then—what?" she blurted out.

"He's a very proud man and didn't want you to know that the business is in trouble. His partner has been skimming money from the till. He was so crafty that Cornell had no idea until he received a notice from the bank." Nate stopped for a moment and took a swallow of tea.

Gladys sat with her eyes wide and her mouth open. Then she whispered, "I can't believe it. They were such close friends. But why didn't he tell me?"

Nate shook his head. "As I said, he's very proud and didn't want you to know that he had been duped, right under his nose. Said he should have seen the signs, but he trusted the man implicitly."

Then she became angry. "What a fool! Didn't he think I would understand? We're life partners."

"Who knows what goes through people's minds? Anyway, the partnership is being dissolved. Cornell isn't going to file charges because the man has promised to repay the money as soon as possible. Gladys, did you know Cornell's partner and his wife are getting a divorce?"

"No! They were such a devoted couple. My God, you never know about people." She grabbed a tissue from the end table and dabbed her eyes.

Emma gave her a hug.

"Did he say what he plans to do?" Emma asked.

"At this point he isn't sure. Said he might sell out to a larger publishing house and work for them, but he is considering an alternative. It will mean less money coming in. I guess he feels he's let you down, Gladys."

"That silly man. Doesn't he remember the promise we made—for better or for worse? He's put me through hell."

"Give him a break," Nate continued. "He feels terrible for the way he's treated you. Right now, he needs your support."

Gladys nodded. "I'll get the first plane home."

Nate held up his hand. "He wants you to wait a day or two. Says he should have things sorted out by then. Please, give him this opportunity. He said he'll call you this evening."

"Okay," she said, letting out a deep breath. "Now that I know the reason, I can relax and stop thinking the worst. But I'm still ticked that he didn't confide in me."

"Now that I've done my good deed for the day, "Nate said, "I'm going to the hardware store."

Emma rolled her eyes. What useless thing would he bring back this time? As the door closed behind him, the phone rang.

"I'll get it," Gladys said, hurrying to pick it up. "Maybe it's Cornell. Hello," she said with a lilt in her voice.

Emma watched as the expression on her friend's face changed from one of anticipation to one of concern.

She put the phone down and turned to Emma. "What a strange call."

"Was it a hang up?"

"No, a muffled voice said, 'mind your own business, or else'."

"Not again," Emma said.

"Have you gotten these calls before?" Gladys asked putting her arm around Emma's shoulders.

"Once. When Nate answers the phone, the caller hangs up. I'm pretty sure it's the same person trying to frighten me."

"By the look on your face, I'd say he or she is doing a pretty good job. Did you tell Nate?"

"No, I thought it might just be a prank call."

"That was no prank call," Gladys said. "That was a warning. But why? What are you going to do?"

"I don't know. Obviously, I'm making someone nervous, June most likely. I'll have to discuss this with my Guardian Angel."

"I think you should tell Nate." Gladys was insistent.

"Let's just see if it happens again. It may not."

"You know better than that, Emma Winberry."

Emma said nothing. She walked out into the atrium and stared at the waves of Lake Michigan tumbling toward the shore. The previously sunny day had clouded over and she heard the distant roll of thunder coming closer. She knew that June wanted her out of the way, but would she resort to threats?

Guardian Angel, what should I do? Be very cautious, her inner voice said.

A streak of lightning slashed across the sky followed by a loud clap of thunder that made Emma jump. She backed away from the windows and slowly closed the door to the atrium.

CHAPTER 24

THAT NIGHT, AFTER A TEARFUL discussion with her husband, Gladys sat down with Emma and Nate. "He won't have to give up the company after all," she said with a relieved sigh. "He is negotiating with another small publisher to combine their companies and the bank has agreed to give him a short-term loan."

Emma took her friend's hand. "I'm so relieved."

Gladys wiped away a tear. "He wants me to come home as soon as possible now that he has things worked out. You were right, my friend, about trust." The women exchanged glances and smiled.

"I'll fire up the computer and check flights for you," Nate said. As he walked into the study, the phone rang.

"Hello," Emma said.

The muffled voice said, "Mind your own business—or else."

"Who is this?" Emma demanded. But all she heard was the dial tone.

"I think you had better tell Nate," Gladys said.

Emma nodded. "Whoever it is doesn't intend to let up."

"Gladys," Nate called, "come in here with your credit card. There's an early morning flight available tomorrow."

Gladys grabbed her purse and hurried into the study.

Emma sat pondering her situation. She felt certain it was June calling, but why? Was she afraid that if Dee regained the power to speak she might say something to undermine June's marriage?

Find out all you can about June Armanetti, her inner voice said.

Who can I ask? How do I go about searching her past? Call Dr. Armanetti's receptionist. She can help you.

* * *

The following morning Emma and Gladys sat in the backseat of the car holding hands as Nate fought the early rush hour traffic.

"Emma," Gladys said, "I can't thank you enough for your support."

"Don't mention it. What are friends for? I loved having you here and you really cheered the clients at the center with you piano playing."

"I'm sorry I won't be here for the program by the chorus members."

"I am, too." Emma gave her friend a hug. "But right now, your place is with Cornell."

"Yes it is." Gladys turned to Emma and whispered, "You will tell Nate about those phone calls, won't you?" Emma nodded. "Promise?"

"I promise."

* * *

On the ride back from the airport, Emma was unusually quiet.

"What is that brain of yours conjuring up?" Nate asked. "You're usually so talkative."

"Oh, I miss Gladys already. It was good having her here but not under those circumstances. I'm glad Cornell got things sorted out but he could have spared her all that worry and anxiety by telling her the truth in the first place."

"I know," Nate agreed. "Some men are funny that way. They don't want the people they love to see them as failures."

"So they put them through hell instead." Emma shook her head. She turned toward Nate. "You're not keeping any secrets from me, are you?"

"No, my dear, all is well. And, if it wasn't, you would be the first to know."

She hesitated for a moment, knew that Nate had always liked women and they, in turn, found him attractive. "You're not drawn to that widow, Yvonne, are you?"

He let out a breath. "We've been through this before. If I meet her in the exercise room, we exchange a few pleasantries, that's all!"

She sat back, satisfied with that answer.

But you are keeping the phone calls secret from him, her inner voice chided.

I'll tell him, if there is one more call, she promised her Guardian Angel.

* * *

The next two weeks went by uneventfully, with no further phone calls. She probably gave up, Emma thought and decided to put it out of her mind.

Dee continued to make progress in her speech sessions as the therapist concentrated on counting. Dee was now able to count to five in Italian and was beginning to use the English words.

Each small improvement made Emma optimistic that Dee would eventually regain her power of intelligible speech.

At that moment, the phone rang.

CHAPTER 25

"OH NATE, WHAT LOVELY WEATHER for the day care center to have their summer festival." Emma extended her arms and danced around the atrium. Her tomato plants and herbs looked as though they were smiling at her from the roof garden.

"I'd better give them a drink before we go," she said waltzing outside with her watering can in hand. When she turned, Nate was standing in the doorway, smiling.

"What are you grinning at?' She asked.

"I swear you would be happy as a farmer. Every seed that pops its head out of the ground sends you over the moon, as they say in the U. K."

She put down the watering can and returned his smile. "I do love to watch things grow. It's a miracle of nature that a tiny seed holds all the information necessary to grow into a magnificent tree."

"What about the birth of a human being? Isn't that just as miraculous?" he asked.

"Now we're getting philosophical," she said. "Time to get dressed."

"I'm ready. Have been for an hour. You're the one who's fussing around."

She gave him a smirk and hurried into the bedroom. Soon she emerged wearing white slacks and a light blue and white striped top.

Nate nodded his approval. "Is that new?"

"Uh huh. I bought it when Gladys and I went shopping at Water Tower Place. Like it?" She assumed a modeling pose.

"Very nice. Now let's get going."

The Sunday early afternoon traffic was light and they reached the center at the same time as the members of the chorus. Emma ran up to them with hugs and greetings and Nate did the same.

She introduced each member to Mrs. Carter, the administrator, and to Sara, the activities director.

Everyone commented on the decorations that the clients had made and hung on the trees: streamers, paper stars and balls. Tiny white and red lights hung from tree to tree and lent a festive air to the place. Annuals, strategically planted in beds around the gazebo and along the perimeter of the building, opened their petals in glorious color to add to the party atmosphere.

Most of the clients and their families had already arrived, but Emma didn't see Dee anywhere. She found Sara arranging plates and silverware on a buffet table.

"Is Dee here?" Emma asked.

"Not yet, but Dr. Armanetti assured me he would bring his mother. Delia is so looking forward to seeing her friends in the chorus." She heard someone calling her. "Excuse me for a minute, I have to talk with Mrs. Carter about something."

The staff members had done a first rate job of organizing everything. Emma went back to where Nate was talking to the chorus director.

At that moment Agnes, the bird-like woman, came up to them. "Hello, forty-five and forty- six. Welcome to the festival."

"Thank you, number one," Emma said as Agnes grinned and went off to greet others.

"Emma," Nate called, "here come the Armanettis."

"Oh good." She walked over to the trio. Mike hovered over his mother as she walked steadily with her quad cane. June, a scowl on her face, shuffled slightly behind the two.

"Hello Dee, Dr. Armanetti, June," Emma said.

"Ma, Ma," Dee said, a lop-sided smile on her face.

Emma gave her a hug then shook hands with Mike. June held her hands behind her back, and gave a slight nod.

When Dee saw her friends from the chorus, she fell into their eager arms. They all talked to her slowly and told her everything that was going on at the Midwest Opera. She began to cry, but, immediately her friends took her in hand and began to sing a simple song. Before long Dee joined in. She stumbled a few times, but soon, sang along with the group.

"Oh Nate," Emma said, feeling a lump in her throat, "isn't it wonderful?" He nodded and slipped his arm around her waist, holding her close.

Soon Sara appeared and announced that the buffet was ready. The clients sat down in appointed chairs at card tables placed on the lawn while their family members prepared plates and served them. Then they went back for their own food.

Emma and Nate sat with the Armanettis, Mike on one side of his mother and Emma on the other. June sat between Nate and Emma. At first Emma sensed some tension, but when Mike saw the happy smile on Dee's face, he began to relax.

Mike and Nate talked briefly about investing then turned to other topics.

Emma tried to engage June in conversation, but she said little and simply toyed with her food, obviously bored with the entire affair.

Emma helped Dee whenever she seemed to need it, but was surprised at how independent she had become, relishing the food. She ate potato salad, sliced tomatoes, and an entire hamburger on a bun and drank a glass of lemonade without spilling a drop.

When the staff came around with cupcakes, Dee shook her head and patted her stomach. Mike laughed. "Look June, Mom hasn't eaten this much since her stroke. Isn't that great?"

June gave her husband a weak smile. "Yeah, just dandy."

Emma noticed that all June had was a salad and a cup of coffee. She sat tapping her foot on the ground, a preoccupied expression on her face. All during the meal she had barely spoken a word. Something's bothering her big time, Emma thought. I wonder what it is. Maybe something in her background? My Guardian Angel did tell me to find out as much about her as possible.

Emma fidgeted, wishing she could read June's thoughts. An idea struck her. "Where did you grow up, June? I've lived in the Chicago area all my life."

The woman scowled. "What difference does it make? We moved around a lot."

Emma prodded a bit more. "I always find it interesting to hear people talk about their past." She smiled, but was met with a glare that seemed to say, "back off." So she turned her attention back to Dee.

While the staff cleared away the plates and silverware, Sara ushered everyone into the day room for the entertainment. When everyone was seated, the pianist took his place and the twelve chorus members sang a few arias, then some songs that were popular in the forties and fifties.

Dee sat on a chair near her friends and joined in. Anyone who wished sang along. Enthusiastic applause issued from the group at the end.

"Would you care for a short tour of the facility, Dr. Armanetti?" Sara asked.

"Very much so," he answered. "Come on June, let's have a look." She sighed and followed.

Emma also trailed behind, not that she hadn't seen the place, but she was curious as to the reaction of the other two.

Mike expressed his approval of the physical therapy equipment and the dining area. "What are all these drawings?" he asked as he examined what looked like children's art work hanging on the wall.

"Art therapy is an important part of our routine. Some of the clients, who aren't able to do much else, enjoy drawing pictures and coloring them with crayons," Sara explained.

"Has my mother done any drawings?"

"As a matter of fact, she keeps making the same squares over and over. Here, this is one of hers." She pointed to a piece of drawing paper with an uneven square in the center and a round circle in the middle of the square.

"What's it supposed to mean?" Mike asked.

"We haven't figured that out yet," Sara answered. "She keeps mumbling something and making motions around the circle, almost as if it's a knob."

"Hmm." Mike examined the drawing and shrugged.

After scrutinizing the paper, Emma's eyes turned to June. Her face had gone white when she saw what Dee had drawn. It obviously meant something to her.

"Does the art therapist have any idea of its meaning?" Emma asked.

"Well, she thinks it may be a door that Delia is trying to open. She may feel that she's locked inside and is trying to get out."

"That sounds reasonable," Mike said. He turned to his wife. "What do you think, June?"

"Don't ask me. I have no idea. "She bit down hard on her bottom lip and frowned.

"Mrs. Winberry, do you have any insight into this?" Mikes asked. "You've been working with Mom."

"I'm not sure. That could be the meaning, but I think she's trying to tell us something. I'll ask the speech therapist next week. We'll try to figure out what the words mean that she's saying. I'm sure that, in time, we'll uncover the mystery."

Guardian Angel, does this have a significant meaning or is it Dee's attempt to unlock the door to her mind?

Watch and listen, her inner voice said.

Emma didn't take her eyes off June. She was obviously disturbed by the drawing, was cracking her knuckles and staring at the strokes.

"Mike, I'm getting one of my headaches," she said, her theatrical persona surfacing. "Isn't it time to go home?"

"I think so. Mom seems to be getting tired, too."

"The chorus members are leaving now," Sara said.

Emma and Nate went to say their good-byes and when they returned, the Armanettis were gone.

* * *

"I thought the whole thing went well, didn't you?" Nate asked as he maneuvered the car out of the grounds and onto the main thoroughfare. "Emma, are you listening to me?"

"Huh? Oh yes, very well."

"Okay, what's going through that active mind of yours?"

"I was just thinking of Dee's drawing and what it might *really* mean."

"I thought that was a pretty good interpretation Sara gave of Dee being locked in and trying to get out. Made sense to me." He stopped at a red light and turned to Emma.

She was frowning. "No, I think it's something else. Did you notice the expression on June's face when she saw it? She seemed disturbed by it."

"No, I wasn't watching her."

"I'll discuss it with the speech therapist next week and see if we can find out what Dee is really trying to tell us."

"There you go, Mrs. Sleuth, always looking for something devious."

Emma was adamant. "There is something going on between June and Dee and I don't think it's good. My Guardian Angel told me to watch carefully."

"And, of course, the Angel always knows best," he said with a note of sarcasm in his voice. Emma didn't respond to his remark, just sat back and pondered the various possibilities.

CHAPTER 26

THE FOLLOWING TUESDAY EMMA EAGERLY made her way to the center. She wanted to solve the mystery of Dee's drawings. She bustled into the Woods Day Care Center right in the middle of a dispute by two of the clients. Agnes, the number lady, was complaining that one of the other clients wouldn't respond to her number.

Sara intervened. "Agnes, you must try and remember that, although you refer to the folks here by numbers, they also have names. And, most of them wish to be called by their proper names."

"But I have my system," Agnes demanded.

Sara put her arm around the distraught woman and sat her down in a chair. "Your system is a result of your work as a physicist many years ago. Do you remember that time?"

Agnes frowned and rubbed her hands over her face. Then she looked up and saw Emma and smiled. "Hello number forty-five. How nice to see you."

"It's good to see you, too, number one," Emma replied, giving Sara a commiserating look. Then Agnes got up from the chair and walked toward the dayroom, humming a tune. "Does this happen very often?" Emma asked.

"About once a week. Now she's forgotten all about it." Sara heaved a sigh. "You need limitless patience for this job."

Sara nodded. "By the way, Diane is here and has just begun working with Delia."

"Oh good. I want to try and decipher the meaning of those squares she keeps drawing."

"Good luck."

Emma hurried into the small room where the speech sessions were held. She stood in the doorway for a moment and observed.

Dee was counting blocks. "*Uno, due, tre.*"

"Very good, Delia," Diane said. "Now can you count them in English?"

Dee pursed her lips and furrowed her brow. "One." She thought hard, but the next number seemed out of reach. "No!" She slammed her hand on the table, scattering the blocks.

"All right, that's enough counting for now. See who's here?"

Dee turned her head and spotted Emma. "Ma, Ma," she said reaching out to her friend.

Emma gave her a hug and sat next to her. "Wasn't that a wonderful festival last Sunday?"

Delia's eyes widened. "*Si, canta, canta.*"

"Yes." Emma turned to Diane. "Too bad you missed it. Dee sang with some of the chorus members from the opera. It went very well. And, she said "*canta*" correctly. That means sing."

"She is making steady progress," Diane said. "I had another commitment that day, or I would have been there."

"Have you seen the drawings she's been working on?" Emma asked.

"I have. Sara pointed them out to me. They're always the same and seem to indicate a closed door."

"I think they mean something else."

"Why do you say that?"

"Just intuition." Emma wasn't about to tell Diane that her Guardian Angel told her. The woman might consider her as daft as some of the clients.

"If it's all right with you," Emma said, "can we ask her now about the drawings?"

"Certainly." Diane went to retrieve one while Emma hummed along with Dee.

When Diane returned, Dee became noticeably agitated. "What does this mean?" Diane asked. "Is it a door?"

"No!" Dee pounded on the table then clenched her left fist. "*Acha ... acha ...* " She struggled to get the words out.

Emma wrote down ACHA.

"Is that something in Italian?" The therapist asked.

"Not really," Emma answered trying to figure out what it might mean. "Perhaps it's part of a word." Mentally she began to put various consonants in front of the four letters. When she came to F, she stopped.

"She might be trying to say *faccia,* which means face." She wrote the word out and put the paper in front of Dee. "Is this what you're trying to say, *faccia?*"

"No! No!" She became more agitated.

"Perhaps we should set that aside for now," Diane said. "We don't seem to be making a connection. "We'll try again on Thursday." She turned to her patient. "How about singing *Santa Lucia* for us?"

Dee shook her head. Then, as Emma began to hum the melody, she relaxed and sang along, loud and clear.

* * *

Dr. Armanetti had gone to his colleague's office next door to confer about a case. The clinic was quiet and Marge took the opportunity to indulge herself in a cup of coffee and a sandwich. Just as she was about to take the first bite, the phone rang.

"Damn," she muttered, then picked it up and resumed her professional persona. "Paws and Claws, how may I help you?"

A high pitched woman's voice said, "I need to speak with Frances. It's an emergency."

The voice sounded familiar, but Marge couldn't place it. "She's on her lunch break. May I take a message?"

"Tell her it's very important—about her mother."

"Just a moment." Marge put the call on hold. She didn't remember Frances ever referring to her mother, but the woman never spoke about her personal life. Marge buzzed the small office that Frances occupied.

"What?" Frances asked in an annoying tone. "You have an urgent call—about your mother."

"My mother?"

"That's what the woman said."

"All right, put it through."

Marge did as she was instructed but her curiosity got the better of her. She inched her way to Frances' partly open door and listened.

"Hello," Frances said.

"I told you *never* to call me here. Somebody might get suspicious. What's the matter?

"What the hell are you talking about?" Her voice took on a menacing tone. "Who is Mrs. Winberry and what difference does it make if the old lady is drawing pictures?"

"Shut up!" Frances almost shouted. Then she lowered her voice. "Meet me at our usual place. I'll leave here at four thirty sharp and be there in fifteen minutes." With those words, she disconnected the call.

Marge pulled back and hurried to her desk. What was that all about? And who was Mrs. Winberry? Marge thought for a moment then remembered the doctor telling her about a woman from the opera who was working with the speech therapist because she spoke Italian. She had called to talk with the doc a couple of times. Of course, the caller was June, trying to disguise her voice.

Marge decided to follow Frances and see just where she and June were meeting. Then she would try and contact this Mrs. Winberry and confer with her. Anything that affected Mike Armanetti also affected her. She would protect him and his mother any way she could.

CHAPTER 27

A T FOUR-THIRTY SHARP FRANCES LEFT the clinic. The afternoon schedule was unusually light and Marge had told her boss she had a dental appointment. She hated to lie to him, but felt this was important. Slipping out the back door, she got in her car and slid down so Frances wouldn't see her. She turned the key in the ignition and waited until the other woman had left the parking lot, then followed at a discrete distance.

In a few minutes Frances tuned into a strip mall and parked in front of a coffee shop. Marge drove around slowly until she found an out of the way spot with a view of the front and waited.

Before long she saw June Armanetti run in and sit across the table from Frances. Marge took out the binoculars she always carried in the car for bird watching. She focused the powerful lenses and could clearly see the two women in a heated conversation. June kept gesticulating with her hands. Finally Frances stood up and moved inches from June's face. She said something, then left the booth.

Marge started her car and drove around the back of the stores. She stopped and let the engine idle until she felt certain that both women had left. Only then did she make her way home.

* * *

As Emma grabbed the ringing phone, she had a nagging suspicion that it would be another threat. "Hello," she answered with some force.

A pause, then the muffled voice. "This is your last warning! Mind your own business."

"Who is this?" Emma demanded. But, as usual, she heard only the disconnect.

She looked up into Nate's frowning face. "Are you going to tell me what's going on? When I answer the phone, the caller disconnects. When you answer, someone says something. Now what is it?"

She sat on the couch, let out a breath, and told him about the calls.

"Why didn't you tell me this before?"

"I thought it was a prank and the calls would stop."

"But they haven't. Do you have any idea who it might be?" The scowl on his face told her he was just as upset as she was.

"It could be June Armanetti. That's why I discounted the whole thing. When she got so visibly upset over Dee's drawings, I began taking her more seriously. There's something she doesn't want Dee to tell us."

"This is harassment! I'm calling the police."

"Oh Nate, I don't think we have to go that far."

"Do you have any other suggestions?"

She screwed up her face. "Not really. But before you do that, let's try and figure out what Dee means by those drawings."

Nate shook his head. "If you and the speech therapist can't understand what she means, what other recourse do you have?"

"A fresh pair of eyes—yours."

"Mine? I don't speak Italian." He held out his hands.

"I don't think it's an Italian word. She seems to be saying face, but when I asked her if that was the word, she adamantly said no."

"Face, face," Nate repeated as he paced the floor. Then his eyes widened. "Turn it around and it sounds like—safe."

"Of course! Oh, Nate." She sprang off the couch and threw her arms around his neck. "You're brilliant."

"Are you just realizing that, my dear?"

"It was staring us right in the face," she said.

"Is that supposed to be a pun?"

"The drawing," she said, "a square with a knob in the center and she kept making a turning motion. We thought it was a door, but it's a safe and someone is opening it. That's what she's trying to tell us."

* * *

A few moments later, the phone rang again. Nate grimaced as he picked it up. "If this is one more of those hang ups, I *will* call the police," he said looking directly at Emma. "Hello."

"Hello, this is Jill Maynard from the Midwest Opera. May I speak with Mrs. Winberry, please?"

"Sure, just a minute." He handed the phone to Emma. "Jill Maynard from the Midwest," he said with a shrug.

"Hello," Emma said, "what can I do for you?"

"Oh Mrs. Winberry, someone called wanting to speak with you. She said it was very important. I told her we didn't give out phone numbers but she left hers and asked that you please call her tonight after eight."

"Did she leave her name?" Emma asked wondering who it might be. "Yes, it's Marge Newman, Dr. Armanetti's" receptionist."

Emma's eyes widened as she waved Nate away. He was standing so close she felt claustrophobic. "Give me the number and I'll definitely call her." Emma scribbled Marge and the number on a piece of paper then thanked the woman and said goodbye.

She turned to Nate. "This Marge Newman is Mike Armanetti's receptionist. She said it's very important that I call her."

"I wonder what that's all about," Nate mused as he rubbed his chin.

"We won't know until this evening. This is obviously her home number, so she doesn't want me to call the clinic. It *has* to involve Dee." Emma shook her head. "It's so frustrating. Something is going on and I have a feeling that it's not good."

* * *

"Shall we go out to dinner?' Nate asked. "I know you're going to be watching the clock and pacing. You're making me nervous already."

"Sounds like a good idea. The hands on the clock seem to be moving in slow motion."

Nate took her hands in his. "Sparrow, time always passes at the same rate. Just because you're eager to hear what the woman has to say, isn't going to make it go any faster." He lifted her chin in his hand and gave her a loving kiss.

"What would I do without you, Nate Sandler?"

"Probably get into more trouble than you do with me. Now, what'll it be: Chinese, Thai, Italian, or just plain American?" he asked with a chuckle.

"I'll settle for American."

"You're on. A juicy burger, greasy fries, and pie. Maybe even add a dollop of ice cream." A short time later they walked out the door to a ringing phone which they both ignored.

It was a balmy early summer evening, a gentle breeze blowing off the lake. They walked the five blocks to The Burger Place and enjoyed a simple meal.

When they returned, there was a message on the answering machine from Sylvia, Emma's daughter. Emma called her back immediately.

"Hi, Mom," Sylvia's cheery voice answered. "Hello, dear, how is the family?"

"We're all fine. The boys are growing so fast I can't keep them in clothes. James and I decided to have a picnic next Saturday—you know, one of those spur of the moment things."

"They always turn out to be the best kind," Emma said, smiling.

"I've called my brothers and they can make it. How about you and Nate?"

Emma glanced at the calendar and saw nothing written for Saturday. "We're free. What can I bring?"

"How about some of your famous muffins? They'll go well with ice cream."

"Fine. What time?"

"Around noon."

"Sounds good. We'll be there."

When she turned to Nate, he had a sheepish expression on his face. "I'm so glad you consult me before making social engagements."

"Oh, Nate. We didn't have anything planned, so I didn't think you would mind."

He laughed. "Emma, you know I love your family like my own. Is the whole clan gathering?"

"Yes, for a picnic."

"Okay. I'll get a couple of bottles of that fine wine James likes so much. Now, it's a few minute before eight and I know your itchy fingers want to call Marge."

"Yes, and don't tell me you're not inquisitive, too. Why don't you get on the extension so I don't have to repeat what she says."

He nodded and went into the den.

Oh Guardian Angel, what does this woman want to discuss with me? I have a bad feeling. You won't know until you call her, her inner voice said.

With trembling fingers, Emma punched in the numbers.

The phone was answered on the first ring with an anxious sounding, "Hello."

"Is this Marge? Emma Winberry calling."

A sigh from the other end. "Oh thank you. I'm Mike Armanetti's receptionist. I've been working for Doc for over ten years. He's a fine vet and a wonderful man."

"Yes, I understand that, but I have a feeling you don't want to talk about the doctor."

"I'll come right to the point. The other day Mrs. Armanetti called to talk to Frances, Doc's assistant."

"Is that unusual?" Emma asked.

"Very—she's never done it before." Marge paused for a moment. "I decided to listen. Now please, don't think that I'm a busybody. I never listen to the doctor's conversations. But I couldn't think of any reason for Mrs. Armanetti to be calling Frances."

"Calm down, Marge. You're talking so fast that I can barely keep up with you. Take a deep breath, then go on."

"You're right." She paused and did as Emma suggested. "That's better. I was very discrete. It was lunch time and there were no clients waiting. Doc had gone out, so I listened at Frances' door. When she heard Mrs. Armanetti's voice, she was furious. Said she was never to call her at the clinic.

"I could only hear Frances' side of the conversation, but it was about someone drawing pictures."

I knew it, Emma thought. Something is amiss.

"Then Frances said they would meet at the usual place after work. I wondered what was going on—don't trust either of them. The doc is so concerned about his mother and I won't let anything happen to her, if I can prevent it."

"I understand," Emma said. "Did anything else happen?"

"I followed Frances—told the doc that I had a dental appointment. I never lie to him, believe me, but I had to see what they were up to."

"Go on," Emma said, as Marge paused again.

"They met at a coffee shop not far away. I stayed out of sight but used my binoculars that I always carry in the car. I'm a bird watcher, you see."

"And what did they do in the coffee shop?"

"They were in a heated conversation. Of course, I couldn't hear what they were saying, but Mrs. Armanetti kept waving her arms around until Frances stood up. I thought she was going to slap her. Then Frances left."

"That's it?"

"I'm afraid so. I wish I knew what they were saying. I probably should have gone into the shop and asked the waitress."

"No, don't call attention to yourself. If they meet there regularly, the waitress might mention that someone is asking questions."

"You're right. I never thought of that. What do you think I should do?"

"Do nothing, but let me know if you see or hear anything out of the ordinary."

"Should I tell the doc?"

"No, not yet. I will be meeting with Delia and the speech therapist tomorrow and see what I can uncover. I'll give you my phone number so you can call me directly."

"Thank you so much, Mrs. Winberry. Anything that affects the doc, affects me, too."

"I understand. You're a loyal employee." Emma gave Marge her number and terminated the call.

Nate walked out of the den shaking his head. "What do you make of that?"

"I have no idea, but Marge will make a good ally."

"She's obviously in love with her boss," Nate said.

"Oh yes, she'll do anything for him. Now to find out who is opening the safe."

"Do you have to wonder?"

"No, it's June, of course. But why? That's the question."

"Perhaps it's merely to retrieve her jewelry."

"No. That wouldn't upset Dee. She's taking out more than jewelry."

CHAPTER 28

WHEN THURSDAY ARRIVED, EMMA WAS so eager to reach the day care center that she almost tripped on the curb.

Be careful, her inner voice said, *you're not a young woman anymore.*

She frowned. Was her Guardian Angel insinuating she was getting old? The years were passing but Emma refused to acknowledge any more birthdays. In fact, no one but her immediate family knew when her birth year was and she wasn't sure herself. Did it really matter?

The buses were running late this particular day as Emma watched the gathering clouds. The meteorologist had predicted heavy rain in the early evening, but she intended to leave the center long before the storm began.

When she arrived, the sky was darkening. That rain isn't going to wait for me, she thought. By the time I leave it will probably be pouring and I forgot my umbrella. Maybe they have an extra one I can borrow.

She greeted the activities director who was in the process of hanging more drawings on the wall. "Hello, Sara. I see the artists have been at work."

"Oh Mrs. Winberry, how nice to see you." A concerned expression crossed her face. "I'm afraid Delia isn't up to par today. Her daughter-in-law said she didn't sleep well and she's been groggy all morning. She barely ate her lunch then lay down to take a nap."

"Hmm, well I suppose we all have our off days," Emma said, but she felt a nagging discomfort. "Do you think she'll be able to interact with Diane? I believe I've figured out what she's trying to say."

"Really. Diane will be delighted to hear that. She's just come in. Let's see if we can rouse Delia."

Sara led the way to a small room containing three single beds where clients could rest. Dee appeared to be sound asleep.

Emma sat on the edge of the bed and gently shook her arm. "Dee, wake up. It's Emma." She had to repeat the words three times shaking more vigorously before the woman opened her eyes.

"Ma—Ma," she mumbled, not the usual wide-eyed greeting with the lop-sided smile. "Wake up, Dee. It's time for speech therapy."

Emma turned to Sara. "Something is wrong. She acts as if she's been drugged."

"Between you and me, I thought the same thing. The administrator is considering calling the daughter-in-law."

Emma frowned. "I suggest you call her son. He may be more forthcoming with answers."

"You're right. He is the more concerned party."

"Ask Diane to come in here and we'll both try to arouse her," Emma suggested.

Sara nodded and a few minutes later Diane entered the room. She sat on a chair next to the bed.

"Come on, Dee," Emma said. "I know what you're trying to tell us." Dee's eyes opened to slits.

"You're trying to say 'safe', aren't you?" Her eyes opened wider. "*Si,*" she whispered.

"How did you figure that out?' Diane asked.

"If you flip the word 'face' around, it sounds like 'safe'".

She turned her attention back to Dee. "Someone is opening the safe, is that what you're trying to say?"

"*Si.*"

"Is it June?"

"*Si.*" Then weakly Dee rubbed her thumb and two fingers together.

"She's taking out money." Emma said. "I wonder if her husband knows."

"My God," Diane said. "We have to tell Mrs. Carter."

Diane went to speak with the administrator while Emma tried to rouse

Dee. She mumbled a few unintelligible words, then went back to sleep.

Guardian Angel, what's happened?

You may have been getting too close to a secret. Find out what's going on between June and Frances, her inner voice said.

How do I do that? When her inner voice didn't answer, she blew out a breath in frustration.

When Diane returned, she appeared worried. "Mrs. Carter called Dr. Armanetti. He said his wife took his mother to the doctor and he may have put her on a new medication. He's going to call the doctor's office as soon as he has time."

She turned to Emma, as if she had the answer, then shook her head. "Mrs. Carter said to let her rest, but keep an eye on her."

"I'll sit with her for a while," Emma promised. She wasn't about to leave Dee alone. She could easily fall out of the bed. Perhaps she had another stroke, Emma pondered, or . . .

June gave her something, her inner voice suggested.

"Oh God," Emma said aloud. "Would she actually do that?"

"Would who do what?" Mrs. Carter asked.

Emma hadn't noticed the woman quietly enter the room. "I was just thinking out loud." Mrs. Carter bent over the sleeping woman, her face set in a frown. "Delia, wake up!" Dee moaned and half opened her eyes.

"It's time for exercise class."

"No-o-o," she whispered.

The administrator shook her head. "Something is wrong with her. I'm going to call her daughter-in-law, right now."

After the woman left the room, Emma prodded Dee and put her mouth close to her ear. "If you don't wake up, they will take you back to the hospital and take away your lucky stone."

"No!" Dee's eyes opened wide. She seemed confused. "Ma—Ma?" She blinked then ran her tongue over her dry lips and clutched at the pouch around her neck.

"Sit up and drink some water," Emma said. At that moment Mrs. Carter returned.

"She's waking up," Emma said. "Help me sit her up. She wants water."

With some difficulty they succeeded to get Dee into a sitting position and she eagerly sipped water through a straw.

"Whatever it was," Emma said, "she seems to be coming out of it."

"That's a relief. No one was home when I called." The frown on Mrs. Carter's face persisted. "If this happens again, we will have to call the paramedics and get her to a hospital for evaluation. She could have had another mini-stroke. I've seen it happen before."

Emma felt that wasn't the problem, but she said nothing. After all, she knew very little about what to expect from stroke patients.

Within the next hour Dee became more alert and even attempted to participate in the exercises.

Emma was reluctant to leave, but the weather was worsening. The wind had picked up and the sky seemed ready to unleash it's fury on those below. She gave Dee a kiss and was relieved to see her acting almost normal.

Then, with a borrowed umbrella, Emma hurried through the grounds and toward the bus stop. She managed to board a bus just as the storm broke. Maybe I should call Nate, she thought, and ask him to meet me where I have to change buses. Or, perhaps, the rain will stop by then.

She remembered he was going to a meeting of the opera board to help plan a fund raiser concert scheduled at the end of summer.

She fidgeted all the way, alternately watching the sky and wondering if June had really drugged Dee. By the time she had to change buses, the rain had slackened to a steady drizzle.

Oh well, she thought, I've been wet before. She got off the bus and was about to cross the street when a car came careening around the corner, missing her by inches and splashing water up to her knees.

Emma felt firm hands pulling her from behind. "Lady, are you all right?"

She turned to see a burly man wearing a mackintosh holding on to her.

"I think so."

"That car almost hit you. It looked deliberate to me."

"Do you really believe that?"

"Nobody drives like that in this kind'a weather unless they're drunk or want to hit someone."

"You didn't see the license number by any chance, did you?" Emma asked.

"No, there was too much water splashing around, but it was a BMW, either dark blue or gray."

"Thank you so much," Emma said. "Oh, here comes my bus."

The man helped her board and made sure she was safe. She smiled and waved at him, but her entire body trembled as she sat down.

* * *

Emma was shaking and soaked to the skin when she got off the bus. She began walking the block to the condo. When she passed a small coffee shop a few doors down, she inadvertently glanced inside. Her eyes did a double take when she saw Nate sitting at a table—with Yvonne Simmons! They were laughing.

No, it couldn't be. Her eyes were playing tricks on her. Should she go inside? As upset as she was, she'd only make a fool of herself. There had to be a logical explanation. She almost ran the rest of the way to the building.

* * *

When she opened the door, she call out, "Nate, are you here?" No response. She was hoping she had been wrong, that it was someone else. But no, it was Nate all right. She needed his level-headed view of the situation. Her hands still shaking, she shed her wet clothes, brewed a cup of tea and sat in the atrium watching the rain pelt the windows. Her poor tomato plants on the roof garden struggled against their stakes. She let out a "tsk" sound as she watched them wrestle with the elements.

Her thoughts turned to the events of the past hour.

Oh Guardian Angel, am I going mad? Did the driver of that car actually try to run me down, or did he or she lose control on the wet pavement?

What do you think? Her inner voice asked.

Emma closed her eyes and tried to visualize the car, but couldn't. The man who pulled her back had said it was a BMW either dark blue or gray. What kind of car did June drive? She had no idea. Sara would know. June dropped Dee off at the center every morning and picked her up in the evening. Surely the staff knew the make and color of the cars that delivered the clients every day.

Should she call? They would ask questions that she wasn't ready to answer. When the phone rang, she debated as to whether or not to answer. And why didn't Nate come home? Because she was so involved with Dee, she was ignoring him. Had she put their relationship at risk?

Hesitantly she picked up the phone. "Hello."

The muffled voice said, "That was a warning. The next time I won't miss." Emma's hand shook so, she could hardly replace the phone on the charger.

"Emma, are you home?"

She hadn't heard Nate's key in the door. In a few seconds his arms were around her trembling body as she began to sob, clinging to him like a drowning victim.

"What happened, Sparrow?" Tenderly he caressed her face and brushed back her unruly hair.

"Sit," he ordered. "I knew the minute I saw the expression on your face that something was wrong. Now tell me everything." He sat next to her on the sofa and held her hands.

Hesitantly she began with Dee's abrupt change in behavior, Mrs. Carter's call to Dr. Armanetti, then her perilous journey home.

Nate's face grew dark, his brows furrowed, his lips pursed. "That's it. You're not going back there. I've found you injured in hospital emergency rooms too often. I don't want to have to identify your body in the morgue." He was trembling as he spoke those words.

"Something else," Emma whispered. "Another phone call." She told him exactly what the caller had said.

"I'm calling the police, right now!"

She didn't try to stop him as he dialed the non-emergency number and explained the situation. "All right," she heard him say. "Give me the address." He wrote something on the pad sitting next to the phone and disconnected the call.

His voice was calmer as he took Emma in his arms. "The first thing we have to do is file a report and take it from there."

Neither one said anything more for a long time. The wind continued to howl as the storm regained its fury. Emma shivered and clung to Nate, still visualizing him in the coffee shop.

Guardian Angel, tell me what to do.

There was no answer.

She felt his eyes studying her. He knew something else was bothering her, could read her like a book.

"Out with it," he said. "There's something else on your mind."

Her eyes closed and she held her hand over her mouth, then whispered, "I saw you with Yvonne Simmons in the coffee shop." A sob escaped her lips.

"What?"

"When I came home."

"Oh dear God." He took her cold hand and held it tight, lifted her chin with the other. "Sparrow, I stopped at the shop for a cup of coffee after the Chapter meeting and—she was there. I couldn't be rude, so I sat and chatted until the rain let up."

"Didn't you drive?" she asked, willing herself to believe him.

"No. I thought it would be easier to take a cab, but, since they were all occupied, I took the bus. End of story. You do believe me, don't you?"

She nodded, wiping away a tear that escaped. "Of course I do."

"Remember, I am not interested in any other woman. *You* are my woman—full time. Understand?" Deep creases formed between his eyes.

"Yes. I'm sorry I doubted you. This whole thing has my mind in a jumble." She remembered Gladys and Cornell and their discussion about trust.

They sat together for a long time entwined in each others' arms, watching the rain,.

CHAPTER 29

AFTER EMMA AND NATE MADE out the report at the police station, they sat in a restaurant trying to pretend this was a normal morning. Emma nibbled on her croissant and Nate pushed his scrambled eggs around the plate, taking an occasional bite.

"The officer filling out the report didn't seem too enthusiastic about getting any results," Emma said.

"I suppose the police are inundated with such things and they take a back seat to more serious issues." Nate took a swallow of cold coffee and motioned the waitress for a refill.

"I think we have to find out more about June. She may have a past, you know." Emma cringed at the angry expression on Nate's face.

He put down his fork and placed both palms on the table. "Now don't go playing sleuth again. It's gotten you nothing but trouble in the past."

Emma heaved a sigh. "Do you want me to just abandon Dee? To refuse to help her?"

"You make me sound like an ogre. I just want you safe. Is that asking too much?"

"No, I suppose not. But I don't feel that Dee is safe, either. I'm afraid for her." She gazed at him with her luminous gray eyes and an expression of supplication.

"Don't look at me like that. I care about what happens to Dee, but I care about you much more."

"I know." She reached over and took his hand. "What can we do?"

"Compromise," he answered. "You go back to the speech therapy sessions for another few weeks, but I go with you."

"Oh, Nate, really? That's so sweet of you. Are you sure you want to spend your time there?"

"That's not the issue. I know how stubborn you are and I simply intend to keep you out of trouble. Besides, then you won't think I'm with Yvonne." His eyes twinkles. "Is it a deal?"

She nodded. "Deal." With that, she picked up her croissant and finished every bite.

* * *

That afternoon when the phone rang, Nate answered, prepared for another hang up. "Hello," he said, a stern note in his voice.

"Hi Nate, it's Gladys."

"Well, how are things going?" He smiled at the upbeat tone in her voice.

"Things are working out, slowly, but on a positive note."

"Let me hand you over to Emma. She's practically tearing the phone out of my hand."

"Hi Gladys, my dear friend, I miss you." Emma settled in her favorite chair in the atrium ready to listen to all the news.

"I miss you, too, and I can't thank you enough for all the support."

"Nonsense. What are friends for? Now tell me everything."

"Well, Cornell and his new partner are merging with another small publishing house. That's the way things go these days. They're expanding into e-books as well as print."

"I don't know what all that means," Emma said. "When I read a book I want to hold it in my hands and turn the pages."

"I know," Gladys agreed, "but technology is taking over our lives."

Emma let out a "humph."

"We're having a garage sale next week. Boy have I accumulated a lot of junk."

"That happens." Emma remembered how she had cleaned out the attic and basement of her old house. "Where do you plan on going? Have you put your house on the market?"

"The realtor is coming tomorrow. Not sure where we'll go just yet, but we'll start looking in one of the areas in New Jersey that's commuting distance from the publishing company."

"That makes sense."

They exchanged family news, and, after they exhausted those topics, Gladys asked how Dee was getting along.

Emma told her everything that had happened, but left out the part of seeing Nate with another woman. She tucked that away, hopefully forever.

"Oh my God," Gladys said. "You're getting involved in something dangerous again."

"No, no, Nate is keeping a close eye on me." Emma lowered her voice.

After Emma terminated the call, she shared everything Gladys had said about their future plans with Nate. He sat listening and nodding in agreement.

"Was that it?" he asked.

"Yes, we talked about the impending move and the kids. Tessa's arm is healing. The cast is off and she's wearing a support. All is well there." Then she got up and walked toward the kitchen. "I'm going to make a cup of tea. Would you like one?"

"Sure," he called after her.

* * *

Later that evening Emma said she felt like taking a walk, needed a few things from the drug store. "Do you want to come?" she asked Nate.

"Huh? I don't think so. This thriller I'm reading is reaching its climax, and I can't put it down."

She let out a relieved breath. "You don't usually get that engrossed in a book." When she got no reply, she grabbed her purse and slipped out the door.

When she was about a half block down, Emma took her cell phone from her purse, checked Marge's number on a slip of paper, and placed the call.

The phone rang six times and Emma was about to disconnect when a breathless voice said, "Hello?"

"Is this Marge? Emma Winberry calling."

"Oh, I just walked in the door. What can I do for you?"

Emma quickly told her of the happenings of the previous day and their visit to the police station.

"Oh my God," was all the woman could say. "What kind of car does June drive?"

"Uh, they have a couple of cars, one is a black SUV, the other is a dark blue BMW."

"That's it," Emma said. "I suspect that's the one that almost ran me down." She hesitated a moment. "How much do you know about June's past?"

"Nothing. All of a sudden Doc said he was getting married again and— there she was," Marge whispered.

Emma heard the bitter disappointment in her voice. She was obviously very much in love with her boss. "Do you at least know what her maiden name was and where she came from? I asked her that once, but she was evasive, didn't seem to want to talk about her past."

"I think I have the name somewhere in my desk. I'll look for it, but I don't know where she's from."

"Can you ask the doctor?"

"What reason would I give him?"

"Tell him you thought you noticed a slight southern accent and did she come from one of the southern states. She's not from Chicago. I thought I heard some remnants of an accent," Emma said.

"Okay, I'll try."

"Get back to me as soon as possible."

After Emma put her cell phone back in her purse, she went to the drug store and bought a few items that she really didn't need. But she didn't want Nate to know what she was up to just yet.

* * *

Nate slammed the book down. "My God, I let Emma go out alone! What was I thinking? Damn!"

He jumped up from his chair and almost collided with her as she walked in the door. "Are you all right?" he asked, examining her from head to toe.

"Of course. Why wouldn't I be?" She shrugged.

He took her in his arms and held her close. "With all the strange things going on, I thought .. ." He didn't finish the sentence, merely held her.

"Maybe you should read more thrillers," she whispered, kissing his chin and feeling secure in his love.

CHAPTER 30

JUNE SLAMMED ON HER BRAKES narrowly missing another car as she carelessly drove into the parking lot. Got to be more careful, she told herself. Can't afford to get into an accident.

When she walked into the coffee shop, Frances stared at her through her snake-eyes. "I saw how you drove in here," she said through gritted teeth. "You'd better not screw up or your fancy life is over. Remember that."

"I know, I know. Listen, I couldn't get any money this week but I'll give you this necklace. It's twenty-four carat gold and worth a lot."

Frances raised her hands. "I don't want anything that can be traced. Cash only."

"But you can sell it. Lots of jewelers are buying gold."

"Then *you* sell it and bring me the money." Frances wasn't pleased and the expression on her face mirrored her thoughts.

"Coffee ladies?" the waitress asked, a pot in each hand.

"Yes, regular," June said pushing her cup forward with trembling hands. "You'd better give her decaf," Frances said. "She's a little nervous today." She looked at June, a question on her face.

"Okay, decaf."

When the waitress walked away, Frances asked, "What's going on with the old lady?"

June shook her head. "I guess I gave her too much Valium Thursday. The center called my husband and asked if there was a change in medication because she was so sleepy."

Frances' brow furrowed and the edges of her mouth turned down in a scowl. "How much did you give her?"

"Just half of a five-milligram tablet."

"Give her half of that. You can't have people asking questions. The change has to be gradual."

"Yeah. My husband asked me if the doctor had added anything new. I told him no, she just didn't sleep well."

That explanation didn't appear to satisfy Frances. She sipped her coffee and continued to stare at June. "What about that Winberry dame?"

"I think I scared her off. Almost hit her with my car when it was raining so hard." She smiled, thinking that would satisfy Frances.

"You idiot! Did she get the license plate number? The color and make of the car? Was anybody else there?"

"It was raining too hard. I just wanted to scare her. Got away as quick as I could."

"Don't do anything else—no more phone calls from either one of us, and take a different car. You've got a couple, don't you?"

"Yeah."

"That woman is no fool. If she reports this to the police, it's eventually going to come back to you. You are a dumb …" She left the sentence unfinished.

"How dare you insult me like that." June balled her hands into fists and scowled.

"You're in no position to accuse me of anything. You're the one in trouble and I hold all the cards. Remember that."

June let out a breath and dropped her head into her hands.

"Now go sell that necklace and bring me the money next week." Without another word, Frances got up and walked out of the coffee shop.

June watched her through hate-filled eyes as her head began to pound. I've got to think of a way to get rid of that woman if it's the last thing I do, she promised herself. And soon.

CHAPTER 31

"GOT EVERYTHING READY?" NATE ASKED as Emma packed the last of her muffins in a plastic carrier and snapped the lid shut.

"All set." She glanced around to make sure she hadn't forgotten anything.

As they drove out of the parking garage, Emma rolled down the window and breathed in the fresh summer air. The meteorologists had predicted a perfect day, sunny and warm, with temperatures reaching the mid-eighties. That was a little warm for Emma but she knew the children would have a fine time in the swimming pool.

Sylvia and James lived on the north side of Chicago in a large Victorian house. The backyard was spacious with plenty of room for an above ground pool and a play area as well.

"Didn't you tell me that they recently got a dog?" Nate asked.

"Uh huh. Sylvia said they went to a shelter and got a medium sized dog."

"Any particular breed?"

"I have no idea, but I'm eager to see the animal. My kids always had a dog. It's good for children to learn responsibility for a pet."

When Emma and Nate arrived, the others were already there. The sound of children laughing and shouting to one another, interspersed with a few barks, brought a smile to Emma's face, and she temporarily pushed her concerns to the recesses of her brain.

Oh Guardian Angel, how lucky I am to have this wonderful family with five healthy grandchildren.

Nurture the youngest, her inner voice said. *She will need your guidance.*

Emma knew that young Robin, only a year and a half, had inherited her 'gift', her sixth sense. It seemed to pass on every other generation. Grandma Lizzie passed it to Emma and, now, she had given it to Robin. It was already evident. Emma heaved a sigh. Life would not be easy for this little one and her parents, but she would give them all the help she could.

"Are you going to stand there all afternoon, or are we going in?" Nate asked taking the container with the muffins from her hand.

"I was listening to the children."

As they walked to the door, Sylvia opened it. "I saw you from the window." She hugged Emma. "We haven't seen you two in a while."

"I know, everyone is so busy."

Nate gave Sylvia a kiss on the cheek and didn't respond to Emma's remark. They walked through the spacious rooms with their high ceilings. Nate nodded approvingly at the new paint job—all the walls a sand color, complementing the polished hard wood floors.

James, Sylvia's husband, came in to welcome them. "Everybody's outside. The day is perfect and the kids are exhausting that poor dog. Come on, Nate, and have a beer."

"What kind of dog did you get?" Emma asked.

"Some sort of terrier mix," Sylvia answered. "She's just the right size for the kids and they adore her."

"What's her name?"

Sylvia laughed. "Lulu. How about that?"

They walked out into the yard and were welcomed by the rest of Emma's family: her oldest son, Stephen and his wife Pat, and her youngest son, Martin, and his wife, Bertie. Their daughter, Robin, toddled up to Emma and grabbed her leg. "Gam—Gam," she said in her baby voice.

"Oh, you sweet thing." Emma lifted the child in her arms and smothered her with kisses. Robin laughed then wriggled out of Emma's arms and toddled off to play with her cousins.

Emma followed to kiss her other grandchildren and pet the dog.

"Can I help in the kitchen?" She called to her daughter as Lulu licked her hands and face.

"Pat and I have everything set. James will fire up the grill, won't you dear?" She laughed.

He and Nate had their heads together in deep conversation.

"Oh sure, honey," James said. "Come on, Nate, give me a hand and we'll continue our talk."

"I swear, sometimes men are worse than women," Sylvia said, laughing. "Every chance he gets, James asks Nate about investing."

"Not a bad idea," Pat said turning to Emma. "That condo you two live in proclaims Nate an authority."

Emma smiled. "I agree. If it were left up to me, we'd probably be living in a hovel."

As Emma sat in a lounge chair watching the children, she overheard Nate and James talking. "A friend of mine has offered to take me and a couple of other guys from the gym sailing on Lake Michigan," Nate said with enthusiasm.

"Wow, I didn't know you were interested in sailing," James said as he lit the coals.

"When Emma and I were in Florida, my son told me about a friend of his who was actually living on a sailboat in the Caribbean. I don't relish the idea of living on a boat, but I would like to do some sailing."

"What does Emma say about it?"

"I haven't told her." He shrugged. "She's so involved with Delia that I do have a lot of time on my hands. I might just give it a try."

"Go for it," James said. "Now these coals have to burn down so let's get another beer."

With that, the men disappeared into the house. Emma froze. Why hadn't Nate said anything about sailing? She was occupied with Dee, but was he hiding it from her? And who was the friend with the sailboat? Could it be Yvonne?

* * *

The afternoon progressed with no fighting among the children and only a few falls and scrapes. Lulu escaped after an hour of being chased and fondled by the children. She found refuge in her crate in the kitchen and fell asleep.

They had just finished their burgers and hot dogs and were eating ice cream and muffins, when Robin came up to Emma, a frown on her tiny face.

"What's the matter, baby?"

Robin started to sing, "Dee–Dee–Dee … "

Emma thought for a moment. Dee had been to Martin and Bertie's house shortly before her stroke. She sang simple songs to Robin and the child had tried to follow along. It had amazed all of them that she was able to pick up the melodies. Was she now trying to say Dee?

"Honey, are you remembering when you and Dee were singing together?"

The child gazed at Emma through huge blue eyes that lit up at the name. Then she sang again, "Dee–Dee–Dee…."

"Yes, you are," Emma said.

Suddenly the child's demeanor changed. She frowned and the sides of her mouth turned down. She pushed Emma's arm, over and over.

"Robin!" Bertie grabbed her daughter. The child was crying with wrenching sobs. "Naughty! You don't push Grandma."

"Wait, Bertie, I think she's trying to tell me something."

Robin had buried her face in her mother's shoulder and continued to sob.

"Robin," Emma said softly, "Are you trying to tell me that someone is pushing Dee?" The child turned to her grandmother and nodded. "Dee—Dee," she muttered.

"I think this little girl needs a nap," Bertie said.

"Don't scold her," Emma said. "She doesn't understand, but I do."

She followed mother and daughter into the house and stayed until Robin fell asleep.

"I was that way as a child," Emma explained to Bertie. "Suddenly I would get upset over something I didn't understand. My mother was at a loss as to how to handle me, but my grandmother understood."

Emma took her daughter-in-law's hand. "Be patient with her and try to associate her behavior with something that's happening. At times it will be obvious, other times … " She shrugged. "I believe that Dee's daughter-in-law may be abusing her. It's possible Robin is picking up on that."

"But she's not even two years old."

"Don't ask me how it works. I've been trying to figure that out all my life."

The picnic ended on a high note when the children played in the swimming pool until their parents dragged them out. The sun sat low in the sky. The women cleaned everything up and they all went home.

As they drove back to the condo, Emma wanted to ask Nate about his conversation with James.

Before she could bring up the topic he asked, "What was that scene with Robin all about?"

Emma shook her head. "That child has my sixth sense. She knew that someone has been pushing Dee. That's what she was trying to tell me by acting it out."

"You really believe that? She's just a toddler," Nate scoffed.

"I do believe it. I remember all too well my childhood—everything I didn't understand. How did I know things that no one else did? I told Bertie about my experiences. Thank goodness my Grandma Lizzie was there to explain it to me. I have to do the same for Robin. I owe it to her."

Emma decided now was not the time to ask questions about sailing, so she tucked it away for later.

CHAPTER 32

ON MONDAY EVENING, NATE ANSWERED the ringing phone prepared for another hang up. "May I speak with Mrs. Winberry, please?" a woman's voice asked.

"Just a minute." He put his hand over the mouthpiece and called, "Emma, for you."

Emma took the phone, smiled, and walked into the atrium. "Hello."

"Mrs. Winberry, this is Marge."

"Oh good, have you found out anything?"

"Well, I did search my desk and found the name—June Foran."

"That's something." A common name, Emma thought, then asked, "Did you find out where she came from?"

Marge snickered. "Doc thought it was a strange question, but I acted curious. We've been together for a long time and he's gotten used to some of my quirks."

That woman is so much in love with Mike, Emma thought. How sad.

"He said she came from the West Coast, somewhere near San Francisco. I didn't try to pin him down any closer. He looked at me kind of funny as it was."

"You did fine, Marge. I'll take it from here. Has anything unusual happened at the clinic?" She winked at Nate who stood with his arms folded across his chest.

"No, nothing." She hesitated. "You will let me know if you find out anything."

"I promise."

When Emma terminated the call, she turned to Nate's scowling face. "What are you up to now?"

"I was going to tell you but I knew you would be angry. I simply asked Marge if she knew June's maiden name and where she came from, that's all."

"And what do you intend to do with that information, Mrs. Sleuth?"

"Gladys' daughter is a computer whiz. She'll simply try to find some information on June's background."

"Why?" He wasn't about to let up.

She put her hands on his shoulders. "That woman has a past, I can feel it. And Frances may be blackmailing her."

He shook his head. "You read too many novels. Do you know how ridiculous that sounds?"

She raised her chin and pursed her lips. "Nevertheless, it can't do any harm. Now I have to give this information to Gladys."

Emma called Gladys as Nate walked away muttering about minding her own business.

"Hi my friend, how are things going?"

"Pretty well. We've been searching for just the right condo. You can't rush these things, you know. We do have someone interested in our house."

"Wow, that was quick."

"This is a prime location and, even though the housing market is down, houses, condos and townhouses around here are selling."

"That is certainly to your advantage." Emma felt relieved for her friend.

"Now I bet you have something on your mind. I can almost hear the wheels turning," Gladys said.

Just like Nate, Emma thought.

"As a matter of fact, I do. Would Nora be able to search for any information on June Armanetti's background?"

"If anyone can, she can," Gladys said with a snicker.

"Her maiden name was Foran and she supposedly came from somewhere in the San Francisco area. I know it's not much."

"We'll see what Nora can do with this. I agree, it's beyond me, but the girl is unbelievable."

"Now, what about the phone calls?" Gladys asked.

"Ever since my close call with that car, the calls have stopped. We'll see if they resume."

"You be careful," her friend cautioned.

"I will. Nate is going with me to the center for the next few weeks."

"Good. Somebody has to take care of you."

They said their goodbyes and Emma looked out over the turbulent water of the lake. Yes, Nate and her Guardian Angel would watch over her, but who is taking care of Dee?

* * *

On Tuesday, true to his word, Nate drove her to the center. When Dee saw Emma she gave her a lop-sided smile and hobbled over to her. "Ma—Ma."

"I'm glad to see you looking so bright today." She turned to Nate. "She's so alert."

"Hello Mrs. Winberry, " Sara said coming up to them. "And Mr. … "?

"Sandler," Nate said. "I've decided to drive Emma here for the next few weeks. The bus ride is rather long and tiring."

"How nice of you. Delia was fine all day yesterday and this morning. Mrs. Carter did talk with her son and there has been no change in medications, so, maybe she was just tired. You never know with these stroke patients."

The speech therapy session went well. Dee was able to count to ten in both Italian and English. Emma was delighted. If she continued this way, Emma would no longer be needed. She was happy for Dee but just a little disappointed. She was enjoying this challenge.

* * *

When Thursday rolled around Emma noticed a change in Dee's response time.

"Diane, what do you make of this?" she asked the therapist when Dee stopped counting at five.

"I don't know. She's slurring her words and slowing down—a big change from Tuesday." She turned to her patient.

"Delia, are you tired now?"

Dee nodded and muttered something neither one of them understood.

"How about a little rest?"

Emma and Diane each took one of Dee's arms and helped her to the room used for rest periods. Within minutes she was asleep.

"I'm going to speak with Mrs. Carter," Diane said. "From Sara's report, she's been bright and responsive until yesterday. Then, as today, her response time was slower. I think something's going on and she needs to be checked out by the doctor."

They both walked over to the director's office but she had left for the day.

"Why don't you go home, Mrs. Winberry? Call in tomorrow and talk with Sara."

"I will."

* * *

Emma was unusually quiet as they drove home.

Oh Guardian Angel, is this something to be expected or is it more serious?

Wait and watch, her inner voice said.

That wasn't much help. What shall I watch for?

No answer. She let out a frustrated sigh.

"Even though you're not talking, I can hear the wheels going full blast in your brain," Nate said.

Emma glanced out the window at people hurrying down the sidewalks, everyone with a destination in mind. Right now, she was in limbo, had no direction, and didn't like it one bit.

"I can't help but feel that this is the calm before the storm."

"Go on," he said.

"Something else is going to happen. I know it and I'm helpless to stop it." She let out a "tsk."

"I've heard all this before. If you don't know what the problem is, you will have to stand back and look at the situation objectively."

"That's business talk," Emma said, a note of irritation in her voice.

"Let's wait until we get upstairs," he said as he pulled the car into the parking garage. "Then we'll make a list of the possibilities and see which is the most likely."

"Hmm, I like that idea."

Nate tapped the side of his head. "Logic."

The first thing Emma did when they walked into the condo was check the answering machine. No messages. Then she walked out into the atrium and surveyed her plants—no heads drooping in need of water.

When she walked into the kitchen, Nate had a sheet of paper and pen in hand. "Sit," he ordered. She complied.

He drew a line down the center of the page. On the left side he wrote "facts", and on the right, "possibilities."

On the left hand column he wrote:

Dee had a stroke leaving her paralyzed on right side. Unable to speak intelligibly.

"Can you think of anything else?" he asked Emma.

"Put down living with Mike and June and attending the Woods Day Care Center."

"All right." He wrote them down, then, possibilities he listed:

At risk for another stroke, minor or major.

Because of instability may be injuring herself accidentally.

He looked up at Emma. "June may be abusing her," she said, "and, or, drugging her."

Nate frowned but wrote them down. "So what can you, Emma Winberry, do about any of these *possibilities?*" He exaggerated the last word.

She shook her head. "I don't know, but I do know that something is going on between June and Frances."

"Again, if that is a fact, what can you do about it? And, if I may repeat as I have so many times, it's none of your business."

She got up from the chair, raised her arms out at the sides, then let them drop. "You're so logical. I suppose you're right. There isn't anything I can do right now. But who knows?"

He stood up and took her in his arms. "Sparrow, just let it play out and see what happens. Dee may still make a full recovery."

Emma nodded. Not as long as she stays with June, she thought, but kept that to herself.

CHAPTER 33

JUNE DROVE TO THE COFFEE shop, her mind conjuring up various scenarios. How to remove Frances from her life? That was her first goal, then to take care of her dear mother-in-law.

She was all sweetness and smiles as she slid into the booth across from Frances and handed the envelope across the table.

"Well," Frances said, "You certainly are chipper this morning. How are things going with the old lady?" She put the envelope in her purse without counting the bills.

"I think I've come up with just the right dose. I'm not giving it to her every day—every other day, and not on weekends. I don't want my husband to notice any change in her behavior."

"Good thinking. And what about that Mrs. Winberry?"

"I think I scared her off. She won't cause any more trouble."

"How can you be so sure?"

June shrugged. "Trust me." She had been muddling over that obstacle, too, and had come up with just the right way to take Emma out of the picture.

"Trust you?" Frances guffawed so loud that people in the surrounding booths looked at them. "You're the last person in the world I would trust."

June simply stared, biting down on her lip and clenching her fists under the table, but she said nothing.

The waitress brought their coffee and asked if they wanted anything else. "I'll have a cinnamon bun," June said.

Frances' eyes widened as she cocked her head to the side. June had never ordered anything but coffee. "Bring me one, too," she said. "Are we celebrating something?"

"Yes." June handed her a folded piece of paper. "Can you get me these supplies?" Frances opened the sheet, read the items, and stared. "Why?"

"None of your business. I'm just asking a favor. You have access. Get them for me."

"I have a feeling you're up to no good. Yes, I can get them, but only once. Don't ask again. If anyone at the clinic sees me, I can get in trouble."

June shook her head. "You're cunning enough to slip them in your bag when no one's around."

Frances laughed. "You and I are so alike in some ways. All right, I'll ask no questions."

"Will you bring them next week?"

"I'll try."

The waitress brought their cinnamon buns and they ate in silence. Then June stood up, dropped some bills on the table, nodded to her cohort, and left.

Frances sat for a while wondering what she was up to. Better if she didn't know. As long as the money kept coming, she was satisfied. But, she would be careful—didn't trust Mrs. Michael Armanetti for one minute.

CHAPTER 34

THE FOLLOWING WEEK EMMA FELT a foreboding of danger. Oh Guardian Angel, something is going to happen. I know it. What can I do?

Share your suspicions, her inner voice said.

Emma frowned. What did her Guardian Angel expect her to do, tell Mrs. Carter that she suspected June of harming Dee? She had no proof. How should she approach this delicate subject?

On Tuesday when Emma and Nate went to the center, Dee was lying down. "What's wrong, Sara?" Emma asked.

The woman shrugged and shook her head. "Again her daughter-in-law said she slept poorly last night."

"What do you think?" Emma asked looking Sara directly in the eye.

"I'm beginning to wonder."

"I've been suspicious for a long time." Perhaps I should share my thoughts now. She turned to Nate.

"Why don't you entertain the clients with your piano playing?"

"Humph. You want me out of your way. All right. The number lady is coming toward us. I'll intercept her and lead her to the piano."

Sara smiled. "You're a fortunate woman to have such an understanding man." The expression on Sara's face spoke volumes

"Indeed I am and I never forget it."Emma didn't ask. She saw no wedding ring and Sara had never referred to a husband or children. It was none of her business. But, she was curious. It was her nature.

"May I speak with Mrs. Carter for a few minutes?" Emma asked.

"I think she's available." Sara led the way to the administrator's office and knocked on the door.

"Come in."

"Go ahead," Sara said. "I'll see you later."

Emma walked into the office and took the proffered chair. "How are you today, Mrs. Winberry?"

"Fine, thank you."

"I presume this is not a social call, so, what's on your mind?"

Emma fidgeted for a moment then confided her suspicions to Mrs. Carter. "I believe that Delia's daughter-in-law is abusing her: the bruises, the falls, and now the unexplained grogginess."

The administrator cupped her chin in her hand and stared out the window for a moment. "To be truthful with you, I've wondered that myself. But we have no proof."

"What do you do in cases like this? Wait until something more serious happens?"

"Adult Protective Services is an agency that investigates suspected cases of abuse, but I don't want to go that far just yet. I received a call from Sam Armanetti, Delia's youngest son. He will be coming to Chicago on a business trip next week. He said he would stop by the Center. I'll speak with him then. I believe he will be staying at the Armanetti home. I'll confide our concerns to him and let him assess the situation. Then, if there is some doubt, I'll call Adult Protective Services."

"That sounds like a great plan," Emma agreed, feeling relieved that, at least, someone would be watching June.

"I really shouldn't be sharing this information with you because you're not a family member, but you do seem to be the most concerned party here and Dr. Armanetti did give me written permission to involve you in his mother's progress. Please keep this between the two of us for now."

"I will, and thank you." Emma left the office with a lighter step. A solution had presented itself—now to wait and see what happens.

* * *

Later that evening Emma received a phone call from her daughter-in-law, Bertie.

"I've been pondering Robin's actions at the picnic. For the last few days she's been punching her teddy bear and saying "Dee—Dee—Dee." When I ask her why she's doing it, she starts to cry. I don't know how to handle this. I need your advice."

Emma shook her head. "I understand completely. No matter what anyone says, that child knows that Dee is being abused. She doesn't understand, but it's upsetting her. As a child, when I behaved in unusual ways, my grandma Lizzie would take me in her arms and tell me it was all right. Then she would try to distract me. Sometimes it worked, other times, it didn't.

"My advice is to hold her and tell her Dee will be all right. Grandma will fix it. Give it a try and let me know."

"Thanks, I will. Being a social worker I've seen all kinds of family problems, but nothing like this, especially with my own daughter."

After they terminated the call, Emma looked out over Lake Michigan. The waves crashed against the shore. A bank of dark clouds blotted out the rays of the sun. Mother Nature was brewing up a storm. Was there one of another type coming into her own life?

Oh Guardian Angel, help me to guide this child and to resolve the problems with Dee. You can only do so much, the inner voice said.

* * *

On the next visit to the day care center, an excited Sara met Emma and Nate at the door.

"Oh Mrs. Winberry, Mr. Sandler, Sam Armanetti is here. What a charmer! He has all the ladies eating out of his hand. And Delia perked up so when she saw him. First she burst into tears and then began singing. He sang right along with her, nice voice, too."

She stopped for a breath. "Too bad he has a wife and three kids. All the good ones are taken." She gave Emma a wan look then said, "Come and meet him."

Emma and Nate followed her into the day room where the clients were drawing pictures under the supervision of the art therapist. Dee was busy making strokes on a piece of paper, a man sitting at her side. He seemed to feel their eyes on him and looked up.

"Mr. Armanetti," Sara said, "this is Emma Winberry and Nate Sandler."

"Ma—Ma." Dee called out. Then she grasped her son's hand. "Mas—Mas."

Sam kissed his mother then rose from the chair to greet them. Emma had to agree with Sara's assessment. Sam had black curly hair and large dark brown eyes with tiny laugh wrinkles at the corners. His full-lipped smile revealed deep dimples, a charmer, indeed.

"I'm so glad to meet you both. Heard how much you've helped Mom. Thank you doesn't cover it."

Agnes came up to them and pointed to Sam, a huge grin on her face. "He's one hundred and one—very special—one hundred and one." She turned and walked away.

Nate laughed. "She's quite a gal."

"So I've heard," Sam agreed.

Emma glanced at Dee's drawing. This one depicted a house with three stick figures standing in front. The center one appeared to be a woman flanked by a man on either side—obviously Dee and her two sons. There was no other figure. She had left June out of the drawing.

"Delia," Diane called. "It's time for our speech session."

"Mas?" Dee asked.

"Your son can come, too."

Dee Sam and Emma accompanied Diane into the therapy room while Nate played a few tunes on the piano to the delight of the number lady.

"All right," Diane said. "Today we're concentrating on practicing a few words in English." Dee nodded holding tightly to Sam's hand.

Diane printed out SAM. "What is this word?"

"Mas," Dee said.

"No, Delia, it isn't. You are saying it backwards. I want you to concentrate on saying SAM—SAM."

Dee tried over and over, but the word kept coming out "MAS." Next Diane tried the individual sounds—still unsuccessful.

Dee turned to her son and caressed his face with her left hand. "Mas, *ti amo.*"

Emma's eyes widened. "She said "I love you" in Italian—correctly."

"That's really encouraging," Diane said. "Now if we can just get her to say more words correctly, her brain may begin reinterpreting them." She glanced at Sam who appeared to be on the verge of tears.

"Mr. Armanetti, these things take time. When certain areas of the brain have to take over the functions of damaged parts, it's a struggle for the patient. This is another breakthrough. I'm very pleased."

Then she turned to Emma. "Perhaps we should concentrate on the Italian words, since that language seems more natural to her."

"Anything that works."

Sam gave his mother a hug. "Listen, Mom, I want you to work very hard and get well. Then I'll take you to live with me and my family if you want to."

*"Si, si."*She kept caressing her son's face and lifting his hand to her lips. She showed more enthusiasm than any of them had seen before.

"How long are you staying?" Emma asked.

"I came straight from the airport. I have a business meeting tomorrow morning downtown. But I must leave by Friday."

"Are you staying with your brother?"

"Yes, that way I can spend as much time as possible with Mom." He smiled at Dee and kissed her forehead.

"Mr. Armanetti," Sara said as she walked into the room, "the administrator would like to speak with you for a few moments."

"Sure. I'll be right back, Mom." He hugged Dee and followed Sara to Mrs. Carter's office. Emma waited with Dee and worked with the speech therapist on counting.

Fifteen minutes later Sam returned with a look of deep concern on his face. He raised his mother's sleeves and examined her arms. A healing bruise covered a good portion of her left upper arm. He frowned and slowly let out a breath.

Dee didn't pay any attention as she concentrated on her numbers.

"Mom, I have to go to Mike's house and get settled in. Do you want to come with me now?" Her eyes widened. "*Si, si.*" She glanced from Diane to Emma.

"Go ahead," the therapist said. "It's about time to finish here and this is a special day." She went to notify Sara that Dee was leaving with her son.

As they made their way to the door, Agnes approached. "One-hundred-and-one—very special."

"Thanks," Sam said giving her an engaging smile. "You're pretty special yourself."

Her face lit up. "Very, very special. I am number one." She grinned and pranced off into the other room.

* * *

On the ride home, Emma decided it was time to ask the question that was nagging her.

"Nate, when we were at the picnic at Sylvia and James' house, I overheard you talking about going sailing. You never mentioned it to me."

"Well, you were so involved with Dee that I considered it. Yvonne's brother is an experienced sailor and has a docked boat on Lake Michigan. She invited me and a couple of the other men from the gym to go out one of these days."

Emma swallowed hard. "Are you going?"

"I've thought about it, maybe sometime later. You have been pretty occupied lately. At times I feel that there's no time for 'us'."

"Oh Nate, no! That's not true. Well, maybe I have been spending too much time with Dee. But I promise that as soon as she's safe, all my time will be yours."

He laughed. "Why my little Sparrow, I do believe you're jealous."

"Do I have any reason to be?"

"Absolutely not," he said, a little too forcefully.

* * *

Later Emma stood on the roof garden watching the sailboats on the lake. They glided by gracefully.

Oh Guardian Angel, am I in danger of losing Nate because of my time with Dee?

Don't try to tether him, her inner voice said. *He will always come back. You must trust him.*

Chapter 35

WHEN EMMA AND NATE WENT BACK to the center, Sam had already gone home. Sara met them as they entered.

"Mrs. Carter had a talk with Sam. He said he watched June very closely. She showed no outward resentment toward his mother and he could find no evidence of abuse. He discussed it with his brother who agreed with him. They decided that all the bruises were accidental." She let out a breath and shook her head.

"June is cagey," Emma said. "Of course she was on her best behavior and you can bet that Dee won't have any new bruises for quite a while. Then Mrs. Carter won't call Adult Protective Services at this point, huh?"

"Nope. We have no cause, unless something suspicious happens."

Emma didn't like that at all. If Dee had a serious accident, she was sure that June would cover it up. She made a mental note to call Gladys and see if her daughter had uncovered anything about June's past.

The speech session went well. Dee was so inspired by Sam's visit, that she worked harder than ever. She was now able to count to ten in Italian, pronouncing the words correctly. The next step was to count in English. Diane was optimistic.

On the way home, Emma told Nate about Dee's progress. "Good. Then they won't need you anymore. Am I right?"

"I suppose." She didn't like the idea of leaving her friend, but Nate was right, as usual. She couldn't impose on him any longer.

* * *

Later that day Emma called Gladys. "Any progress?"

"I'm afraid not. She can't find any June Foran in the San Francisco area fitting that description. She even checked birth certificates. Nothing that fits the age of your lady."

"How did she do that?"

"I don't ask, but I think birth and death certificates are a matter of public record. She has a computer nerd friend and I sometimes wonder if everything they do is above board."

Something Gladys said triggered a thought. "Ask her to check the death certificates. It wouldn't be the first time someone assumed the identity of a deceased person."

"I never thought of that," Gladys said. "Of course, with all the mysteries you read … " She left the sentence unfinished.

"I wouldn't want her to get into any trouble with this search though," Emma said.

"Oh she won't, believe me. She's very careful. Besides, she works for an Internet company and does all kinds of research. I wouldn't be surprised if she ends up working for the CIA." Gladys laughed, deep and hearty.

"I'm glad to hear you laugh again, my friend. Things are going well, I take it?"

"Yes. We've found a condo in Montclaire that fits our needs and, as I told you, someone is interested in this house. So—I'm in the process of getting rid of more stuff that I don't need any longer. Such a good feeling."

They talked for another half-hour. When they ended the call, Emma turned to Nate. His eyes bore into her.

"Why are you staring at me like that?"

"What was that all about?"

She told him about the condo and the impending move.

"The part before that," he persisted.

Emma plopped down on the couch. "Her daughter hasn't been able to uncover any information about June. I think she's lying about her past."

"Let it go," he warned. "If you keep digging, you'll only get yourself in trouble again." He stood staring down at her, his arms folded across his chest.

"I wouldn't know where to start," Emma said, "so I'll have to let it go."

"Good. Now how about some dinner?"

* * *

That night Emma received a call from Marge.

"Mrs. Winberry, you told me to call if anything unusual happened."

"Yes."

"Well, today Dr. A got a phone call. He looked so angry that his faced turned a dark red. I was rather concerned as I watched him out of the corner of my eye. When he finished the call, he told Frances to take care of the clients and call the vet next door if there was anything serious.

"Then he said he would be back as soon as he could and stormed out of the clinic."

"Do you have any idea what happened?"

"No. If it involved his mother, I'm sure he would have said something."

"How was he when he returned?"

"Very quiet. To me he looked kind of—sad. I asked him if I could do anything and he said no. He could handle the problem. He finished the day but didn't talk much."

"Thanks, Marge. Let me know if you hear anything else."

"So, what now?" Nate asked as Emma terminated the call.

"Dr. Armanetti got a call from someone that, obviously, upset him. Marge said he was gone for awhile and said nothing when he returned."

"So?"

"I'll bet it involved June," Emma said lifting her chin. "So?"

"I know. It's none of my business."

"Exactly." He went back to reading his newspaper.

Emma walked out onto the roof garden. She surveyed her plants with a keen eye, picked off a dead leaf here and there, then sat in a lounge chair and surveyed the placid lake.

Oh Guardian Angel, this is so frustrating, not knowing what's going on. Does it involve Dee?

Be patient, her inner voice said. *Dee is safe—for now.*

Emma frowned. She didn't like that answer at all. Had June gotten into some kind of trouble? If it didn't involve Dee, what was it all about?

CHAPTER 36

JUNE INCHED HER WAY INTO the coffee shop, her head down, a scowl on her face. Slowly she sat across from Frances.

"What?" Frances asked.

"I got in trouble."

"I'm waiting." Frances tapped her fingers on the table and glared at June.

"I was caught shoplifting."

At that moment the waitress approached and poured their coffee. "Anything else?" she asked.

Frances shook her head and motioned for her to leave. "So what happened?"

June raised her head, her eyes blazing. "I can't take any more money. My husband will know something is wrong." She gritted her teeth and shook her head. "I was desperate and felt sure I could get away with it, but the saleswoman saw me slip the diamond bracelet off my wrist and into my purse."

"You are a stupid bitch!" Frances whispered, her snake-eyes slits, her fists clenched. "Did store security call the police?"

"No, they called my husband. He spends a lot of money there and the manager didn't want to embarrass him. Mike came down, paid for the bracelet, and assured them it wouldn't happen again." She sat quietly as she relived the episode with her husband.

The silent ride home, the icy stare—worst of all was the hurt tone in his voice as they walked in the front door.

"Why?" He demanded. "They could have arrested you!"

She shrugged. "I don't know what came over me," she lied. "I didn't realize what I was doing." She tried to sound contrite but knew she wasn't convincing.

"Come on, June, I've given you everything you've asked for, haven't I?" He grabbed her shoulders and shook her, hard.

"Owe, you're hurting me," she wailed.

"Sometimes I wonder why I ever married you." He dropped his hands and walked away.

"Are you going to tell me what he said?" Frances asked.

June lifted her head, realizing where she was. "I'm afraid he'll divorce me if I pull anything else or ask for any more money."

Frances shrugged. "Okay, then I'll mail this information to him and that will help him make up his mind." She smiled, but with her lips only.

June leaned across the table and grabbed Frances' shirt with both hands. "I should kill you."

A man approached their booth. "Ladies, is there a problem here?"

Frances took June's hands in hers and held them tight. Then she gave the manager a weak smile. "My friend and I are having a minor disagreement. She was just leaving, weren't you—dear?"

With her eyes glued to the floor and her cheeks blazing, June hurried out of the shop. She ran to her car and drove, with no destination in mind. She had to come up with a plan before it was too late.

CHAPTER 37

"NATE, CAN WE GO TO the day care center for just one more week?" Emma widened her gray eyes and held out her hands in supplication.

"I suppose, if it will ease your mind." He snickered. "I do enjoy that number lady. She comes up with some unusual remarks."

Emma threw her arms around his neck. "You are a dear. I can't help but feel that something is going to happen. I don't think Dee is out of the woods yet."

"Okay, with your history of premonitions coming true, I won't argue that point. I guess I can handle another week."

* * *

Later that day Gladys called. "You were right. Nora found a death certificate for a June Foran in the county office that encompasses the San Francisco area. She died in 2003 at the age of twenty- five."

"Hmm." Emma rubbed her forehead. "So we have no idea who the woman who calls herself June Armanetti really is."

"I'm afraid not. That's as far as she can go without access to police files. The woman may have a criminal past."

"I wouldn't doubt that for one minute. Tell your daughter I appreciate all the work she's done." Emma felt deflated. She was hoping to find more information about June, but, this route was a dead end.

She and Gladys talked for a while longer, about family and the impending move. Cornell and his new partner were busy revitalizing the publishing company. His previous partner had set up a payment plan to restore the funds he had taken.

Before they terminated the call, Emma said, "There's something I have to ask you."

"By the tone of your voice I'd say it's personal."

"Uh huh."

"Ask away."

Emma told her about Yvonne Simmons and Nate's discussion with James about possibly going sailing with her brother.

"You're jealous," Gladys said with a throaty laugh.

"Am I being foolish?" Emma asked.

"Yes. Nate loves you, but he is a virile man. Never forget that." Emma blushed at her friend's words.

"Remember, as you told me when I was with you, you have to trust your partner. I suspected Cornell of having an affair, and it was totally unfounded. You must trust Nate. But, on the other hand, don't give him a chance to get involved with anyone else. Okay?"

"Thanks, my friend. I do feel better."

* * *

The following day Emma and Nate drove to the center under a blanket of dark clouds.

"It'll probably be pouring when we leave," Nate mumbled.

Emma felt the energy of the approaching storm, and it left her apprehensive. Something was wrong. She wanted Nate to drive faster, but kept her thoughts to herself.

When they arrived, Sara met them at the door. "Mrs. Winberry, I'm so glad you're here."

"Is something wrong?"

"Delia is showing the same symptoms she did a few weeks ago: lethargy, instability and slurring of speech. She's just not herself."

"Let me talk to her." Emma followed Sara into the day room where Dee sat slumped in a wheelchair, her chin resting on her chest, a safety belt strapped around her waist. Nate was close behind.

"Dee, it's Emma. Can you talk to me?"

With difficulty she lifted her head and struggled to open her eyes. "Ma—Ma," she mumbled. Emma grasped her hand and squeezed it, but there was no response. She turned to Sara.

"What does Mrs. Carter say?"

"She has a call in to Dr. Armanetti. She feels Delia should see her doctor for a workup."

"Do you think there's any possibility Dee is being drugged?" Emma blurted out.

"By whom?" Sara asked.

"That's a good question. I don't know, but the thought keeps popping into my head." She decided to keep her suspicions about June to herself.

Mrs. Carter came out of her office and walked toward them. "I just talked with Delia's son. Her doctor told him to bring her to the emergency room. He has called for a private ambulance to take her to Northwestern Hospital where her physician will see her." She shook her head.

"Is this common?" Emma asked.

"Some of these patients do regress, just when you think they're on the road to recovery." Emma held Dee's hand, talking to her, seeking a response. But it was minimal.

Within a short time, the ambulance arrived. The paramedics checked Dee's vital signs then placed her onto a stretcher. They hooked her up to an EKG monitor, placed an intravenous line in her arm, and loaded her into the ambulance.

Emma was frantic. "Nate, can we go to the emergency room with her, please?"

"Of course. I'm not going to abandon our friend when she needs our support."

They heard a rumble of thunder in the distance. "Come on, let's go before that storm hits." He hustled Emma into the car just as the wind began to blow.

"Northwestern, right?"

"Yes, that's what they said."

By the time they reached the hospital, heavy rain pelted the windshield.

"Here," Nate said. "I'll let you off at the entrance and then park the car."

"Don't forget the umbrella," Emma called after him as she hurried into the emergency entrance. She waited impatiently until Nate joined her, holding the unopened umbrella in his hand. Rain dripped from his head and face. She glanced at him, shook her head, but decided to say nothing. It must be a man thing, she thought. They would rather get wet than stop to open an umbrella.

Nate wiped his face and forehead with a handkerchief as they walked up to the desk. The receptionist was answering two phones at once and attempting to pass a chart to a nurse.

Emma swayed from one foot to the other, waited for a pause in the activity, then asked, "Delia Armanetti. She just came in by ambulance."

The woman examined a sheet of paper before responding. "You'll have to wait. The doctors are examining her now." She pointed to an area marked WAITING.

Nate hustled Emma away from the desk before she could ask another question.

"Why are you rushing me?" she complained.

"Can't you see how busy the woman is? No use asking questions she can't answer.

She frowned. "I guess you're right."

They sat in the crowded waiting area. Emma noticed Nate's discomfiture. He had an aversion to hospitals, especially emergency rooms. They had too many experiences with these places in the past few years.

Nate picked up a newspaper sitting on a table and buried his face in it. Emma examined the other people in the room: a teen-ager with a bandage wrapped around his arm, grimacing in pain, a woman attempting to comfort him; an older man holding a wash cloth against his forehead, spots of blood seeping through; a mother trying to quiet a fretful child.

Oh Guardian Angel, so many people in pain.

Before she could recognize any response, she saw Mike and June walk into the room. Mike gave her a surprised smile while June greeted her with a scowl. Nate stood and the two men exchanged greetings.

"What did the doctor say?" Emma asked.

"He doesn't know much," Mike answered. "She is responding, but minimally. They've taken her for a CAT scan to see if she may have had another stroke." He rubbed his hand across his face. "I just don't know."

"Did they draw blood to rule out over medication?" Emma blurted out.

June blanched. "Why would you say that?" she demanded.

Emma shrugged. "I've read that older people don't always excrete medications as completely as younger ones and they can build up in the body."

Mike nodded. "I think the doctor said something about that. They have to rule out every possibility."

"That's a waste of time and money, if you ask me," June was quick to respond. "She hasn't had any problems before."

She gave Emma a look that said, "Stay out of this."

While the Armanettis waited for the results of the scan, Emma and Nate went down to the cafeteria to get something to eat. When they were seated, each with a ham and cheese sandwich and coffee, Nate asked, "How long do you intend to stick around here?"

"I don't know." Emma put down her sandwich. "Can we just wait 'till she comes back from the scan?"

"I suppose." He took a generous bite of sandwich. "This is pretty good. By the way, did you notice how quickly June said that the blood tests were a waste of time—a little too quickly." He took a swallow of coffee.

"I agree," Emma said. "And she certainly had a concerned expression on her face, and it wasn't over Dee, either. I think it was guilt."

"Do you really believe she's drugging Dee?"

"I do, and so does my Guardian Angel."

Nate said nothing about Emma's celestial guardian. She knew he didn't believe in spirits, but she did, with all her being.

When they went back to the waiting room, they saw Mike pacing, while June sat with a bored expression on her face, paging through a magazine and bouncing her foot. She put down the magazine as the doctor walked up to them directing Mike to a private corner.

Emma strained to hear the conversation.

"Good news. From the preliminary findings, there has been no further damage to your mother's brain."

He heaved a sigh of relief. "Thank God for that."

"But, we don't have all the results of the blood work yet. There may be some imbalance. Everything so far is within normal limits, but some results won't be back until later."

"Thank you, Doctor." Mike grasped the man's hand.

"We want to keep her overnight, just to be sure."

"Of course." He turned to his wife. "I want to see her before we leave."

"Go ahead," June said picking up the magazine again and suppressing a yawn.

Emma and Nate were about to leave when they heard a soft moan from June. She dropped her head in her hands.

"What's wrong?" Emma said sitting next to her and grasping her shoulders. She was pale and trembling.

"I don't know—light-headed—all of a sudden."

"Put your head down between your knees. Nate, call the nurse." Emma steadied the woman as she did as she was told.

Soon the color returned to June's face. "Better now?" Emma asked.

"Uh huh. I don't know what happened."

A nurse hurried in and took June's vital signs. "Everything appears normal."

As Mike was coming toward them, he was alerted by the nurse that his wife felt faint and should be worked up. June's stage persona took over. "I'm all right. This has all been too much for me." She heaved a theatrical sigh and turned to her husband. "I think I'm getting one of my migraines. Please, take me home."

She turned to the nurse, her eyes blazing.

At that moment an emergency ambulance pulled up to the ER and the nurse ran to help. "Come on, honey," Mike said as he helped her up. She leaned against him and stumbled out the door.

* * *

As they drove home, Nate asked, "Do you think that entire episode was an act?"

"I'm not sure. She was pale and trembling, but that passed very quickly. That last bit was an act for Mike's benefit."

"Poor man, I certainly wouldn't want to be in his shoes."

"Don't worry, dear." Emma cuddled close. "I'm not that good an actor. You would see right through me."

"You're right about that," he said laughing. "You've tried to tell me fibs in the past and failed every time."

"I never." Then she remembered a few times that she hadn't told him everything. He always guessed that she was holding back. "I suppose I have to always tell you the truth, Nate Sandler."

"Yes, you do. And, I'll do the same."

CHAPTER 38

THE FOLLOWING DAY MIKE ARMANETTI was especially busy at the clinic. He knew his mother was well cared for at the hospital and tried not to worry.

"Doctor," Marge called, "you have an important phone call."

"Can you take a message? I'm rather busy at the moment."

"It's Doctor Morrison calling from the hospital."

"Okay, I'll take it in my office." He excused himself to the client and hurried into his office, closing the door behind him.

"Hello, Doctor, how is my mother today?"

"She's much better. In fact, you can take her home."

"That's good news. But I have a feeling you called to tell me something else."

There was a pause at the other end. "You're right about that. We found benzodiazepines in one of the blood samples the lab tested, a high enough concentration to cause the symptoms she's been having. Everything else is normal."

Mike frowned. "Exactly what does that mean? Aren't those anti-anxiety drugs?"

"Yes. Apparently someone has been giving her a drug like Valium. And I have not prescribed these medications for your mother."

Mike sat forward in his chair and let out a breath. "But—who?"

"That's what you have to find out. At that concentration a woman in her condition can easily have a serious fall. I suggest you call the administrator of that center where your mother spends most of her time."

Mike rubbed his hand over his forehead. "I checked that place out thoroughly. They have a spotless reputation."

"I hate to say this, but the only other explanation is that someone at home is giving it to her. At first I thought it might be contamination, so I ordered more testing. The findings are conclusive."

"I see. Thanks Doctor. I'll pick her up as soon as I close the clinic."

"Fine. I'll get the discharge paperwork in order."

Mike returned to his client. Who would do something like that?

After he closed for the day, Mike drove aimlessly for a long time, his mind mired in suspicion and disappointment. He went over and over what the doctor had said. He really didn't believe that anyone at the center had drugged his mother. That left only one person—June. He refused to believe she would do such a thing, but he had to confront her.

* * *

That evening June was unusually solicitous toward Dee. Mike watched her every move. During dinner she made sure Dee's food was cut up and placed conveniently at her left side. She wiped up any spills without reprimanding the woman and even gave her an extra serving of custard.

After Dee was in bed, Mike took June's hand and sat her down in a chair. "We have to talk." He couldn't read the look in her eyes. Was if fear, guilt, or something else?

"I have something to tell you," she blurted out.

"Can it wait?"

"No. I'm pregnant."

"What?" He couldn't wrap his mind around this unexpected disclosure.

"I said, I'm pregnant. That's why I got faint at the hospital." Her voice dropped to a whisper.

She turned her head to the side, her mouth agape. Her actor's persona took over. "Are you sorry?"

He grasped her hands. "Of course not. But you said you couldn't have children. When the time was right we were going to adopt."

"The doctors were wrong. I've been feeling light-headed and my period is late so I took one of those pregnancy tests—and it was positive." She gazed at him with soulful eyes. "You did say you wanted children, didn't you?"

"Yes, yes." He took her in his arms, suddenly feeling very protective. She was carrying his child. How could he ever suspect her of doing something so heinous as drugging his mother.

She smiled and smoothed his curly hair. "I hope it's a boy and he looks just like you," she purred. "Now, my darling, what was it you wanted to talk about?"

"Nothing important." He would speak with Mrs. Carter tomorrow. It had to be someone at the center, perhaps another client.

"I'm going to bed," June said yawning. "Are you coming?"

"In a few minutes. Go ahead. You need your rest. Tomorrow make an appointment with the doctor. I don't want anything to go wrong." He kissed her and watched as she slowly climbed the stairs, clutching the banister.

His mind was a whirl of thoughts. Caring for his mother was certainly too much for a pregnant woman. Maybe that was the reason she took that bracelet. Didn't the sudden hormonal changes cause women to react erratically?

To ease his mind he searched the medicine cabinet but found only the drugs Dr. Morrison had prescribed. It wasn't June. Of that he was certain. He went into the study, poured himself a glass of brandy and considered his options: either hire a live-in care giver for his mother, or send her to a nursing home. That thought didn't sit well with him. Sam had said he would take her to live with his family if she was independent enough. That might be the best solution. He sighed, knew he would get little sleep tonight.

* * *

The following evening, Emma received a call from Marge. "Mrs. Winberry, you told me to call if I heard anything suspicious."

"Yes, Marge, what do you have to tell me?"

"Well, she paused for a moment, "I don't want you to think that I regularly listen to the doc's phone calls, but he asked me to get Mrs. Carter at the center. I couldn't help wondering what he wanted to say to her, so, I listened at his door."

There was another pause and Emma could feel the woman's discomfort. "Go on," she urged.

"It seems that someone has been giving the doc's mother Valium and he thinks it may be somebody at the center."

"That's an unfounded accusation," Emma said, feeling angry. "Why would he suspect someone there?"

"I don't know. From his side of the conversation I gathered that Mrs. Carter was very upset and assured him she would look into the situation."

"Hmm," Emma said. "Thanks, Marge. I think I'll speak with Sara, the activities director. Keep your eyes and ears open. Something doesn't smell right about this whole situation."

"I agree with you, Mrs. Winberry, and I will."

Emma turned to Nate who had heard her side of the conversation and filled him in. "That's a ridiculous accusation," he said. "The first suspect should be his wife."

"I agree, but she must have convinced him that she's innocent. I wonder what she told him."

* * *

June walked into the coffee shop with a determined step. She had come up with a plan and would put it in action if Frances forced her hand.

As she slid into the booth, Frances looked at her with half closed eyes. Neither woman said a word as the waitress poured their coffee and then left.

"Well?" Frances raised her eyebrows in expectation.

"Well what?" June responded.

"I don't see an envelope in your hand."

"I need more time," June said, a note of confidence in her voice.

"Why? Won't the doc give you any more spending money?"

"I'm pregnant."

Frances' eyes narrowed and she half shook her head. "I don't believe you."

"Do you want a statement from the gynecologist?" June saw the doubt and suspicion on Frances' face.

"I've had a few attacks of light-headedness and my husband is beginning to realize that I can't take care of his mother and a baby at the same time."

"I seem to remember that a pregnancy takes nine months. A lot can happen in that time."

"Exactly. You can't ruin my life with a child at stake." As soon as the words were out June realized how theatrical they sounded.

"Huh!" Frances laughed out loud. "So what's this grand plan of yours?"

"I'm just putting it together now. Please, be patient a little longer. You will get everything that's coming to you."

Frances sat for a moment. "I don't like the way you phrased that last statement."

"I meant the money, of course."

Frances heaved a sigh. "All right. I'll give you the benefit of the doubt. Another month and that's all!"

"That's all I need." June left without touching her coffee, a smile of satisfaction on her face.

CHAPTER 39

A S SOON AS SHE COULD, Emma called Sara at the Center. "Hi, it's Emma Winberry."

"Oh Mrs. Winberry, hello." Her voice was low and devoid of its usual exuberance.

"What is it Sara? Dr. Armametti's accusation? I know that he called Mrs. Carter about the possibility of someone drugging his mother."

"No one, I mean *no one* would ever drug a client." Her voice rose with each word.

"I'm certain of that," Emma agreed. "Is there any possibility that it could be another one of the participants?"

"I don't see how. Only the staff has access to the kitchen and most of our clients are not—well—how shall I put this—not "with it" enough to do something like that."

Emma heard Sara let out a deep breath.

"The most likely person is her daughter-in-law," she said.

"I thought the same thing," Sara agreed.

"I wonder why Dee's son doesn't suspect her," Emma pondered.

He has a reason to protect her, the inner voice said.

Emma frowned. Now why would her Guardian Angel suggest such a thing? What could be the reason? It was obvious that June disliked Dee. Even Mike must see that. She is an actor, but not good enough to conceal her true feelings all the time.

"Mrs. Winberry, are you still there?" Sara asked.

"Oh yes, sorry, I was distracted for a moment. Is Dr. Armanetti going to send Dee back to the center?"

"He told Mrs. Carter that if she is positive it was no one here, he would consider it."

"All right. Let's keep in touch. I hope he does. She was making such great progress."

Emma said goodbye and terminated the call. She turned to see Nate examining the mail. A furrow appeared between his eyes.

"Look at this. We're invited to a mass at Holy Name Cathedral next Sunday."

"What's the occasion?"

"It's for the recovery of Delia Armanetti."

"Oh, well I'd like to go to that. How about you?"

"Sure, why not? Can't hurt."

"I know you don't believe in a higher power, Nate Sandler, but I do," she said, hands on hips.

"I didn't say anything. I love looking at old cathedrals." He smirked and chucked her under the chin.

* * *

On Sunday morning Emma dressed in a summer outfit appropriate for a church service—a sleeveless linen print dress with a turquoise short jacket. She adorned herself with pearls and earrings to match.

When Nate emerged from the bedroom, she gave him an appraising look. "My, aren't you the handsome one." He wore dark gray slacks with a gray and white striped shirt and a lighter colored gray jacket. He had opted not to wear a tie. People were dressing less formally these days.

"Do you think I'll turn the ladies' heads?" he asked.

"Of course. But I will stake my claim."

They both laughed as they left the condo. When the elevator stopped at the third floor, Yvonne Simmons entered wearing a clinging black sheath and an outrageous pink hat. It suited her perfectly.

Emma frowned. I could never wear a hat like that, she thought. I'd be a laughing stock. She smiled and greeted them, laying a hand on Nate's arm.

Emma frowned as she noticed that Nate didn't pull away. "You look festive," he said.

"I'm going to a christening. And you look very dapper."

Emma gritted her teeth and tried to smile, but her lips refused to move.

"Oh, Mrs. Winberry, your outfit is lovely," she said as an afterthought.

"Thank you."

Yvonne exited on the main floor with a two finger wave and Emma and Nate rode down to the garage in silence.

When they were seated in the car Emma said, "That woman is after you."

"I must admit that it *is* flattering, but my heart belongs to you, my Sparrow."

"Is that a mocking tone in your voice?"

"Forget about her. She flirts with all the men in the exercise room. The next few hours should prove much more interesting."

Traffic was light and they reached the cathedral a half hour before the scheduled mass. Nate parked in the designated lot across the street and escorted Emma to the massive bronze doors.

They stood open, welcoming the faithful to worship.

Emma gazed up at the huge gothic arches. She grabbed Nate's arm to keep her steady. The many stained glass windows fractured the light into its spectral colors.

"This certainly is a spectacular building," Nate whispered. "Look at the length of those pipes on that organ."

As they walked toward the sanctuary, a number of people began arriving for the eleven o'clock mass. Nate took Emma's hand and they slid into a pew about the center of the church. Before long, Nate spotted Mike and June Armanetti. He pointed them out to Emma.

"Where's Dee?" she whispered.

"She probably couldn't make those stairs," he said.

"But there's a ramp."

He shrugged.

Why did they leave her out of this? Emma wondered.

Soon the priest came out and the service began. When it was time for the reading, the priest announced that this mass was being offered for the recovery of Delia Armanetti.

After the mass concluded, Emma and Nate waited to speak with the Armanettis. "Just look at her," Emma said, a scowl on her face. "She's so full of herself."

"I take it you don't like the woman," he answered, suppressing a grin.

"Humph." Emma's lips spread in a smile that never reached her eyes as Mike and June exited the church.

"Mrs. Winberry, Mr. Sandler, how good of you to come," Mike said. "Join us for a cup of coffee."

June didn't look pleased but quickly changed her expression to a theatrical welcome.

What a phony, Emma thought, then quickly turned her attention to Mike. "Where is your mother?"

"We thought it best to leave her home with a sitter. These stairs, and even the ramp, would be too much for her."

Emma agreed. Dee was not ready for such a challenge.

When they were seated in a small restaurant, each with a cup of coffee and a Danish, Mike looked at them and smiled. "I must share our good news with you two."

June frowned. "It's a little too early, darling," she chided.

"I know, but I'm just so happy. We're going to have a baby!"

Emma's eyes widened, her mouth agape. "That's wonderful," was all she could say. Nate simply looked from one to the other.

Emma examined June and watched her fingers twitching. She's dying for a cigarette, then decided to rub it in a little.

"So how are you managing with the smoking?" she asked innocently.

"Oh," Mike said proudly. "She quit cold turkey as soon as she realized she was pregnant."

"That's good," Nate said. "Not an easy thing to do."

"I wouldn't do anything to put our child at risk," June said.

"Of course you wouldn't," Emma said, never taking her eyes off June. "When is the baby due?"

"When?" June appeared confused for a moment. "Oh, my due date is around the beginning of February—yes February."

Mike put his arm protectively around her shoulders. "You see, June was told she could never have any children, so we planned to adopt, when the time was right. Now this wonderful surprise." He beamed down at his wife.

"That indeed is a blessing," Emma said trying desperately to restrain herself. "By the way, are you going to send Dee back to the day care center? She was making such great progress."

A frown crossed Mike's face. "I don't know what to do. Mrs. Carter assured me that no one there would ever drug my mother." His eyes met Emma's. "You've spent a lot of time there. What do you think of the staff?"

"I think they are all beyond reproach," she said staring directly at June. Then she turned back to Mike. "Have you considered that the pharmacy may have made an error in filling one of her prescriptions?"

"I never thought of that."

"That's got to be it," June jumped in, a little too quickly. "The pharmacy made a mistake."

"We'll look into it. In the meantime, I'll send Mom back to the center." Mike turned to his wife. "June, dear, after you drop Mom off tomorrow morning, take her prescription bottles to the pharmacy and ask them to check the contents. Are you up to that?"

She sighed, and dramatically stroked his cheek. "I think I can manage."

* * *

As Nate navigated the traffic on their way home, Emma sat quietly rehashing the conversation. "Do you actually think the pharmacy might be to blame?" Nate asked.

"Of course not. But June jumped at the possibility." Emma made faces as she thought about the situation. "I really think Mike suspects her, but he's conflicted with the possibility of a baby on the way."

"You don't believe she's pregnant. She was pale at the hospital and did complain of light- headedness."

"Remember, she's an actor. Anyone can feign light-headedness. And the pallor—well I have to admit, her skin was pretty colorless. I think she' putting on a pretty good show. Did you see her fingers twitching? She was dying for a cigarette. I'm sure she took the first opportunity to satisfy her craving. My concern is Dee. June will probably convince Mike that she can't possibly care for his ailing mother and a child at the same time. What will happen to Dee now?"

Nate shook his head. "Time will tell." How Emma hated those words.

CHAPTER 40

EMMA COULDN'T WAIT FOR TUESDAY. She was eager to see Dee and try to determine her feelings about the pregnancy.

Nate had a meeting of the opera board to attend; he was becoming more and more involved in the planning for the next two years. James was delighted to have the benefit of his expertise in the business world. Emma was glad he was away from Yvonne Simmons and she had some time to herself.

When Emma arrived at the center, she met a smiling Sara. "Oh, Mrs. Winberry, Dr. Armanetti has apologized for his accusation. He is investigating the pharmacy." She gave Emma a sideways glance. "They don't usually make mistakes like that."

Emma shook her head. "It's not the pharmacy. I'm convinced it's June, but now that she claims to be pregnant, he will never blame her."

"He told us the news. He was so elated. Don't you believe it?"

"Let's just say, I have my doubts. It's a little too convenient. Now I must see Dee."

She found her friend in the exercise class. "Ma—Ma," Dee called, her face beaming in a lop- sided smile. Emma gave her a hug and joined in the class.

When it was time for the speech lesson, Emma accompanied her friend and greeted Diane. "Delia, I'm so happy to see you back here and ready to continue our lessons."

Dee nodded, "*Si, si.*"

"Mrs. Winberry, welcome. I'm glad you're back, too."

Emma nodded then sat to the side and observed. They went through the numbers from one to ten. Dee hesitated at first, but after a few tries, managed to say them in English in the proper order.

"Excellent," Diane said. "If you keep progressing like this, I feel confident your speech will return."

She turned to Emma. "Perhaps not as it was before—she may hesitate while she searches for the words—but she should be able to make her needs known and even carry on a conversation."

"Oh, I'm so glad," Emma said. Then she felt it was necessary to voice what was on her mind. "Did you know that Dee's daughter-in-law is pregnant?"

"No," Diane said. "I hadn't heard that. What do you think about it, Delia?"

"No!" Dee slammed her left hand on the table. "No!"

"I don't think she's too thrilled with the idea," Emma said.

Dee shook her head and searched for the words. Then she used her left hand to mimic a pregnant woman's belly while shaking her head and continuing to say, "no." She became more agitated with every movement.

"Settle down, Dee," Emma said. "Are you trying to tell us that June is not pregnant?"

"*Si, si.*"

"But how do you know?"

Dee frowned, then picked up a crayon and began to form letters on a piece of paper. She started on the right hand side of the paper and made a T. Next to it she placed an A, then an M. the word spelled MAT.

Diane and Emma exchanged glances and tried to interpret the meaning.

Remember, she's writing backwards, Emma's inner voice said.

"Of course, she's been writing things backwards. Let's turn it around." She wrote TAM. "Is that what you wanted to write, Dee?"

"*Si, si.* She nodded vigorously.

"But that doesn't tell us anything," Diane said.

Finish the word, the inner voice said.

"Perhaps it's only a partial word." Emma thought for a moment, then suddenly realized what Dee was trying to tell them and added the letters PON.

"*Si! Si!*" Dee said excitedly.

The word read TAMPON. "So what do you want to tell us about tampons?" Emma asked, but she was pretty certain she already knew.

Dee hesitated then pointed to Emma's purse. "June has them in her purse?"

Dee nodded.

"No pregnant woman carries tampons around with her," Diane said.

"Did you actually see her put them in her purse?" Emma persisted.

"*Si! Si!*" Dee pounded on the table with her left hand.

"All right," Diane said, "Calm down. It's okay. We believe you." Dee sat upright, a satisfied expression on her face.

* * *

When Emma left the center she felt that her suspicions were confirmed. What purpose did June have in pretending pregnancy? In a few months it would be obvious.

But that is enough time to rid herself of Delia, her inner voice said.

Exactly. Emma was totally frustrated. Her hands were tied. She couldn't tell Mike. That would definitely be inappropriate. She decided to call Gladys and discuss it with her. Besides, she wanted to know how her friend's planned move to the new condo was going.

* * *

That evening Emma settled herself in her favorite chair in the atrium, a cup of herbal tea on a small table at her side. She placed the call to Gladys and was rewarded with her friend's throaty voice.

"Emma, we must have a psychic connection. I've been meaning to call you, but with all that's happening, I've been working my buns off."

"So when does the actual move take place?"

"We closed on the condo last week; sold our house to a nice couple with two kids; and we move in three days."

"Wow! That was fast." Emma visualized the frenzy her friend was experiencing. "Do you need some help?" Now what made me say that? She bit her lip, afraid that Gladys would take her up on the offer.

"No thanks, The girls are here and almost everything is packed. In fact, we're living out of boxes. But things are falling into place and I thank you for the offer."

"I wish I could do more," Emma said, with a sigh of relief.

"By the way, I have some information for you about that June person," Gladys said. "Now where did I put that in all this confusion?" she muttered. "Oh there it is, on the fridge door. Heaven knows it would get lost anywhere else around here." Eagerly Emma waited for anything Gladys could tell her.

"Let's see," Gladys said. "As I told you before, Nora found a death certificate for a June Foran."

Emma knew Gladys was overburdened, but did she have some further information? "Anything else?"

"There was something, but I can't seem to remember."

"That's all right. I know you've got a lot on your plate right now." But Emma was disappointed.

"It'll come to me in a minute."

Emma heard Gladys muttering to herself, something she did regularly.

"Got it. Nora searched the newspaper archives for the time the woman died. No evidence of foul play. She succumbed to leukemia. Sorry, but that's it."

"Thank Nora for all she's done. It raises more suspicions. I wonder why June assumed her identity. Possibly to cover her own past." Now what made me say that? Emma wondered.

It's a distinct possibility, her inner voice said.

"One of Nora's friends is a San Francisco detective. She can ask him to look for any criminal record for a June Foran. But who she really is remains a mystery."

"Now I have some interesting news," Emma said and told Gladys about the pregnancy.

"Wow, that was convenient."

"I thought so, too."

"Sorry to cut this short, Emma, but I have to go. I'll send you the new address and phone number. In the meantime, if you have to call me, use the cell. Bye."

The cell number, where was it? She had it somewhere. Emma decided not to bother her friend until she was settled in her new place.

Now Emma had another piece of the puzzle, but what good did it do her? How could she protect Delia?

Guardian Angel, please give me some guidance. I don't know what to do next.

Wait and see, was the only answer she received and Emma wasn't satisfied with it—not at all.

CHAPTER 41

THE PEKINESE YIPPED IN PAIN. "No!" the owner called. "Stop, you're hurting her."

Mike hurried into the treatment room, a deep furrow between his eyes. "What's the problem here?"

A woman held a shaking little dog in her arms, blood dripping from its paw. "She cut her!" she complained. "She cut my Suzie."

Mike glared at Frances standing next to the treatment table, a pair of blood stained nail clippers in her hand.

"I was only cutting her nails, when Mrs. Collins jerked the dog. I accidentally cut into the quick." She shrugged. "It happens."

Mike clenched his fists, annoyed at her irresponsible attitude. "I'll take over from here.

"Frances, please restack the shipment of supplies that arrived today."

Frances tossed the nail clippers in the sink and stomped out of the room.

"I'm sorry about this, Mrs. Collins. Let me take a look." Hiding his displeasure he examined the injured paw. Frances had cut deep. There was no excuse for such incompetence. He applied styptic powder to stop the bleeding.

"I don't want that woman ever touching my Suzie again. This isn't the first time she's handled her so roughly," Mrs. Collins said as she murmured soothing sounds to the animal.

"Believe me," Mike said, "she won't be handling the animals anymore."

Suzie licked his hand as he finished trimming her nails. Then he gave her a treat which she greedily chewed. Her big brown eyes mirrored trust as she wagged her tail.

"There you are, Suzie, all done." He held the dog for a minute then handed her back to her owner. "There shouldn't be any problem but, if the nail begins to bleed again, put some of this powder on it." He filled a small jar and handed it to his client.

"Thank you, Doctor."

Mike preceded her out of the room and said to Marge, "There will be no charge for Suzie's visit today."

Mrs. Collins smiled with satisfaction and walked out of the office.

Mike turned and hurried into the stock room. "Frances, we have to talk."

"It wasn't my fault, Dr. Armanetti. She jerked the dog."

He shook his head. "This is not the first complaint I've had about you from the clients. I'm giving you two weeks' notice. During that time you will *not* have any contact with the animals. You can do the ordering, stocking, and whatever else needs to be done."

"You *can't* fire me," she said, fear registering on her face.

"I can and I am. I will not endanger my practice with incompetence." He left the room and closed the door behind him.

Frances panicked. This was the third job she'd lost because of similar situations. Who would hire her now? And what kind of recommendation could she expect from the good doctor? She grew more resentful and angry as she finished stocking the shelves. It wasn't her fault. None of the instances had been her fault. It was time to get even, with both him and June. She retrieved her belongings from her locker and took out a manila envelope. She kept it with her for just the right time. And this was it.

Frances stomped out to the waiting room where the last patient was just leaving. She turned to Mike and, with venom in her voice, said, "You have no right to fire me. I've been a good employee. I'll see my lawyer and sue you."

Mike opened a drawer and retrieved a folder. "This is a record of your "competence." Complaints from Mrs. Dobry, Mr. Evans, Mrs. Collins. Do you want me to go on? There are more."

Her breath came in dry gasps. She stared at him through narrow cruel eyes. "I'm leaving—now!" She threw the envelope and her keys on the desk with such force that they fell into Marge's lap. "You haven't heard the last from me. You'll be sorry, mark my words." She left and slammed the door behind her.

Mike stood for a moment breathing heavily. "Cut her a check for two weeks' pay and put it in the mail, return requested. If she does see a lawyer, I don't want to give her any ammunition to use against me."

Marge turned frightened eyes to her employer. "Do you think she might do something like try to blow up the clinic?"

He smiled at her. "Don't worry. The only thing she's blowing is smoke. I'll be in my office for a while working at the computer. You can close up and go home. Let's try to forget this unpleasantness."

Marge picked up the envelope that had fallen to the floor. She was about to give it to Mike then decided to see what was inside. She put it in her bag, finished her chores, and left the office.

CHAPTER 42

LATER THAT EVENING EMMA RECEIVED a call from Marge. "Oh Mrs. Winberry, there was such a disturbance at the clinic today. I don't know where to start."

"Calm down," Emma said. "Start at the beginning and tell me what happened." She heard Marge take a swallow of something.

"Okay. I heard raised voices, one of the clients and Frances. While she was trimming the client's dog's nails, Frances cut into the quick. That's painful and results in a lot of bleeding, you know."

Emma didn't know, but that wasn't important just now.

"Then Dr. Mike went into the room and I heard more arguing. Pretty soon Frances went into the storage room. I had a glimpse of her face. She looked furious." Another swallow. "You must forgive me. I'm so upset that I'm drinking a glass of wine."

"That's all right. Take a deep breath and let it out slowly. Good. Now another one. What happened next?"

"Well, there have been a number of complaints about Frances, how rough she is with the animals and how curt she is with their owners. So Doc fired her right then and there—gave her two weeks' notice. She stormed out and said she wouldn't be back and he would be sorry."

Emma heard a sniffle followed by another swallow. "Do you think she would do anything—drastic?" she asked.

"I really don't know," Marge continued. "She's a vindictive woman. But that's not all. As she was leaving she threw the keys on my desk along with a manila envelope with Dr. Mike's name on it. It fell on the floor. He never even noticed it. So I picked it up and took it home with me." A long pause and more swallowing.

"What was inside the envelope?" Emma asked, her curiosity piqued.

"Newspaper clippings from a paper in San Francisco dated five years ago. A woman named Lyla Winters was suspected of poisoning her husband. She was arrested and went to trial, but the evidence was sketchy and she was acquitted."

Another pause. There must be some relevance to this situation, Emma thought, but I wish she would get to it.

"The picture of the woman is a little grainy and she had dark hair, but I'm certain it's the doc's wife, June."

Now Emma was speechless. When she gathered her thoughts she said, "That puts a whole different light on things. I wonder if Frances was blackmailing June over that?"

"Could be. I followed Frances twice and saw the two of them meet in the same café."

"What do you plan to do with the envelope?" Emma asked.

"I don't know. Should I give it to Doc?"

Emma thought for a moment. "Not just yet. I have a friend who is good at digging up information. Let's see if we can find out any more before alerting Dr. Armanetti."

"All right, if you think that's best," Marge said, a relieved tone to her voice.

"In the meantime, keep your eyes and ears open for anything out of the ordinary."

"I will and, thanks for the advice."

After terminating the call, Emma relayed the new development to Nate.

"You're getting embroiled in something that's none of your business, again," he said, his arms folded across his chest, a frown on his face.

"I just want to protect Dee, that's all. She's helpless against a woman like June."

Emma placed a call to Gladys. Cornell answered the phone.

"Hi Emma, we're getting settled in our new digs." He laughed. "Moving is exhausting."

"Oh I know," Emma said in commiseration. "I wouldn't bother you if it weren't important. May I speak with Gladys?"

"She fell asleep and I really don't want to wake her unless I have to."

"No, don't. Just give her a message. Please write down this name: Lyla Winters from San Francisco."

"Okay, what about it? Who is she?"

"Ask Gladys to give the name to your daughter, Nora. She'll know what to do with it."

"Sounds kind of mysterious," he said.

"No, I'm just meddling, as usual." From the corner of her eye she saw Nate nod at those words. "Sorry I bothered you and, thanks Cornell."

Emma walked into the atrium and gazed out over the lake. If Mike found out about June's past, what would he do? If she had really killed her first husband, would she hesitate to do away with Dee? *Oh Guardian Angel, show me how to handle this.*

* * *

When Mike got home that night, the first thing he did was pour himself a drink. He downed it in one gulp then poured another.

"Hey," his wife said, "what's going on? You never start drinking as soon as you walk in the door." She snaked her arms around his waist and rested her head on his shoulder.

He held her close for a moment then patted her flat abdomen. "Bad day." He groaned and let out a breath. "I fired Frances."

"What?" She pushed away from him, her eyes wide, her mouth pressed in a thin line. "Why?"

"I don't want to discuss it in front of Mom," he whispered. He walked over to Dee who sat at the kitchen table ready for dinner, a bib around her neck. She gave him a crooked smile. "Mike, Mike." She had mastered his name as well as a few other words.

"How was your day, Mama?"

She shrugged her left shoulder and gave him another smile.

"I take it that means it went well." He kissed her cheek. She grasped his hand and pressed it to her lips.

He turned to June who was standing in the same spot. "Let's have dinner, honey. I'm beat."

She went through the motions of serving the spaghetti and meatballs. While taking the salads out of the refrigerator, her trembling hands dropped one. "Oh dear, look what I did."

"Easy, easy," Mike said. "Why are you so uptight? Sit down, I'll clean this up."

As she watched him clean up the mess, June tried to compose herself. She felt Dee's eyes boring into her. She clasped her hands together to stop their trembling. How she wanted a cigarette right now. If he had really fired Frances, would she make good on her threat?

Mike sat and said grace. Then he cut up his mother's spaghetti and meatball and handed her a spoon.

June played with her food, but every bite stuck in her throat. She washed it down with a glass of water, finally pushing the plate away.

"Why aren't you eating?" Mike asked.

"You're not telling me what happened today, so I'm worried. In my condition I can't afford to get upset." There was a petulant tone to her voice.

"I'm sorry. I shouldn't burden you with problems at work, especially now." He covered her hand with his and gave it a squeeze.

June glanced at Dee. The woman's expression seemed to say, *you liar. I know what you're doing and it won't work.*

She pulled away and covered her face with both hands, feigning sobs. "Your mother hates me, and the baby, too."

"How can you say such a thing? Mom loves kids. She'll be a great grandmother, won't you Mom?" He turned to Dee but her face was an unreadable mask.

"See," June almost shouted. "No smiles, nothing."

"You're making a mountain out of a mole hill. I guess it's the hormone rush. I'll put Mom to bed while you clean up the kitchen. Then we'll talk."

Later Mike and June sat on the couch. He nursed another scotch.

"So," she said, "why did you fire Frances? What did she do that was so terrible?"

"It was the last straw. I have been keeping a folder of complaints by the clients. Today she injured a Pekinese while clipping her nails. The client was livid and said she didn't want Frances to touch her dog again."

"I'm sure she didn't do it deliberately," June said in an attempt to defend the woman.

"It was carelessness." Mike's face took on a hardened expression. "One time too many. I gave her two weeks' notice but she stormed out and said I would regret it."

June froze. She knew exactly how Frances would retaliate. Couldn't allow that. She would have to stop her—now.

"If she thinks she'll get a reference from me, she's sorely mistaken," Mike said, beginning to slur his speech.

"You're upset, I know," June cajoled. "Go up to bed and get some sleep. I'll be up in a little while."

She watched her husband slowly climb the stairs. Before she joined him, she had to make a phone call. The sooner the better.

* * *

June listened to the quiet house; the only sound she heard was the ticking of the grandfather clock. How she hated that thing, announcing every hour. Perhaps one day she could convince Mike to sell it. But she had more important things on her mind right now.

She pulled a cell phone from her purse, one she had purchased for an occasion like this—use it once and throw it away—no trace—no way to connect her to the call.

She opened the patio door and walked out into the balmy evening air. June shivered as a black cat slinked its way across the yard, a feral thing, hunting to survive. Right now, like the animal, her survival was at stake.

She opened the phone, consulted a small address book, and punched in a local number. The phone rang and rang until an answering machine picked up. "Not home. Leave a message."

"I know you're there," she said softly. "Pick up the phone. It's important."

After a long pause, a gruff voice answered. "A nightmare from the past. Where are you?"

"I'm in Chicago. It's payback time. Got a job for you."

"You need it done right, huh? Okay. I owe ya. But this is the last time. Give me the details." She told him what she wanted done and gave him the necessary information.

"No sweat. That's an easy one."

"It has to be tonight, is that clear?"

"Yeah. Then the slate is clean and I don't ever want to hear from you again."

"You won't," June said. "You can count on it."

She pressed the disconnect, folded the phone and threw it on the cement patio. She stomped on it until it was nothing but a bunch of useless pieces. Then she picked them up, put them in a baggie and sealed it up. Tomorrow she would toss it in a dumpster.

CHAPTER 43

THE FOLLOWING AFTERNOON EMMA RECEIVED a call from Marge. "Mrs. Winberry, we just had some distressing news. The police came to see Doc."

"Why? What happened?"

"Frances was in an auto accident—in Intensive Care—on life support."

"Oh my God! What a shame, but what does that have to do with your employer?" Emma heard sniffling sounds.

"Doc told them he had to terminate Frances because of client complaints."

"Marge, you're not telling me what happened. Please, get a hold of yourself and start over."

"All right. It seems that the brakes on Frances' car failed and she collided with a tractor-trailer."

Emma cringed at the image this brought to mind. "Go on," she urged.

"Apparently she had gone to the dealer for a maintenance check only a few weeks ago. It was a fairly new car. I remember her telling Doc about it and that everything was in perfect working order. She was fussy about her car, treated it like her child."

"So why were the police questioning Dr. Armanetti?" Emma wasn't following.

"The police think the brakes were tampered with. They found a hole in the line and the fluid had all drained out."

"Uh huh," Emma said, starting to pace. "So since the car was just checked out by the dealer and given an okay, the police suspect foul play."

"Exactly," Marge said letting out a breath. "Mrs. Winberry, do you think I should give that envelope to the doc now?"

"That information makes June the prime suspect," Emma said. "You have to or you will be withholding evidence."

"It'll kill him," she said with another sniff.

"Your other option is to destroy it, but I don't think you should do that. There may be another copy somewhere in Frances' things and the police are bound to find it, sooner or later. If June is involved in Frances' accident, that makes her a danger to Delia and even the doctor himself."

"Oh no!" Marge hesitated for a moment. "I'll tell him I found it on the floor where Frances may have dropped it. Don't want him to know I took it home."

"That's the right thing to do," Emma said. "Did the police question you?"

"Yes, they asked if Frances had any enemies that I know of. I said no, didn't know her that well. Should I have told about following her and seeing her meeting June?"

"Absolutely not! Just give Dr. Armanetti the envelope and let him take it from there. Don't get any more involved than that."

"All right, I'll give it to him tomorrow."

Oh Guardian Angel, what a mess. I'm sure June was responsible for tampering with Frances' car. She must have someone working with her. What can I do?

Dee is in danger, and so are you, her inner voice said. *Warn her son, and be careful.*

* * *

"Emma where are you?" Nate called coming in from the exercise room.

Emma took two deep breaths and tried to compose herself. "I'm right here, in the kitchen."

"How about going out to a concert at Millennium Park tonight? We haven't been there yet this summer." He had a towel around his neck, his face dotted with perspiration, his tee-shirt damp with sweat.

"You look like you had a good work out," she said without meeting his gaze.

"Yeah, I need a shower." He stood waiting for her to raise her eyes. "Sparrow, what is it?"

"Oh, Nate, I can never keep anything from you."

"I don't want us ever to keep anything from each other, is that clear?" He took her chin in his hand and raised her head until their eyes met.

"Sit down," she said. Within a few minutes she had told him about the phone call and what happened.

Nate swore under his breath. "Can't we have any peace in this house?" He got off the chair and stormed into the bathroom.

Emma heard the shower running. She tried to come up with a plan, but her mind remained a blank.

* * *

When Nate came out of the bedroom, showered and dressed, Emma was sitting in the recliner attempting to read a book. He walked over and planted a kiss on her forehead. "Sorry I was such a grouch."

"I understand. I get too involved in other people's business." She closed the book and gave a slight shake of her head.

"I know you can't help it, Sparrow. It's both endearing and, sometimes—aggravating." He laughed. "Otherwise, life might just be dull. Let's go for a walk and then out for dinner."

"I thought you wanted to go to the concert at Millennium Park."

"We can have dinner first. Okay?"

"I'll be ready in a jiffy." She hurried into the bathroom.

Within minutes Emma had changed and put on a little makeup. She vowed to put all her concerns on the back burner and enjoy her time with Nate.

As they walked out the door, the phone rang, but they chose to ignore it and let the answering machine pick up.

* * *

Emma and Nate returned hours later, after a thoroughly enjoyable evening. After a light supper, they had gone to the concert. It was wonderful—an all Beethoven program—under the stars on a balmy summer night.

Emma felt relaxed. "Sometimes it's good to do things on the spur of the moment," she commented.

"Yep," Nate agreed. "Looks like we have a few messages." He pressed the play button and they heard Gladys' voice.

"Emma, call me. Nora found out quite a bit about your mystery woman and none of it is good."

"Oh dear." Emma checked her watch, eleven o'clock. It was midnight on the East Coast. She would have to wait until morning.

The next message was from Bertie. "Emma, Robin is acting very strange. She keeps calling "Dee, Dee, Dee," and throwing her teddy bear down the stairs. Do you think that means anything? Call me."

Emma felt a chill down her spine. Dee was in danger but, again, she would have to wait until tomorrow.

Nate shook his head as he walked into the bedroom.

Emma went into the atrium and stood for a long time watching the waves of Lake Michigan flowing toward shore.

Oh Guardian Angel, what does this all mean? I have a bad feeling that this dilemma is coming to a head.

No response from her celestial guardian confirmed, in her mind, that some disaster was brewing.

CHAPTER 44

EMMA COULDN'T WAIT FOR THE sun to show itself. She tossed and turned, listening to Nate's snores. *Why can't I sleep like that?* Of course she couldn't, as long as she worried herself into a constant state of wakefulness about other people's problems. But Dee was her friend, and, right now, she was helpless and at June's mercy. Emma was eager to find out what Gladys' daughter had unearthed about the woman.

When the sky began to lighten, she quietly got out of bed and brewed a pot of coffee.

Walking from room to room, she waited until the hands of the clock approached seven. It was an hour later in New Jersey and Emma knew Gladys would be up. She placed the call and paced until her friend answered.

"I knew it was you. No one else calls at the crack of dawn on a Saturday morning." Gladys' throaty laugh lifted Emma's spirits just a little.

"What did Nora uncover?" she asked.

"So, no hi, how are you? How's life in the big city?"

Emma heard the teasing tone in her friend's voice. "Oh, Gladys, I'm so worried. I know Dee is in danger and I'm powerless to help her." She told her about the call from Bertie and Robin's unusual behavior.

"Yeah, you said the child has apparently inherited your—'abilities'."

"Also," Emma interrupted, "Frances was in an accident; seems as though someone tampered with her brakes."

"Is she dead?"

"No, but she's on life support."

"Wow, but from what Nora uncovered, I wouldn't be a bit surprised if June was involved.

"My inquisitive daughter and her computer nerd friend might, sometimes, be doing things that are considered—hacking. I certainly don't want to know.

"When you told me about the newspaper articles, I asked her to investigate further. Apparently some newspaper files are backed up on the computer. If one knows where to look, *voila*, there they are.

"Okay, here goes. In September of 1994, Lyla Winters was picked up for shoplifting, not once, but a number of times. She was given probation and community service.

"The following year, it happened again. This time she injured someone trying to escape. She spent a few months behind bars for that little stint." Gladys took a breath and a swallow of something. "Also, she kept showing up in emergency rooms with vague complaints.

"Then, an investigating reporter wrote an article for a magazine describing Munchausen Syndrome. He reported the symptoms and Lyla appears to be a classic case."

"What in heaven's name is that?" Emma asked. She walked out into the atrium and stared at the lake as if the answer would materialize in the waves.

"It's pretty interesting. These people actually hurt themselves or feign an illness and show up in the emergency rooms on a regular basis. Sometimes it's excessive laxative use, vomiting, migraines, cuts and bruises. Some of them even pretend to be pregnant." Gladys laughed. "The nurses refer to them as "frequent flyers." In and out all too often."

Emma took in an audible breath. June complained of migraines all the time and now she said she was pregnant. She remembered reading an article on false pregnancy. Was she going to use that to her advantage? Of course.

"Why do they call it Munch—Munch, whatever you said?" By now Emma felt totally confused.

"Because a Baron Munchhausen in the eighteenth century exhibited these kinds of symptoms. He did it as an attention getting mechanism. In 1951 an article in *The Lancet* identified this group of symptoms and called it Munchausen Syndrome."

"My God," Emma said, "people will go to any lengths to gain attention. June certainly fits the picture."

"It seems so, but I'm not finished yet. Lyla had psychiatric treatment. Then, a few years later, her husband died in an automobile accident. The police suspected her but there was no hard evidence and the coroner deemed it an accidental death. Get this, the brakes on his car failed."

"Does that sound like coincidence to you?"

Emma couldn't speak. She stood like a stone statue.

"The woman is evil," Gladys said. "Shortly after she claimed the insurance, Lyla Winters disappeared from the face of the earth and June Foran surfaced."

"Oh God, this is like a horror movie," Emma almost sobbed. "The woman has to be stopped. Both Dee and Mike are in danger."

Don't forget yourself, the inner voice reminded her.

"I would say so. Let me know the next chapter in the story."

Emma thanked her friend profusely and, again, offered to pay Nora, but Gladys said the girl loved delving into other people's secrets, might even become a writer someday.

* * *

A fog of fear and indecision surrounded Emma. What should she do? What *could* she do?

Oh Guardian Angel, please give me some direction.

The Internet, came the answer.

Emma's fingers pecked away at the computer, the tip of her tongue protruding from her lips.

She was so preoccupied that she jumped when the sound of Nate's voice interrupted her concentration.

"What are you researching there?"

"False pregnancy."

He ran his hand down her flat abdomen. "Emma, you're not … ?"

Her hands stopped typing and poised above the keyboard. "Don't be ridiculous!" She turned to him with a smirk. "You may be good, Nate Sandler, but not good enough to get a woman my age pregnant."

He clasped his hands and raised his eyes. "Thank God!" They stared at each other and broke into peals of laughter.

"Seriously," he said pulling up a chair beside her, "Why are you interested in false pregnancy?"

"Well, I'm just wondering if June is really expecting a child or is making it up. Or, she may really think she's pregnant when she isn't."

"I don't understand the relevance," he said rubbing his chin.

"I remember reading an article on the subject some time ago. See?" she pointed to the screen. "It lists the symptoms and causes. It's called *pseudocyesis* and usually affects women in their thirties and forties. They have all the symptoms of pregnancy, but—no baby." She turned to Nate who was reading intently.

"Interesting, but didn't you say Dee saw June with tampons?"

"She could have been mistaken, but, it says here, that these women can have irregular periods. One of the causes is psychological." Emma turned off the computer and faced Nate.

"What do you think?"

He shook his head. "I haven't the foggiest. Remember, I'm just the sperm donor. The rest is up to the woman." He grinned.

"Very funny, now let me tell you what Gladys' daughter found out. This will blow your mind."

He grabbed onto the chair in mock alarm. "I'm listening." Nonstop, she told him everything she had learned.

"Whew," he said. "That's quite a story. Presume that, since it was reported in the newspapers, it's, at least, partially true. You know how the media exaggerates. But it is possible that June, or whatever her name is, does have this Munch—whatever syndrome."

She nodded, and turned her eyes to him beseeching an answer. "Do you have any suggestions?"

He put his arm around her shoulders and held her close. "Ordinarily I would tell you to mind your own business, but this sounds serious." He thought for a moment. "Why not follow up with Bertie and see if Robin is still so upset?"

She took his face in her hands and kissed the cleft in his chin. "You really believe she's inherited my—ability?"

"Sparrow, living with you, I have come to accept almost anything."

"I love you, Nate Sandler," she whispered.

"I love you, too. Now don't get maudlin. Call Bertie."

Before Emma reached for the phone, it began to ring. She pulled her hand back, almost afraid to answer.

Nate grabbed it. "Hello."

"Hi, Nate, it's Bertie. Is Emma around? Robin is still acting strange and I need her advice."

"She's right here." He handed the phone to Emma and mouthed Bertie.

"Hi, what's my granddaughter doing?" She was afraid to hear the answer but knew she had to follow through.

"She's still throwing her teddy bear down the stairs and saying, "Dee, Dee, Dee." When I tell her that Dee is all right, she shakes her head and starts to cry. I'm really starting to worry."

Emma heard the strain in Bertie's voice. "This behavior has been going on for a couple of days now, right?"

"Yes. I distract her for a while with a game or some toys. She plays fine with her friends, but after a while she starts all over again. What does it mean?"

"It means that Dee is in danger. I'll look into it right away and get back to you." Nate frowned as Emma said goodbye.

"How do you plan to look into it, hmm?"

"Let me think." She closed her eyes for a moment. "I know Mike has the clinic open on Saturday morning. That leaves Dee alone with June. Today Dee may have an accident. She'll fall down the stairs." Emma shivered at her own words. "Don't ask me how, but I know it, and so does Robin."

Emma picked up the phone again and called the clinic. When Marge answered, she asked how long the doctor would be there.

"He has quite a few clients today, Mrs. Winberry. He'll probably be here until at least two this afternoon. Why?"

"His mother is in danger. Don't ask questions but tell him to phone home, now, and make sure she's all right."

"But what reason will I give him?"

Emma heard the confusion in Marge's voice. "Uh, tell him that a neighbor heard shouting coming from the house and was concerned."

"Okay, if you think it's important."

"I don't think, I know. Do it, Marge, now."

She turned to see Nate walking into the study. "What are you going to do?" she asked.

"I'm going to Google the Armanetti's address. There's no point in going out if we don't know how to get there."

"Oh Nate, you're a dear." Emma threw her arms around his neck and kissed the cleft in his chin.

"Yeah, yeah, I know. This will only take a minute. Give me the address."

* * *

Marge hesitated, unsure of how to proceed. When Mike finished with the cat he was treating, she called to him.

"Dr., I received a strange phone call from someone who identified herself as one of your neighbors. She said you should call home."

"Why?"

"Well, she said she heard shouting, or something like that, coming from your house." Marge hated to lie but Emma had been insistent.

"That's not possible. I have over an acre of land and no houses are that close." He frowned. "Who would make such a call?"

Marge shrugged and held out her hands.

"I'm up to my ears here with Frances gone and no temporary assistant starting until next week. Please call my wife and see if everything is all right." With those words, he returned to the treatment room and the next client.

Marge picked up the phone and punched in the numbers to the doctor's home. It rang and rang until the answering machine kicked in. She left a message to call the clinic. Okay, she thought, I did what I was told to do. But something was wrong with the whole picture. Before long she was inundated with calls and appointments and put the entire scenario out of her mind.

CHAPTER 45

A S NATE BATTLED THE SATURDAY afternoon traffic, he swore under his breath. Emma knew he hated to drive on weekends trying to avoid SUVs filled with women and children and groceries. He called them weekend warriors. But this was an emergency.

"Tell me where to turn," he said as they neared their destination.

She studied the printout carefully and frowned. Her sense of direction was none too accurate. "Uh, next light, turn left."

"Are you sure?"

"Reasonably." She squinted at the tiny map on the page.

"What's the name of the street?"

"Fourth Street," she answered.

"There appears to be a no left turn at Fourth Street. It's one way," he said, frustration mirrored in his voice.

"Oh dear, no—no, Fifth. That's it, Fifth. Why do they print these things so small?" She blew out a breath.

Nate made the turn and found the subdivision. "Okay, now all we have to do is find the house. All these damn mini-mansions! I'll never know why anyone needs such a big house."

Please, Guardian Angel, get us to the right place. I have a bad feeling. You'll be there in time, her inner voice said.

"There it is, Nate, that house on the corner."

"How can you be sure? I don't see any numbers."

"It is, trust me." She just knew, but, with his logical mind, he wouldn't accept that.

Nate pulled into the driveway and caught the number on the mailbox. "Okay, you're right. This is it."

Emma jumped out of the car as soon as he stopped and ran to the front door. She rang the bell, heard it, and waited. She pushed it again, but no answer. By now Nate had joined her and was peering in a window.

"Do you see anyone?" she asked.

"No, but since there is a car in the driveway, there must be someone here. Why don't we go around the back?"

He grabbed Emma's shaking hand and led her down the walk to the backyard. There they saw June lying on a lounge chair wearing headphones. She wore dark sunglasses and moved her feet in time to whatever music that assaulted her ears. A cigarette dangled from her right hand.

"June," Emma called.

No response.

She walked over and shook the woman's arm.

June jumped, pulled off the earphones and dropped the cigarette. She stared at Emma and Nate, a quizzical expression on her face. Then recognition dawned.

"What are you doing here?" Her tone was far from inviting as was the expression on her face.

"It's nice to see you, too," Emma answered, a note of sarcasm in her voice. "We came to see Dee."

"Just like that, huh? Why didn't you call? She's sleeping, taking a nap. Don't want to disturb her—was up all night." June kept up a staccato rhythm, but was noticeably uncomfortable. She began cracking her knuckles.

Emma winced, but her thoughts turned back to her friend.

"Maybe she's awake. We'll just take a look." Emma turned to the patio door.

"Wait a minute. You can't simply walk into my house uninvited." June jumped off the chair and planted herself in front of the door.

"Is there some reason why you don't want us to come in?" Nate asked, giving her an intimidating stare.

"Of course not. I—I'm sorry. I haven't been well—morning sickness." Her face became noticeably pale. Nate grabbed her as she began to waver.

"We'd better get you inside so you can lie down," he said encircling her waist with his arm.

Emma slid open the patio doors and Nate guided June to a couch while Emma went to check on Dee.

"Nate! Come quick!"

He left June and rushed to the bottom of the staircase where Dee lay, a pool of congealing blood under her head.

Emma knelt next to her friend, calling her name. She felt for a pulse and breathed a sigh of relief when she heard Dee moan. "Oh, thank God. She's alive."

Nate grabbed his cell phone and called 911, giving them the particulars and the address.

Then he turned to June. She was now sitting up, her face a mask. "Do you know what happened?" he asked.

"She must have got up and fell down the stairs."

"By the appearance of this blood, she's been laying her for some time. When did you last check on her?"

June's demeanor changed, her eyes became slits. "You have no right to question me like that. You're not the police! How dare you make insinuations?" She was standing now, her lips pursed, her fists clenching and unclenching as her nails dug into her flesh. She jumped at the sounds of sirens in the distance.

"For God's sake, June," Emma commanded. "Get me a wet wash cloth so I can wipe this blood off her face. She has a deep gash on the side of her head."

With hesitant steps, June did as she was told without any further comment.

Within moments the paramedics arrived, assessed the situation, put a protective collar around Dee's neck and took her vital signs. They then started an intravenous drip, and hooked her up to an EKG readout.

"Which hospital, Ma'am?" the one in charge asked Emma. She pointed to June.

"Huh?"

"We can take her to any of the surrounding hospitals. Where is her doctor on staff?"

"How the hell do I know?" June responded waving her hand. "Take her anywhere. Just get her out of here."

The man shook his head and turned to Emma. "We'll take her to St. Frances in Evanston. It's the closest."

Emma nodded. "Where is that?"

He gave the information to Nate then called the hospital.

Carefully they moved the patient to a stretcher and then into the ambulance.

"Come on, Nate," Emma said, "we'll follow in our car. June, do you want to ride with us?"

"Uh, no, I feel sick." She flopped back onto the couch.

"Before you get too sick," Nate said through gritted teeth, "I suggest you call your husband." Then he and Emma hurried out the door.

CHAPTER 46

NATE FOLLOWED THE AMBULANCE AS close as he dared without exceeding the speed limit. "Do you think June called the good vet?' he asked.

"Who knows. I think I'll call the clinic and ask Marge." Emma pulled her cell phone from her purse and fiddled with it until she had a signal. With a sigh of satisfaction she punched in the number to the clinic.

"Paws and Claws, may I help you?' Marge answered.

"This is Emma Winberry. Did June call the doc about Dee?"

"She did call him. They're talking now. Is everything all right?"

"Absolutely not! We went over to the house and found June sunning herself in the backyard and Dee lying at the bottom of the stairs, unconscious."

"Oh my God!"

"We're following the ambulance to St. Frances Hospital in Evanston. In case that fool, June, didn't remember which hospital, you might tell Doc that I called and we'll meet him there."

"Thanks, Mrs. Winberry. I'll tell him right away."

* * *

Emma and Nate ran into Mike as they entered the emergency room. He acknowledged them and hurried to the desk. Emma overheard the receptionist ask for the insurance information then directed him to the waiting room.

He turned to Emma and Nate, a bewildered expression on his face. "What happened? June was hysterical when she called and I couldn't make any sense out of what she was saying."

"Sit down," Nate said, taking the man's arm. "Do you want to tell him?" He directed his question to Emma.

She nodded. "Mike, I sometimes have premonitions about people in trouble. Don't ask how, because I don't understand it myself, but I *knew* something was wrong with your mother." She took a breath, and continued. "I called the house repeatedly and got no answer, so Nate and I drove over there."

"But where was June?" He held up his hands. "She was supposed to be watching Mom."

"She was in the backyard sunning herself, listening to her Ipod, and smoking a cigarette."

Emma couldn't keep the distain from her voice. "She said Dee was sleeping but I insisted on seeing her. That was when we found her at the bottom of the stairs."

"Oh, God." He sat with his head in his hands and gave a soft moan. After a moment he lifted his head and looked directly at Emma. "Where is my wife now? Is she on her way here?"

"She's at home, said she wasn't feeling well."

"This pregnancy seems to be taking a lot out of her," he said unconvincingly. Emma wanted to say more, but she felt Nate squeeze her hand.

"Do you want some coffee?" Nate asked.

"No, no thanks. I was told to wait here until the doctors do their initial examination. I'll never forgive myself if something serious has happened to Mom."

"It's not your fault," Emma said with more force than she intended.

"I should have hired a professional to care for her and not relied on June."

This was the first statement he made insinuating that his wife might be at fault. Again, with difficulty, Emma held back what she really wanted to say. Had Marge given him the information that Frances left for him? She wondered, but dared not ask.

They sat in silence. Mike appeared to have aged since Dee's stroke. Poor man, Emma thought, this is all too much for him to cope with.

After an hour, the doctor came out and spoke to the trio. "Dr. Armanetti, your mother's condition is serious but not critical."

They all breathed a sigh of relief.

"She has a fractured left arm which we will cast as soon as the swelling goes down. In the meantime we have applied a soft brace. She also has a mild concussion and a number of bruises. The cut on her head didn't require stitches, just some surgical glue. How far did she fall?"

"There are twelve stairs with a railing. They're carpeted, but the floor at the bottom is hardwood." Mike grimaced with every word.

The doctor raised his eyebrows. "She's very lucky she didn't sustain more serious injuries. It will be a problem now since she's paralyzed on the right side and her left arm will be casted.

"We'll keep her in the hospital until we're certain that she's stable. Then you'll have to make arrangements for either a rehab center or a full time caregiver and physical therapy at home. You can discuss that with social services before she's ready for discharge."

"May I see her?" Mike asked.

"Certainly, right this way."

"May I come, too?" Emma asked.

Mike nodded and the doctor waved her on. Nate chose to stay behind.

As Emma walked into the cubicle where her friend lay, she fought back tears. Mike sat in a chair next to his mother and wept openly. "Mama, Mama."

An intravenous line fed fluids into her right arm. Her left eye was swollen shut, the entire side of her face bruised and abraded. Her left arm lay in a supporting brace, the fingers only visible, fat as sausages. The regular blip, blip of the electrocardiographic tracing on the machine above her head was the only encouraging sound.

"Dee," Emma called softly, "it's Emma and your son, Mike. Can you open your eyes?" Dee moaned and struggled to open her right eye. "Ma—Ma," she said softly. "Mike—Mike."

A crooked smile crossed her lips.

"Oh, Mom, please get well. I'll never leave you alone again." Mike's tears fell on his mother's cheek. He tenderly wiped them away and kissed the bruises.

Dee gave them a puzzled look, as if to ask what happened.

"You fell down the stairs," Emma said. "Do you remember anything?" Dee slowly moved her head from side to side. "Nos—nos," she whispered. "What is she saying?" Mike asked.

"She wants her lucky stone. It's probably with her things."

"I'll ask the nurse." Mike got off the chair and left the cubicle.

This is my opportunity, Emma thought. "Dee, were you trying to say that you didn't fall?"

"*Si.*"

"Did someone push you down those stairs?"

"*Si.*"

"Who was it? June?"

No answer. She moaned and closed her eyes, as if the effort had been too much for her.

Mike returned with the pouch containing the lucky stone. Gently he and Emma placed it around her neck. She partially opened her right eye and smiled.

"We're ready to transfer her to a room," the nurse said. "The number is 642. Let us get her settled and then you can come up." Emma was reluctant to leave Dee alone, but she knew Nate was waiting for her in the lobby. His aversion to hospitals pulled at her. She kissed Dee on the forehead—no response.

"I'll be back tomorrow," she whispered. Still no response. Emma sighed and quietly left the room.

If it had been up to her, she would have stayed the night, but that was out of the question. When she reached the lobby, she searched the area—no Nate. Where could he be? Perhaps the bathroom. She stood near the exit shifting her weight from one foot to the other. After a while she became impatient. They had agreed to meet here. He certainly hadn't remained in the Emergency Room waiting area.

After fifteen trying minutes, she heard his voice talking to someone and—laughing. Then she recognized a woman's voice. Who was it?

Nate and a tall, attractive woman came into the lobby. Something about her was familiar. A pang of jealousy shot through Emma. She had been upstairs at the bedside of their seriously injured friend and he was socializing with a woman.

"Emma," Nate called. "Look who I ran into, Sandra Andrews from the opera chapter." He took the woman's arm and led her toward Emma.

"Oh, yes." Emma forced a smile and held out her hand.

"Nice to see you," Sandra said in a musical voice. "Nate and I have been having a nice chat."

"This is an odd place to run into acquaintances," Emma said.

Sandra's smile faded. "My husband is upstairs in the Coronary Care Unit. He's had a third heart attack. This one is extremely serious."

Then what are you doing down here laughing with Nate? Emma thought, but held her tongue.

"I'm waiting for my daughter," the woman said. "It was refreshing to meet Nate. He helped me think of something else for a little while."

"Glad I could be of service," Nate said with obvious gallantry. "Now are you ready to go, Emma? You know how I feel about hospitals."

"Yes, I'm ready. Nice to see you, Sandra, but I wish it were under different circumstances." They said their goodbyes and left.

Emma was unusually quiet on the ride home. She knew Dee was looked after, but something kept nagging at her. However, she also knew she must spend more time with Nate, especially when she saw him with other women. The last thing she wanted was to jeopardize their relationship.

"Shall we go out to dinner tonight?" she asked.

"That's a good idea. You need to get your mind off Dee and her problems. She's Mike's responsibility and I'm sure he'll put her somewhere safe."

The words, 'put her somewhere safe', bothered Emma—as if the woman were a family heirloom instead of a fellow human being. She knew Nate didn't intend it to sound that way so she said nothing and promised herself to enjoy the evening.

* * *

When Mike left the hospital, his mind was in a whirl. He would have to make provisions for his mother's safe care. A nagging suspicion crept into his mind. Could June be responsible for the fall? No, it was unthinkable. She was his life companion, the mother of his unborn child. He refused to harbor such thoughts.

But he could no longer ignore the articles in the envelope Frances had left for him. The woman in the pictures did resemble June, but they were grainy and unclear. He desperately wanted to believe it was someone else. His rational mind told him that anyone can change their appearance: hair and eye color, plastic surgery. Was it possible? Could June have also orchestrated Frances' accident? Was he living with a woman with a split personality? He would have to confront her—today.

As he pulled into the driveway, he felt a chill, then shook it off as the result of nervous exhaustion.

"June," he called walking in the front door. "June, where are you?"

"In here," a weak voice answered.

He hurried into the living room to see her sprawled on the couch, one arm and one leg dangling over the side.

"What's wrong?" He knelt down beside her, all thoughts of confrontation gone, as he took her in his arms. "My dear, tell me what's wrong."

"Sick ... cramps ... afraid I'll lose the baby."

"Oh no! I'll get you to the hospital right away."He held her closer, felt her heart beating rapidly, her body bathed in sweat.

"No!" Her voice was stronger now. "Get me to bed. The doctor said if I have any cramping, to go to bed and take the pills he gave me. No hospital, please, unless it gets worse."

Against his better judgment, he half dragged, half carried her up the stairs and put her to bed. After sponging her face and arms and giving her the mild sedative the doctor had prescribed, he sat next to her until she fell into a restful sleep.

Mike sat for a long time attempting to view the entire situation objectively. Did he really trust his wife? Could she handle a sick woman and a baby at the same time?

No, of course not. What should he do now?

CHAPTER 47

JUNE CHECKED THE SMALL PHONE book she carried in a zipped compartment of her purse. She thought for a moment, then punched in the numbers with such force that she almost dropped the phone.

"Hullo?" a sleepy voice answered.

"Hi, Sis, I'm glad to hear you're bright and cheerful, as usual."

"Lyla? Is that you?"

"Not Lyla. My name is June, June Armanetti."

"Huh! That's a laugh. How did you come up with that moniker?"

June's mood changed dramatically. "That's not important. Are you working?"

A yawn from the other end. "I got laid off, so to speak. Was working in a bar and the boss caught me with my hand in the till, so, he fired me."

June heard the woman take a drag on a cigarette. How she wanted one. But she didn't dare smoke now. Mike would smell it and give her hell. "I've got a job for you, if you want it."

"What do I have to do?"

"Not much—just a slight injury to someone who's getting in my way."

"You don't want me to off anybody, do you? I don't do that sort of thing."

"No, no. Like I said, just a slight injury to keep this woman out of my face for a while." June took a sip of cold coffee then dumped the rest. "Where are you, anyway?"

"Minneapolis."

"Hop on a plane and I'll pick you up at O'Hare."

"I can't do that. I'm broke." Another drag on the cigarette.

June shook her head. Her sister would never change. "All right, I'll get you a ticket."

"Where are you getting this money—June?"

The tone of her voice took on a superior note. "My husband is Dr. Michael Armanetti, a veterinarian. He's doing very well."

"How can you be married when … "

"Shut up!" June shouted into the phone. "Don't ask any questions, and, by the way, what name are you using?"

"Vicki Smithson. Pretty classy, huh?"

"It's okay. I presume you have identification."

"Don't I always?"

"I'll get back to you as soon as I tell my husband that my sister is coming for a visit. I was overjoyed to hear from her."

"Will he be okay with that?"

"Of course. I know just how to handle him."

* * *

"Your sister?" Mike's expression mirrored his surprise. "You told me you didn't have any family."

"Well, Vicki got into some trouble—was in drug rehab for a while—and we lost touch. But she's cleaned up now and has a job interview in Chicago." June gave him a pleading look but wondered if Mike was buying her story. She was glad her mother-in-law wasn't around. The old lady was beginning to understand. She had to be careful around her—very careful. But she knew just how to take care of *that* problem.

Mike still appeared confused. "How did she find you?"

June had her answer all ready. "Through my Facebook page, on the Internet. I had my maiden name on it, as well as my married name. You know, in case old friends want to get in touch." Did he believe her?

"Do you feel well enough to entertain anyone? I'm still worried about you and the baby."

"I'm fine, now. Vicki's call really helped. All the cramps are gone. When I called the doctor, he had me come in for a checkup and said all I needed was rest and relaxation." She cocked her head to the side like a child.

Mike leaned back and smiled. "Good. I'm glad you've reconnected with your sister. Family is important."

* * *

A few days later, when June picked up Vicki at the airport, she noticed the hard lines on her sister's face. Even though she was younger, the years had not been kind.

"Okay," June said, driving her BMW into the three car garage, "this is it." Vicki's eye widened, but she simply nodded her approval.

They walked into the spacious living room with furnishings out of Better Homes and Gardens. The long floor to ceiling windows bathed the room in light. A stone fireplace took up half of one wall; an original oil painting of a peaceful landscape hung above it.

Vicki ran her fingers along the marble mantle sporting a bronze sculpture of a nude woman. "Geesh, nice digs. You did okay, Sis."

"Just don't do or say anything to throw a monkey wrench into my life. I have to warn you about something." She saw the questioning look on Vicki's face.

"My mother-in-law is temporarily living here. She had a stroke and I'm not sure how much she understands. Right now she's in the hospital—fell down the stairs, poor thing."

June pursed her lips, sticking out the bottom one as much as she could. "She's cagey, can't talk anything but gibberish and some Italian words. It's only temporary. I got plans. She's starting to talk in Italian. That makes me real nervous. And there's this busybody who understands her. She's the problem right now, the one I want out of the way."

June led her sister up the long flight of stairs and into one of the smaller of the four bedrooms. Vicki dropped her bag on the plush moss-green carpeting.

"This room is bigger than the dump I was living in." She walked to the window and gazed out at the lush lawn and the well tended rose bushes around the periphery. "I got to admit, you did good for yourself this time—June." She drew out the name slowly.

June's eyes narrowed as she came within inches of her sister's face and grabbed her shirt. "And nobody had better interfere with what I got, and that includes you."

Vicki stepped back and held up her hands. "Hey, I'm glad for you. I'll do my job, take my pay, and get out of your hair."

June relaxed her grip on Vicki and took a breath. "Okay. But that's *all* I want you to do."

She pointed to an antique chest of drawers. "You can put your stuff in there and this is your bathroom." She opened a door to a room with all the amenities of a five star hotel.

"How'd you meet this guy, anyway?" Vicki asked as she stuffed clothing into the drawers.

"Humph, he was a sitting duck. I was in a bar having a drink and scouting the territory. Remember when we used to do that?"

"Yeah, I do."

"Anyway, I spotted him—good looking with dark curly hair. He was talking to another guy and shaking his head. He definitely didn't seem happy. So—I pulled the usual—accidentally bumped into him and spilled my drink on my dress. Lots of cleavage showing, of course."

June remembered how helpful Mike had been when she apologized. He had asked the barman for a towel and carefully wiped her dress, never taking his eyes off of her ample breasts.

"He bought me another drink and I sat with the two men for a while. Then the other guy left and Mike and I stayed. We got to talking about our lives. I gave him a sob story, don't even remember what I said. We were both pretty drunk by then. He said his wife was always getting involved with volunteer work and didn't have time for him. The marriage was on the rocks. That's all I had to hear."

Vicki laughed. "You shifted into high gear then, huh? How long did it take to seduce him?"

"We got a hotel room that night. Then I teased him along until he divorced his wife and married me."

"I gotta admit, Sis, you were always good at that sort of thing. But this time you struck gold." Vicki closed the drawer and snapped her case shut.

* * *

Later they sat on the patio, each with a cup of coffee.

"One more thing," June said. "I'm pregnant."

"Get out. I don't believe that for a minute." Vicki laughed, a hard guttural sound.

"I said, I'm pregnant. I don't care if you believe it or not. Mike does, and that's all that matters." Her eyes narrowed sending her sister a message that the subject was closed.

"Give me a cigarette."

"Are you supposed to smoke?" Vicki asked.

"I'll change and brush my teeth before Mike gets home. I can't stand watching you smoke without having one myself."

"Okay."

June lit the cigarette, took a deep drag, held it for a moment, and let the smoke trail out of her nose. "Heaven."

Vicki sat forward and fixed her eyes on June. "Now that you've had your fix, tell me why I'm here and what you want me to do."

For the next hour, June told Vicki the whole story and what she expected of her. They went through two packs of cigarettes.

* * *

That evening June ordered out from the local Chinese restaurant. She chilled a bottle of white wine and set the table in the dining room.

"This looks pretty formal," Vicki said as she set out gold rimmed plates and linen napkins.

The silverware that June retrieved from a cabinet was sterling.

"We're celebrating. My long lost sister and I are reunited." June laughed, a hard, ugly sound. "Just remember, if you cross me ... "

"Don't worry. I'm here for you, Sis." Vicki made a move to embrace June, but thought better of it.

"Don't touch me." Then the theatrics took over. "Remember, I'm in a delicate condition."

At that moment, they heard the door. June hurried to greet her husband. She threw her arms around his neck and nuzzled close. "How was your day, baby?"

"Not too bad. I stopped at the hospital this morning. Mom was kind of tired. The therapists are working with her at the bedside, but she's still pretty weak."

June ran her hand over his furrowed brow. "Poor dear. I'm so sorry, but you know modern medicine can do miracles these days. She's a strong woman."

He slid his arm around her waist and planted a kiss on her cheek. "Now I want to meet this sister of yours."

Vicki walked gracefully into the room dressed in a new outfit of June's. She held out her hand.

Mike took it and studied the woman's face. "You two resemble each other quite a bit, except for the hair color and the eyes. I'm so glad you and June reconnected … ?"

"Vicki, Vicki Smithson."

He gave her a kiss on the cheek and June gave her a warning look. During the meal, June remained on guard. She never did trust her sister.

"So where is your job interview?" Mike asked.

Vicki was about to open her mouth when June jumped in. "At the corporate office of McDonald's in Oak Brook. I'm going to drive her there tomorrow."

He nodded approvingly.

The women exchanged glances. They had rehearsed this, but June was afraid Vicki would say the wrong thing. With everything she had at stake, she could take no chances.

"I've heard that's a great place to work," he said, "potential for advancement. Where are you staying?"

"Well, if I get the job, I'll look for an apartment in the area."

"In the meantime, stay here," Mike said. "We have plenty of room."

"You certainly do. This is a great house."

"It's a little big for us, but, with a little one running around—did June tell you?" His eyes brightened.

"I did," June said. "And she's delighted that she's going to be an auntie. Aren't you?"

"You have no idea how much."

Again the women communicated with their eyes. They had learned to do it as children when they weren't allowed to speak at the dinner table.

"Say, I just had an idea," Mike said. "Maybe you can help June when the baby comes." He turned to Vicki, a smile on his handsome face.

"Sure, I'd love that."

June kicked her under the table, but Vicki ignored it.

"There's plenty of time before we have to make those plans," June said taking her husband's hand. "Now I'm feeling a little light-headed. Mike, please help me to the couch. I need to lie down for a few minutes."

"Of course."

Vicki watched the drama unfold as Mike tenderly helped his wife to the couch then covered her with a flowered throw.

Yep, she thought, Sis's got it made. Now how can I cash in on some of it?

CHAPTER 48

A FEW DAYS LATER EMMA received a call from one of the members of the opera chorus.

"How is Delia progressing?" the woman asked. "Everyone here is eager to have her back."

"I'm afraid that isn't going to happen any time soon. She's had a setback. Fell down the stairs." Emma winced every time she spoke the words.

"Oh my, how badly was she injured?"

"Nothing that won't heal, thank goodness, but her left arm is broken; that's her good side, so she's virtually helpless." Emma paced, feeling just as impotent as her friend.

"That's terrible news. I'll get a few of the other singers together and we'll pay her a visit. What hospital is she in?"

"St. Frances in Evanston, but wait a few days. She's also had a concussion and is still a bit groggy. I'm sure that a visit from friends will perk up her spirits."

"Thanks, Emma. I'll rally the group. Bye now."

"Who was that?" Nate asked walking into the room.

"One of the members of the chorus. She plans to get a few others together and visit Dee."

"Sounds like a good idea. But is she ready for many visitors yet?" Nate smoothed down a few unruly hairs that stood out from behind Emma's ear.

"I told them to wait a few days and, yes, I need a haircut."

"I didn't say anything, did I?" He gazed at her innocently.

"You didn't have to. I know I look a sight."

"You'll always be my Sparrow." He took her in his arms and began waltzing around the room. Before long, they collapsed on the couch, laughing.

"Remember when we first met? We used to go dancing a lot," Nate said, a hint of nostalgia in his voice.

"Uh huh."

"Why don't we do that anymore? We're in a rut."

"No," she said, "not a rut, just a comfortable lifestyle." She kissed the cleft in his chin. She had always been attracted to men with dimpled chins.

"Yeah, in between the adventures that you keep getting involved in. So what do you plan to do now about Delia? I can hear the wheels turning in your head."

"She's totally helpless. I've been thinking this out."

"Oh, oh, I see trouble ahead." He held out his hands at his sides and shrugged.

"Hear me out—please. If June orchestrated Frances' accident to prevent her from telling Mike about her past, it proves that she will go to any length to hold onto the nice lifestyle she has." She held up her hand before he could interrupt. "So, if she *did* push Dee down the stairs, and I have no doubts about it, she will do something drastic to keep the woman quiet. What better time than when she can't defend herself."

"Do you actually think that June will go into a hospital room and do something to Dee?"

"I do. She's ruthless. What would it take to smother a helpless woman? A pillow, that's all."

Nate shook his head. "You read too many mysteries. She's not that bold."

"I think she is, and so does my Guardian Angel; so there."

"I guess I'm outnumbered." He held up his hands and shook his head. "I'm going to the gym for a while."

"Does Yvonne use the machines much?" Emma asked innocently.

"Sometimes. Why do you want to know?" He gave her a mischievous grin.

"Just curious, that's all. I thought I would go to the hospital this afternoon, if you don't mind."

"Go ahead. I have an article to write for the investment journal. I'll work on that. But remember, tonight is that Rachmaninoff concert at Millennium Park. I don't want to miss it."

"I'll be back in time, never fear."

At that moment the phone rang. "I'll get it," Nate said. "Hello. Oh yes, Sara, she's right here." He handed the phone to Emma. "Sara from the day care center."

"Hello, Sara, did Dr. Armanetti call you about Delia?"

"No, what happened? Mrs. Carter has been trying to reach him these past few days when Delia didn't show up, but there was no answer. She asked me to call you rather than bother him at the clinic."

"Well, there's been an accident." Emma proceeded to tell her the entire story, leaving nothing out.

"My God, what a tragedy. I'll tell Mrs. Carter and I'm sure she'll send flowers to the hospital. Will you keep us updated, please?"

"I will," Emma promised, then said goodbye.

* * *

When Emma walked into the hospital room carrying a bouquet of flowers, she heard music playing and Dee humming along. That was surely a good sign. A nurse was in the room straightening up. A pin on her uniform said Cindy, LPN.

"Hello there," Cindy said in a cheery voice. "Mrs. Armanetti is doing much better. And you are?"

"I'm so glad to hear that. I'm Emma Winberry, a good friend."

At the sound of Emma's voice, Dee opened her eyes as much as possible and gave her a crooked smile. Then she said, "Em-ma."

Emma couldn't contain her excitement. She turned to the nurse. "This is the first time she's been able to say my name correctly."

Cindy nodded. "That's encouraging. Her son stopped by this morning on his way to work and brought the CD player and asked us to play music for her."

"Excellent. She's a member of the opera chorus and a fine singer."

As if on cue, Dee sang a few bars from the opera *Carmen* along with the soprano on the CD.

Emma sat down on a chair at her bedside. "Oh, my friend, you're going to get well, I know it."

Dee began to hum along with the music.

"When will the doctor be able to cast her arm?" Emma asked. "I see that her fingers are much less swollen."

"I believe that will be sometime this afternoon. There are a few more tests scheduled and, if they're normal, she'll be moved to rehab."

"My, that's quick."

"The longer she stays in bed, the more muscle tone she'll lose. Today the physical therapist will work with her at the bedside and then, get her up in a chair."

"Yes, I see the need for getting her moving." She turned to her friend. "Dee, you have to work very hard—no slacking off."

Dee continued to sing.

"I'll bring a vase for those flowers," Cindy said.

She returned in a moment with a vase, then went to answer a call.

Emma went into the bathroom to arrange the bouquet. She felt encouraged at the sound of Dee's voice. It was a positive sign.

As Emma began arranging the flowers, she heard someone enter the room. She presumed it was Cindy until she heard June's voice.

"Hello, my dear mother-in-law. I hear you're improving."

"No! No!" Dee said.

Emma hid herself behind the door. She was curious as to what June was up to. She strained to hear the voice say in a low venomous tone, "If you get your speech back, it might not be good for you. Do you understand me? Remember, you tripped and fell down those stairs. As long as you stick to that, everything will be fine. Understand?"

Emma could restrain herself no longer. She casually walked out of the bathroom with the vase of flowers. "Oh, hello June, I thought I heard your voice."

June pulled herself back, a startled expression on her face. Immediately she relaxed and slumped into a chair and reverted to her theatrical persona.

"I'm so tired these days. Just wanted to see Mother D for a moment."

Emma put the flowers on the bedside table. She noted the expression of concern on her friend's face.

"Em—ma, *bugia, bugia.*"

"Everything is all right," she assured her, patting her shoulder. "What's she saying?" June asked abruptly.

Emma shook her head. "Just rambling. It doesn't mean anything." But Dee had clearly said the word "lie".

At that moment the physical therapist came in to work with her patient. Emma and June walked out together.

"So, how far along are you?" Emma asked as they waited for the elevator. June thought for a moment. "About two and a half months."

"In the first trimester the body is making a lot of adjustments—lots of hormone changes. I remember feeling wretched. But, I'm sure that you'll feel better soon."

June frowned. This was obviously *not* what she wanted to discuss. "I hope you're right," she said with a sigh.

When the elevator doors opened, she grabbed the rail and pulled herself inside.

Emma wanted to laugh and tell her what a phony she was, but that wouldn't help the situation.

When they exited the hospital, June almost sprinted toward her car. Emma watched for a moment before walking to the bus stop. She saw June light a cigarette before getting into her car. *Buggia* is right.

Watch her. She's dangerous, her inner voice said. A chill ran up Emma's spine.

CHAPTER 49

"**N**ATE, SOMEONE IS KNOCKING AT the door," Emma called from the kitchen.

"Okay."

She heard him open the door and greet Claude, their next door neighbor. Though she could hear their voices, she couldn't make out what they were saying. Quickly she rinsed her soapy hands, dried them and arranged a plate of cookies. She walked into the living room and greeted their neighbor.

"Claude, how nice to see you."

"Emma, my dear, you grow younger every day." He made a slight bow then kissed her on the cheek.

"I have some of your favorite cookies. Do sit down and visit for a while. We haven't seen much of you and Thomas lately."

Claude sat gracefully, his long legs stretched out in front of him, the back of one hand to his forehead. "Alas, Thomas is gone on a business trip, and, you know how lonely I get."

Emma and Nate exchanged glances, each repressing a smirk. They were used to Claude's theatrics. He had been in ballet for many years and was now the choreographer for a ballet troupe at the Performing Arts Center. Thomas, his partner, was doing well in interior design.

"You must come for dinner," Emma said.

"Thank you so much." His graceful fingers curled around a cookie and he raised it to his mouth. He took a bite, chewed and swallowed, an ecstatic expression on his face. "Dear lady, you should open a bakery. These are heavenly." He quickly finished it and took another.

Emma saw Nate's frown and winked at him. "I think I have enough to do without that burden, Claude. I want to thank you again for taking such good care of my plants while we were gone."

"It was a pleasure." He furrowed his brow. "But now, I have a favor to ask of you."

"Name it," she said.

"Oliver is having a birthday in two weeks and Thomas asked me to shop for him. I do need some guidance, Emma. Could you possibly take an hour or two to assist me? The only experience I've had with children is my contact with Oliver."

He gave her a supplicating look that almost made her laugh. She remembered the shy boy, Thomas' son by an unfortunate marriage. The birth had been difficult and the boy's mental development lagged behind his physical growth.

"How old is he going to be?" Nate asked.

"Eleven. But, you know, he has the mental capacity of a five-year-old."

"I'm sure you and Emma can do a super job shopping for the boy," Nate said. "Why don't you go right now? But Claude, please keep a careful eye on Emma. She tends to get in trouble, as you well know."

He bowed from the waist. "I will guard her with my life."

Emma glanced at Nate with suspicion. "Are you trying to get rid of me? What are you going to do? Why don't you come with us?"

"No Sparrow. I'm going to the gym and work out. You keep baking these delicious confections, so I must burn off the calories. And don't worry about Yvonne. She went sailing with her brother."

Emma heaved a sigh of relief and turned to Claude as he devoured the last cookie on the plate. "Let's go."

"Thank you, from the bottom of my heart."

* * *

Emma and Claude chose three shirts, one with a baseball logo, one football, and one basketball. That way, they had all the sports covered. As they waited for the clerk to wrap the parcel, Claude whispered, "That woman over there is watching us. Do you know her?"

Emma glanced behind them and made eye contact for just a moment before the woman turned away. "There's something familiar about her, but I can't recall a name or where I might have met her."

"I've seen her before," he said, taking the package and nodding to the clerk. "Where?"

"A couple of days ago. I was standing in the foyer waiting for a cab. That same woman walked by the building and checked out the address. Then she stood for a while reading the names on the doorbells."

Emma felt a tingle up her spine. "Then what did she do?"

Claude shrugged. "Just walked away, so I presumed she had the wrong address. Then my cab arrived and I thought nothing of it. But now, there she is again. And she was watching you." He turned to her with a concerned expression. "Is there any reason someone would be watching you?"

"It's probably coincidence." She wanted to placate Claude, but she knew there were no coincidences. She promised herself to be cautious and, if she saw the woman again, to confront her.

"Do you think we should follow her?" Claude asked raising his eyebrows.

"Don't you remember what happened when we followed that stranger in the opera house?" Emma asked.

Claude shuddered. "Don't remind me. I retract that statement."

* * *

When Emma called the hospital the following day, she asked to speak with Cindy. "Hello, Mrs. Winberry, I'm afraid Mrs. Armanetti's had a setback."

"Oh no! She didn't fall, did she?" Emma pictured the helpless woman on the floor.

"No, nothing like that. Since Dr. Armanetti did put your name on the information list, I can tell you that she has a urinary tract infection. She's running a high fever, so her transfer to the rehab ward will have to be postponed for a few days. She'll be on IV antibiotics until the infection is under control."

"Oh dear," Emma said, "That will weaken her, won't it?"

"I'm afraid so, but she will still have bedside physical therapy and, as soon as her fever comes down, perhaps we can get her to the therapy department."

"Thanks, Cindy. I'll visit later."

When Emma replaced the phone on the charger, she turned a distraught face to Nate.

"Bad news?" he asked.

She related what Cindy had said.

"Well," he raised his hands, "all the reports say that a hospital is a good place to get an infection. That proves them out."

"I guess so."

That leaves her vulnerable that much longer, the inner voice said.

* * *

Emma entered the hospital with a heavy heart and a slow step. What would she find? Would June be there? Then the vision of the woman in the store popped into her mind. Where had she seen her before? She racked her brain, but the answer remained out of reach.

Guardian Angel, who is she?

Beware of that woman, the inner voice said.

Emma searched her surroundings to be sure the mystery woman wasn't following her. She hadn't said anything to Nate, but if she saw her one more time, she would certainly tell him.

She found Dee sleeping peacefully. Soft music issued from the CD player. She sat at the bedside for a while, hesitant to wake her friend.

Cindy walked by, saw Emma, and motioned to her to come into the hall. "Is she any better?" Emma asked, hands clasped tightly together.

"Not yet. It takes about twenty-four hours for the antibiotics to do their work. But don't worry." Cindy took one of Emma's hands and gave it a squeeze.

"Has she had any visitors?" Emma asked.

"Her son dropped by this morning, but no one else."

"Thanks, Cindy, please keep an eye on her and tell her I was here."

"I sure will." With that the busy professional scurried down the hallway to answer a buzzing light.

It's wonderful that there are such dedicated people to care for the sick, Emma thought as she walked toward the elevator. Again, she examined her surroundings searching for the mystery woman. Who was she?

CHAPTER 50

NATE OPENED THE MAILBOX AND retrieved the bills, junk mail, and a check he was expecting. He smiled as he turned to see Claude approaching.

"Nate, I have to talk to you," Claude said in a half whisper.

"What's the matter?"

Claude scanned the area then said, "I saw that woman again."

"What woman?"

"The one who's been walking by the building, the same one Emma and I spotted at Water Tower Place when we were shopping." He drew back and put his hand over his mouth. "Emma didn't tell you."

"I guess it slipped her mind. So you saw this woman how many times?"

"Three."

"Did she appear suspicious?"

"The first time she was reading the names on the doorbells. The second time she was staring at Emma."

"And this last time?" Nate wanted to pull the words out of the man's mouth.

"She was standing on the corner at the bus stop. I thought she might live in the area. When the bus came, she didn't get on, just studied all the people who got off. What do you think?" He wrung his hands.

"I think I need to have a talk with Emma. Apparently she *forgot* to inform me of the mystery woman. Thanks, Claude."

Nate didn't wait for the elevator but climbed the six flights of stairs instead. He was winded when he reached his door, but had worked off his frustration and annoyance. He opened the door, went straight to the kitchen and downed a glass of water.

"You look like you've been exercising," Emma said.

"Walked up the stairs."

"Why in the world would you do that? And why are you frowning at me?"

"Sit," he commanded. He tossed the mail on the table then sat across from her. "I met Claude downstairs."

"Oh?"

"Why didn't you tell me about this woman who seems to be showing some interest in you?" His tone reflected his irritation.

"I thought it was merely a coincidence. I saw her in the store and something about her seemed familiar. That's all there was to it."

"Well Claude saw her a third time, at the bus stop, examining the people getting off. That makes three sightings by our neighbor. With everything that's going on right now, I would view this woman as suspicious."

Emma's eyes widened. She folded her arms across her chest. "What do you expect me to do? Sit in the house all day with the door locked? She may have recently moved into the neighborhood. It's possible."

"And she may be stalking you." He leaned his hands on the table and brought his face close to hers.

"That's ridiculous." But Emma rubbed her arms and pulled back.

"I see by your reaction that it's not as strange as it sounds. When were you planning to tell me about it?" He drummed his fingers on the table.

"Okay, you're right. If I spotted her again, I was going to tell you."

He let out a deep breath. "I don't want you to go anywhere without me for the next week. If this woman surfaces again, I *will* confront her. Is that a deal?"

"I'll go along with that." She caressed his cheek with her hand. "You are a dear man."

He took it gently in his and kissed the palm. "I don't want any harm to come to you."

* * *

"What do you mean she saw you?" June tapped her foot and glared at her sister.

"She was with this guy buying stuff. We just made eye contact, and I turned away." Vicki shrugged.

"What did the guy look like?"

"He was tall and skinny. Acted kind of fruity. You know what I mean?"

"Doesn't sound like the one she lives with. Are you sure you had the right woman?" About now, June was sorry she had called Vicki. Wasn't sure she was up to the job.

"I'm sure. I been trailing her for three days now."

"Just to be on the safe side, you'd better wear a disguise. I've got a few wigs in different colors, and wear dark glasses. And you better hurry up. Mike told me that the doctors have my dear mother-in-law's infection under control and she'll be transferred to rehab by next week. I want Emma Winberry out of my hair—soon."

* * *

Emma called the hospital every day. Finally Cindy said the infection was beginning to clear up, but Dee would remain on the ward for a few more days until a bed was available on the rehab unit.

Emma breathed a sigh of relief. If June was going to try something, she would probably have done it by now. Perhaps she was worrying for nothing.

This is not the time to let your guard down, her inner voice said.

Emma couldn't shake the feeling of foreboding that haunted her. She knew June was planning something, but didn't know what or how to prevent it. On a hunch she called Bertie.

"Hi, Emma, I was just thinking about you," her daughter-in-law said. "Hello, my dear, how is the family?"

"Well, Robin has a bad cold and you know what that means. Besides, she's cutting two molars, walking around gnawing on her fingers and fussing."

"Poor baby. Is there anything I can do to help you?"

"Thanks, but I just put her down and I think I'll put my feet up for a few minutes. I'm bone weary."

"You do that, but I have one question. Has she shown any more anxiety about Dee?"

"Not really, but this morning she kept saying, 'No, Gam, no Gam'. I have no idea what she's trying to tell me."

"It's probably nothing," Emma tried to reassure her. "Go lie down while you have the chance and we'll talk soon."

Now Emma was more upset. Gam was what Robin called her. Was she trying to warn Emma? I'm overreacting, she thought. A child not two years old can't possible foresee danger, or can she.

* * *

When Nate came up from the exercise room, he found Emma baking. "Okay, what's up? You just baked yesterday and now you're at it again." He stood with his hands on his hips as she furiously kneaded bread dough.

"I thought I would try out this recipe for old country bread."

He opened the freezer compartment to the refrigerator. "There are three loaves of bread in here already. Do you intend to fill it up, or are we expecting company?" A sarcastic note reflected in his voice.

She heaved a sigh and plopped the dough in a bowl, covered it, and set it aside to rise.

"Will you stop worrying?" he said. "There is nothing you can do, and Delia is safe in that hospital."

She hadn't told him about the veiled threat she heard June make the previous day. "I think I'll call and see if they've transferred her to the rehab ward yet," she said wiping her floury hands on a dish towel.

Nate shook his head and walked into the bathroom.

Emma placed the call to the hospital and asked for the nurses' station on the sixth floor. "May I speak with Delia Armanetti's nurse, please?"

"Just a moment, I'll call her," the ward secretary said.

A few minutes later a cheery voice came on the phone. "This is Cindy. May I help you?"

"Oh Cindy, yes. This is Emma Winberry. Have they scheduled Delia's transfer yet?"

"There will probably be a bed for her the day after tomorrow. The Ortho service casted her arm this morning and sent her to x-ray to make sure it was in the proper position. Her IV antibiotics will be finished by tomorrow evening. Then we'll remove the IV and she'll be ready."

"Thank you so much and, is she still singing?"

Cindy laughed. "More than ever. Some ladies from the opera chorus came earlier and serenaded the entire ward. It was great."

"Has her daughter-in-law been there today?"

"No, just her son, before he went to work."

"Thanks so much, Cindy. I may be over later."

* * *

That evening Marge called.

"Hello, Marge, has something happened?" Emma felt a tinge of discomfort.

"You said to call about anything out of the ordinary."

"Yes, I did."

"Well, the doc told me that June's sister is visiting. He seemed happy about it."

"Did you know that she had family?"

"No, and apparently, neither did the doc. June said that Vicki, that's her name, made contact on June's Facebook page."

"Oh, did he say how long she was going to stay?"

"No, only that she had applied for a job in the area and was waiting for a second interview."

"Thanks, Marge. Keep me posted."

"You were making faces," Nate said after Emma terminated the call. She gave him a confused look.

"What is Facebook?"

"That's a strange question."

"June's sister contacted her on Facebook and came for a visit."

"Hmmm. Facebook is a social network site on the Internet where people post things about themselves. Some have gotten into trouble giving out too much personal information."

"You don't have one of those, do you?" she asked, raising her eyebrows.

"No,. my dear, I see no need for anything of that sort." He rubbed his hand over his chin. "But I'm curious about this so-called sister of June's. I wonder what she looks like?"

Suddenly the light bulb went on in Emma's head. "Oh my God! That's it. I told you the mystery woman seemed familiar. She resembles June, only with dark hair." Emma walked into the atrium so Nate wouldn't see the worried expression on her face.

Oh Guardian Angel, is June trying to harm me? She got Frances out of her way, didn't she?

CHAPTER 51

"EMMA, HERE ARE THE TICKETS for *Hamlet* at the Shakespeare Theater," Nate said, opening the mail.

"Huh?"

"*Hamlet*, remember? We discussed it a few weeks ago, so I ordered the tickets." He held out the envelope to her.

"Oh yes, I remember now. When is it?"

"Tomorrow night. Starts at seven. We can have dinner at Riva's right near the theater. They have great seafood there. Look, we even get a discount because we're going to see the play. Can't beat that."

Emma envisioned the crowds of people at Navy Pier on a lovely summer evening. Would the mystery woman be there, stalking her? Nonsense. What could she do with all those people milling about? Just go and have a good time, she told herself. You deserve it. Besides, she had resolved to pay more attention to Nate. That Yvonne woman had her eye on him.

"Why do you have that concerned expression on your face?" he asked.

"No reason, just being foolish." She gave him a coy smile.

He circled her body in his arms and kissed her neck, then smiled as he felt the goose bumps on her arms.

"You know what that does to me, Nate Sandler."

"Yes, that's why I do it. And I don't want you to worry about the mystery woman. I'll be watching and protect you from all the bad things."

She nestled in his embrace and inhaled the masculine smell of his body. Here she felt safe.

Don't get complaisant, her inner voice said.

For now, Emma ignored the warning.

* * *

Nate wore a light summer suit while Emma dressed in a long sleeved pantsuit. She remembered how chilly it was in the Shakespeare Theater, even on a hot summer night.

Instead of driving to Navy Pier, Nate decided to take a cab. It would be less hassle and probably get them there faster. When they arrived they joined the milling crowds, some outdoors, others indoors, perusing the shops and waiting in line for the I-Max Theater.

They made their way to Riva's where Nate stopped at the lobster tank. "Look at these great lobsters," he said eying the sea creatures lumbering around the tank, their claws taped shut. "We can choose any one we want."

Emma cringed. "Oh Nate, I would never be able to eat those poor things. Just the thought of dropping them in a pot of boiling water … " She didn't finish the sentence but grabbed his arm and clung to him.

He hugged her and grinned. "All right, my squeamish one, we'll order something from the menu that's probably been frozen."

She smiled and nodded.

They ordered Tilapia served with baked potato and fresh asparagus. It was cooked to perfection and delicious. A glass of Pinot Grigio settled her frazzled nerves, but she found herself periodically scanning the room, studying the other diners.

"Relax," Nate said. "I've already checked everyone out. No one remotely resembles June." Emma took a deep breath, but didn't feel much better.

* * *

Vicki drove to the parking garages. She wore a red wig and had padded her clothing, giving her the appearance of a woman twenty pounds heavier.

Now, where would they be? She had seen them hail a cab and followed as close as she dared.

But when they disembarked at the entrance to the Pier, she had no clue as to where she might find them.

If I screw this up, Lyla won't pay me. Got to find them. Vivki saw the sign indicating parking for the Shakespeare Theater and figured people their age might be headed there. She parked the car as close to the exit as she could. *Might need to get out fast.*

She went to the box office and saw that the performance wasn't scheduled until seven o'clock. She checked her watch and saw that it was only six, so they must be eating somewhere.

Vicki purchased a ticket and sat on a bench to wait. *This might be a waste of money,* but since it wasn't hers, she didn't care. That was the price of doing business. If they didn't arrive by the time the play started, she would have to look somewhere else.

Damn that sister of mine, she cursed. *Why did I listen to her? She wouldn't tell me what she's planning, but it's something bad. I know her too well. Even when we were kids, she was devious and cruel. I remember how she enjoyed making fun of the kids who were slow. She hasn't changed one bit, maybe has gotten worse. If I can pull this off, I'll take the money and start over somewhere far away.*

A few patrons had arrived, but not many. Vicki took the opportunity to scout out the place. She went into the ladies' room and noted that there were two exits. That might come in handy.

She asked about the stairway and was told that there was seating upstairs also. *Swell,* she thought. *If they sit up there, I might not spot them.* After she had taken in the lay of the land, she sat next to a window and gazed out over the lake.

Pretty nice place. Wouldn't mind living around here if I could afford it. Maybe I'll hop on that excursion boat afterwards and take a ride. Nobody will search for me there, especially after I ditch the wig and this padding.

People began trickling in and Vicki carefully studied each couple. It wasn't difficult to weed out the 'not thems.' Emma was very thin, so she skipped over all the over-sized women and those with walkers and canes.

Geesh, lotta old people come to this stuff. Vicki had never seen a Shakespeare play and had no desire to sit through this one, either. But a job was a job.

A couple standing at the doorway caught her attention. She looked closely. The woman scanned the room appearing nervous, while the man held her arm.

That's them all right. She's scared, I can tell. Must be on the look out for me. Gotta be careful. That woman's no fool. She sat back but noticed where they were at all times.

Surveillance was a skill she had perfected through the years.

When the doors opened to the seating area, Vicki made a mental note of which one Nate and Emma entered. Then she took her seat. It was at the back of the theater. That was good. She could see them with no problem and began to compose her moves.

* * *

"Sparrow, will you relax? Your body is as tight as a drum." Nate held her arm firmly as he guided her to their seats.

"I can't help it. I feel as though we're being watched."

"You're just keyed up. I'm looking around and don't see anyone remotely resembling the mystery woman."

"She may be wearing a disguise," Emma said clutching her playbill.

"I'll say it again. You read too many mysteries. I'm here. Nothing is going to happen to you."

Watch carefully. She's here, the inner voice said.

This time Emma felt the goose bumps crawl up her arms and it had nothing to do with the temperature in the theater.

CHAPTER 52

HOW CAN PEOPLE WATCH THIS stuff? Vicki squirmed in her seat as the play progressed. *I don't even know what they're talking about.* At one point she closed her eyes for a moment and nodded off. She lifted her head with a jerk. *Gotta stay awake.* Applause filled the theater and the house lights came on for intermission. Vicki's eyes searched out Emma and Nate and saw they were standing, preparing to exit the theater.

She jumped up and scurried out of her row, stepping on people's feet and pushing them aside.

"Ow ... be careful ... what's your hurry?"

"Sorry ... sorry," Vicki said as she jostled her way into the lobby. *Where are they?* She spotted Emma going into the restroom. Nate stood in the hallway, arms folded across his chest, scanning the crowd.

Gotta be careful of that guy. He's watching for me. She kept her head down as she joined the queue for the ladies' room.

"Excuse me," she said politely. "I really need to go. Do you mind if I step ahead of you?" Vicki wore a distressed expression on her face.

Most of them smiled and nodded.

Vicki pushed inside the door. Two women stood in front of Emma and two behind her, one leaning on a cane. *This might be my best chance.* No one paid any attention as she slid the knife out of her purse. Emma was next in line. It was now or never.

At that same moment, Emma dropped her playbill and bent over to pick it up. Vicki twisted her body and sank the knife into the arm of the woman with the cane.

A scream—the woman staggered and fell against Emma.

Damn! Vicki dashed out of the rear exit to the restroom, as women shouted and called for help.

Emma grabbed the injured woman. Someone handed her a bunch of paper towels. She held them against the wound to staunch the flow of blood.

"Oh, oh, she hurt me," the woman moaned. By now three women had helped her to the floor. Her head was cradled in Emma's arms.

"I don't think it's too bad," Emma said, trying to console her. "Help is coming."

Oh Guardian Angel, that was meant for me. And I know you knocked that playbill out of my hand.

Within minutes the manager entered. "Everyone out, please. In here, doctor."

A staff member brought in the emergency kit and turned to Emma who was spattered with blood.

"Are you hurt, Ma'am?"

"No, she fell against me. I'm fine."

"All right. If you go out into the lobby, security will want to question you." An usher escorted Emma to a secluded area. Nate rushed to her.

"Sparrow, what happened ?"

"Don't worry. It's someone else's blood, but I'm certain it was supposed to be mine."

Nate held her tight. "I promised to protect you and I failed."

"I'm all right. Did they catch the woman?"

"I don't know. Security is searching the theater. They have all the doors locked."

"Did you recognize her?"

She shook her head. "I'm sure she was wearing a disguise." Emma heaved a sigh. "She's long gone. You can be sure of that."

* * *

Vicki pulled off the red wig, threw it in a trash can, and ran her fingers through her hair. She sprinted down the stairs and out onto the Pier. Two policemen ran toward the theater.

Stay cool. Mingle with the crowd. She heard people talking and asking each other what happened. The bloody knife was still concealed in the folds of her skirt. *Gotta get rid of it.* Without calling attention to herself, Vicki went inside, and found a restroom. She removed her outer garment along with the padding, wiped her prints off the knife, and wadded the clothes around it. She dumped it all in another trash can.

Glancing in the mirror, she fluffed her dark hair, and washed her hands and face. She smiled at the reflection. No one would recognize her as the heavy-set, red-headed woman. Her smile turned into a frown as she realized that Lyla wouldn't pay her now. No second chances from her sister. Vicki knew that from experience. Had to get on a bus and get out of town.

Within a few minutes she was in the grassy area making her way to the streets filled with Sunday traffic.

* * *

Emma fidgeted as she waited for the security guard to question her.

Oh Guardian Angel, I know Dee is at risk. This attack was a diversion to keep me away. Hurry, her inner voice warned. *There isn't much time.*

She put her hand to her head and moaned. "Are you ill, Ma'am?" the usher asked.

"This has been too much for me. I must get home and lie down. I have a—condition."

Nate frowned. "What are you doing?" he whispered, as the man went to speak to someone in authority.

"We have to get to Dee as soon as possible. You know as well as I do that attack was meant for me. If we tell the security guard what we know, he'll detain us until the police get here. We're wasting precious time. It may already be too late." She gave him a commiserating look.

"All right. I'll see what I can do." Nate walked away and returned in a few moments. "I gave the man in charge our information. If the police want to question you, they'll call." He took her arm and she leaned heavily against him.

As soon as they were out on the Pier, Nate had to hold her back. She wanted to run to the taxi stand. He shook his head and followed.

CHAPTER 53

"CAN'T YOU GO ANY FASTER?" Emma urged the cab driver. He had noted the dried blood on her clothing. "If you needed an ambulance lady, you should have called one. I'm going as fast as I can. There's closer hospitals, you know."

Nate checked his watch. "By now visiting hours are about over. Just keep going, please," he told the driver.

When they arrived, Emma sprinted to the front door as Nate paid the cab driver. Visitors were leaving in droves.

"I'm sorry, but visiting hours are over," a security guard stationed at the entrance told them.

When he examined her, he said, "Maybe you should go to the ER. That looks like blood."

"I can't explain now, but please," Emma begged. "I must see my friend. It's a matter of life and death." She knew that sounded melodramatic but the feelings were so strong she wanted to bolt right past him.

"We'll only be a few minutes," Nate said.

"Wait a minute. I have to call security."

Emma ignored the man and ran, Nate right behind her.

An elevator opened disgorging passengers. Emma wanted to pull them out faster, but all she could do was wait. Nate held her, trying to calm her down.

Finally they entered the empty elevator and Emma pushed the button twice. It seemed to take forever to get there.

The elevator stopped an inch above the floor before it leveled itself and Emma stumbled trying to rush out.

"Be careful." Nate grabbed her as she lost her balance.

At the nurses' station Emma spotted Cindy. She must be working a ten-hour shift, she thought.

"Cindy," she called. "How is Delia?"

"Oh, Mrs. Winberry." She's okay. Why are you here so late? Visiting hours are over." Suddenly her expression changed. "Is that blood on your clothes? Are you hurt?"

"It's not my blood. I don't have time to explain now. I must see Delia."

"She's been singing but she's quiet now."

"May we go in for just a moment?"

"I guess so." The girl sat down to finish her charting. "But only for a few minutes. The supervisor gets after us if we let visitors stay too late."

At that moment they heard Dee's voice loud and clear. *"Maladetta!"* She called. *Aiuto....aiuto ..."*

"What's she saying?" Cindy asked, an alarmed expression on her face.

"She's calling for help!" Emma was already at the door of her room, Nate right behind her.

'Aiuto! Aiuto!"

A figure clad all in black stood over the bed, holding a syringe, poised to strike. Dee tried to fight back with her casted left arm.

Emma flew at the intruder, knocking the syringe to the floor. The figure batted Emma across the face knocking her against the metal bedrails.

Cindy pushed the Code Blue button on the wall as Nate grappled with the would-be assassin; long fingernails raked his cheek.

Within seconds the room filled with personnel. One young doctor restrained the black clad figure while Nate pulled off the ski mask revealing a disheveled June.

"Well, if it isn't Lyla Winters," he spat.

"Take your hands off me," she shrieked, kicking and biting.

Two security guards rushed into the room and grappled her to the floor. Nate turned to Emma. "Are you all right?"

"Yes, she wacked me on the side of my face is all. The woman is a demon."

Cindy tended to Dee, who was upset, but unhurt.

Someone went to pick up the syringe.

"Don't touch that," the security guard said. "That's evidence. The police will take it to the lab and check for prints and whatever's in there."

June screamed. "My baby!" Blood began pouring from one of her pant legs.

"Is she pregnant?" a guard asked.

"Supposedly," Emma answered. Perhaps she really was.

"Let's get her to the ER, but keep her restrained."

June sat back as someone pushed a wheelchair into the room. She continued to cry and moan about her baby.

* * *

Before long Mike came rushing into the room. His hands shook as he cradled his mother's face. "*Figlio mio*," she whispered.

"*Mama mia*," he said, tears streaming down his cheeks. He turned to Emma and Nate. "What happened?"

Emma sat with a cold pack on the side of her face. Nate sported a few band aids on his cheek.

"You'd better sit down," Nate said. Then, as unemotionally as possible, he told Mike exactly what happened, starting with the episode at Navy Pier.

The man sat unmoving, his eyes wide. "I can't believe this. These things happen in the movies, not to ordinary people like us." He motioned to his mother lying helpless in the bed. "I refused to believe the material Frances left for me. I convinced myself it was someone else. And how convenient that her sister showed up when she did. What a fool I've been." He held his head in his hands.

At that moment Cindy walked into the room. "They want you in the ER, Dr. Armanetti." She stooped down and picked up some debris left by the doctors.

"Nate, go with him," Emma said. "I'll stay here with Dee."

"Thank you," Mike mouthed, unable to speak.

Nate practically lifted the man from the chair and escorted him to the elevators. He leaned most of his weight against Nate, dragging one foot after the other.

When they reached the ER, Nate sat him in a chair, afraid he would pass out. Mike's face was white and covered with perspiration.

"Are you all right?"

He shook his head. "I don't know."

Nate waved over a nurse who took one look at Mike and instructed him to put his head down between his knees. She and Nate held him until his color returned. Then she checked his vital signs and nodded.

"Mike, Mike! Where is my husband?" June called from a cubicle nearby.

A doctor came out and sat beside the two men.

"Has she lost the baby?" Mike asked, an expression of pain bathing his face.

The doctor took a deep breath. "She was never pregnant."

Mike's eyes widened. "What? But they told me she was bleeding."

"Your wife had a pouch of theatrical blood attached to her underwear. All she had to do was squeeze it. She fooled all of us, that is, until I examined her."

"Get away from me, you bitch!" June screamed. "Mike, where are you? I did it for us. Your mother was coming between us. Mike ... " Her shouts ended in a moan.

Mike sat with his head in his hands, his shoulders shaking with the sobs. "Oh God," he whispered.

Nate put his arm around him for support.

"Do you want to see her?" the doctor asked. "The police are ready to take her to the station."

Mike raised his head, narrowed his eyes and gritted his teeth. "I never want to see that woman again."

The doctor nodded in understanding and returned to the cubicle. "Mike ... Mike ... " the cries continued.

"Let's go back upstairs," Mike said to Nate. "I can't bear this."

Nate helped him up and, as they walked toward the elevator, the cries became fainter and fainter until they could no longer hear them.

* * *

Back in the room, Dee was asleep. Cindy had given her a sedative and she appeared peaceful. "May I stay here tonight?" Mike asked.

"Certainly. This recliner is comfortable. Lots of family members sleep very well on it," Cindy said.

"We'll be going now," Nate said. "Is there anything you need?"

"How can I thank you both for saving my mother's life?"

"Thank Emma. It's her sixth sense that did it."

"No thanks necessary," Emma said. "Dee is my friend. I do whatever I'm told." The two men looked at each other, but neither responded.

They said goodnight and left Mike to sort out his life.

CHAPTER 54

EMMA MADE SURE SHE VISITED Dee every day. The woman made remarkable progress. It was as if, whatever force had been holding her back, was gone. Emma saw the relief on her friend's face. Her speech was gradually returning, hesitant, but intelligible. Better yet, the sensation in her right hand improved daily.

"At this rate," the physical therapist told Emma, "she'll be ready for discharge soon." But discharge where? Emma decided to talk to Marge.

She placed a call to the clinic. "Paws and Claws, veterinary clinic," a male voice answered. "Is Marge there?"

"She's assisting the doctor," the man answered. "Do you want to leave a message?"

"No, don't bother her. I'll call back later." Huh, Emma thought. Had Marge been promoted to assistant? She knew the woman would like nothing better.

"Are you poking your nose in other people's business again?" Nate asked.

"I was concerned about Mike. This entire mess has turned his world upside down. I don't want to ask him directly where Dee will go when she's discharged from the hospital, but Marge might know." She gave him a condescending smile.

That evening, Emma called Marge at home.

"Oh, Mrs. Winberry, I have so much to tell you. Can we meet for lunch tomorrow? Doc is closing early. He's going to a discharge planning meeting for his mother."

"That sounds great."

They set a time and place. Then Emma sat in the atrium and made a mental note of everything she wanted to ask. She had to put this matter to rest.

* * *

The following day Emma dressed conservatively in a simple summer dress and gave Nate a kiss on the cheek.

"Do you want me to go with you?" he asked.

"Nope. She'll talk more freely if it's just 'us girls'."

"All right. I'll spend some time in the workout room. The women around here have been noticing my trim figure, especially Yvonne."

Emma pursed her lips and frowned, remembering Gladys' words about trust. Nate laughed and kissed her. "I only have eyes for you, my Sparrow."

"I won't be late," she said. With that she walked out of the room, promising herself to spend more time with Nate. And, if he really wanted to go sailing, she *would* go with him, whether she liked it or not.

When Emma arrived at the restaurant, she recognized Marge sitting in a rear booth. Even though they had never met in person, Emma knew who she was. The woman wore a satisfied smile on her face. She gave Emma a hesitant wave.

"Marge? It's good to see you looking so happy," Emma remarked.

"Doc has made me his new assistant," she said, preening. "I've helped him before when he was under a lot of pressure. He said that since we work so well together, he offered to teach me everything I need to know."

"That's wonderful."

The server came up to the table, poured coffee for each and handed them menus. Emma scanned the sandwiches and ordered a ham on rye. Marge ordered the same.

"So, how is Mike doing?" Emma asked taking a sip of coffee.

"He's handling the situation better than I expected. He doesn't talk about June, but she's been charged with attempted murder. Do you know what was in that syringe?" Her eyes widened.

"What?"

"It was filled with Euthasol. That's what we use at the clinic to euthanize animals. It would have been a fatal dose if she had managed to inject it into the IV." Marge took in a breath and blew it out of her mouth.

"But how did June get a hold of that?"

"I'm sure she got it from Frances before Doc sacked her."

"So she was planning all this well in advance." Emma frowned. "What a diabolical woman."

"And," Marge continued, "Doc found out that June, or Lyla, is still married to Jack Winters. So Doc and June aren't legally married. He has his lawyer working out the details."

"But I thought her husband died and she was a suspect," Emma said.

"That was her first husband. Don't know what his name was. Then she married this Winters fellow. No one seems to know where he is. I wish Doc had never ... " She looked down at her hands. "Too late now."

"I think he'll be more cautious from now on. By the way, did they ever find June's sister?"

Marge shook her head. "Not that I know of."

"Maybe it's better that way."

At that point the server placed their sandwiches in front of them and refilled their coffee cups.

Emma simply shook her head. "June, or Lyla, was a better actor than I gave her credit for."

"You can say that again." Marge took a generous bite of her sandwich and swallowed before she continued.

"Doc hasn't gone back to the house—says he's going to sell it and buy a townhouse or condo closer to the clinic."

"That sounds like a good idea," Emma agreed. "He needs time to heal and a change of scene will be good for him."

"Uh huh." Marge was obviously enjoying her meal as well as keeping Emma up to date.

"What about his mother?" Emma finally asked. "Has Mike said anything about his plans for her?"

"Yes, Sam is planning to take her to live with his family. They have a large ranch home and Doc said his brother's having it equipped with handrails."

"I'm so relieved," Emma said with a sigh. She realized she hadn't touched her sandwich and now ate it with relish.

"That seems to tie up all the loose ends except for Frances. Do you know anything about her?"

"The last Doc heard, her family was considering taking her off life support and donating her organs. There's no brain activity at all."

Emma sighed. June had ruined so many lives.

"Oh, one more thing," Marge said swallowing the last bit of her lunch. "Doc said that if I want to become a licensed veterinary assistant, he'll send me to school, and pay for it."

"Are you going to do it?" Emma already knew the answer.

"Absolutely! With training, I can take on more responsibility."

"I'm happy for you, Marge. You've been waiting a long time for this." Both women knew the implication in that statement.

CHAPTER 55 - THREE MONTHS LATER

EMMA SAT WITH DEE AT the rehabilitation center where she had been since her discharge from the hospital. The cast was off her left arm and she wore only a sling for support.

"You look wonderful, my friend."

"I—feel—*buono*—good. I can—talk, and—see?" She slowly lifted her right arm about a foot.

Emma swallowed hard. "Your broken arm is healed and soon you'll be as good as new."

Dee shook her head. "No new—but better."

"So you're going to live with Sam and his family."

Dee nodded. "Mike needs his," she struggled for the words, "own—life."

"I can understand that," Emma agreed.

"House is for—uh—selling."

"Where is Mike living now?"

"In. ." She shook her head in frustration, unable to retrieve the words.

Emma spotted a brochure on the night stand. She picked it up and studied a rendering of a new townhome community in Lincolnwood.

Dee nodded and pointed to the picture. "So he bought a townhouse here?"

"*Si, si.*" Dee smiled. "Close to—work."

"Excellent. And how is he feeling?"

Dee shrugged her left shoulder, slightly lifting the right. "Sad. But he—*forte.*"

Emma took her friend's hand. "You're both starting a new phase of your lives: you with Sam and the children, and Mike enlarging his practice. I've kept in touch with Marge. She's his assistant now, you know."

She noted the twinkle in Dee's eyes. "Good woman."

"Yes, she is that, and faithful. She'll always be there for Mike. And, who knows, in time they may get together. There's nothing she wouldn't do for him."

Dee sighed and nodded.

"We get stronger by these experiences, my friend, and we learn to adjust." That's enough of that, Emma thought. She told Dee about the grandchildren, and pulled two CDs from her purse.

"These are for you. The staff says you sing all the time and entertain the other patients."

"Grazie," Dee said examining the titles.

Reluctantly Emma stood. "Nate is expecting me home. We're leaving tomorrow on vacation."

"Where?"

"Seattle and Vancouver. There are beautiful gardens there, the Bouchart Gardens, and this is the best time of the year to visit."

She hugged Dee but failed to stem the flow of tears that mingled with those of the other woman.

"Arrividerci, my friend. We will see each other again."

Dee didn't speak, simply clutched her lucky stone that still nestled in the pouch around her neck.

ABOUT THE AUTHOR

Helen Osterman lives in Homer Glen, a suburb of Chicago. She has five children, nine grandchildren, and two great-grandchildren. She received a Bachelor of Nursing degree from Mercy Hospital-St. Xavier College and later earned a Master's Degree from Northern Illinois University. Throughout her forty-five-year nursing career, she wrote articles for both nursing and medical journals. She is a member of Mystery Writers of America, and Sisters in Crime and The Authors' Guild.

Helen is the author of the Emma Winberry Mystery Series:

The Accidental Sleuth - 2007
The Stranger in the Opera House - 2009
The Elusive Relation - 2011
Emma Winberry and the Evil Eye – 2012
Locked Within - 2013
Rogue Wave - 2015

Other books by Helen Osterman

Notes in a Mirror, a paranormal/historical - 2009
Song of the Rails, a love story - 2011
Maker's Mark, a cozy mystery - 2012
Danger by Design, a cozy mystery - 2014
Dipped in Danger, a cozy mystery - 2016

Visit Helen at www.helenosterman.com

AUTHOR'S NOTE

I HAVE TAKEN SOME LITERARY liberties with privacy concerns. I'm certain my readers understand this was necessary for the story content.